the Best *of* Good

the Best *of* Good

A Novel

Sara Lewis

ATRIA BOOKS

New York   London   Toronto   Sydney   Singapore

ATRIA BOOKS

1230 Avenue of the Americas
New York, NY 10020

ISBN: 0-7434-3671-7

First Atria Books hardcover edition December 2003

10 9 8 7 6 5 4 3 2 1

ATRIA BOOKS is a trademark of Simon & Schuster, Inc.

For information regarding special discounts for bulk purchases,
please contact Simon & Schuster Special Sales at 1-800-456-6798
or business@simonandschuster.com

Manufactured in the United States of America

To my sisters, Maggie Lewis Thomas
and Susannah Lewis-O'Dea, and my
brother, Evan Lewis, with love

the Best *of* Good

o n e

I was in my sister Ellen's bathroom, drilling through tile. The first try, a couple of days ago, resulted in a cracked tile, which of course I had to replace. I had never put a single tile in the middle of a wall of them, so I had to hunt down a knowledgeable Home Depot employee and listen carefully to his instructions. I had to buy grout, new tile, a special drill bit and so on. A small square of plain white tile is not as easy to find as you might think. There are all kinds of variations on white, white shadow, off-white. The possibilities are endless. And the size has to be the same. So start to finish, getting the new shower curtain rod put up, which was what my sister had asked me to do for her in the first place, ended up taking three days and costing more than expected. But as I put the final screw in the wall, my sister standing in the doorway with the shower curtain in her hands, I was almost sorry to see it end. After all that work, what she had in her bathroom was what she had before the little suction cups on the old rod gave up—a functional shower curtain. It didn't seem like enough.

"Great, Tom!" She started to snap the plastic curtain hooks over the rod. "Thanks so much for doing this. Sorry it turned out to be such a hassle."

I took the other end of the curtain and started hooking it from the opposite direction. "Is that all you want me to do?"

"That's it."

"Sure you don't want, maybe, a shelf unit there above your hamper?"

"No, thanks," she said.

"Or, maybe—I know! What about a mirror right here?"

"Really," Ellen said. "I have enough in here. It's the best-equipped bathroom I've ever seen!" She looked at herself in one of the mirrors, fluffing up the front of her hair. I didn't want to tell her that this didn't make the gray strands any less noticeable. My sister was only four years older than me, but she had all the gray hair.

I surveyed the room. There were hooks I'd put up for her towel and robe. Two mirrors, a shelf unit beside the medicine cabinet. "How about another towel bar right over here?"

"Well, see, I just don't need to hang up any more towels. I've already got room for four. Two here, one there, and one over here. And since I live alone, I don't really—"

"Yeah," I said. "You're right." I walked into the bedroom. "Any other repairs? What about bookshelves? Want some more shelves somewhere?"

"Thanks, but I think you've built me more shelves than the public library down the street has."

"Well," I said, "it's not a major branch." I was still looking around the condo, checking for things that needed repairs, places where racks or shelves or hooks could be added.

"I have everything I need," she said. "Let's eat. I made that spaghetti sauce you like."

"You did? All right!" I said. "I'll wash the dishes."

"Deal," she said. "But, Tom, this time would you mind waiting until after we've finished eating the food that's on them?"

"Ha, ha, ha," I said.

Of course the sauce was excellent and so was the salad. While I was eating, I was looking around the place, hoping to find something broken or loose or worn that I could fix for her. Unfortunately, everything was in pretty good shape. I owe my sister a lot, and I am always on the lookout for ways to repay her.

"Hey!" I said, looking up from my spaghetti.

"What?"

"Maybe you need a spice rack!"

She pointed. Next to the stove there was a set of little wooden shelves, just right for a medium-sized spice collection.

"Oh," I said. "Right, yeah. I guess I made you one already."

"What about your place, Tom?"

"What about it?"

"Don't you think you should put up some shelves there? Build *yourself* a spice rack?"

"No," I said. "My place doesn't matter. And what would I do with a spice rack? I don't cook."

"I'm just saying that you put so much time and energy into fixing up my place, but maybe you should focus some of that effort on your own."

I looked at her. "What for? What would be the point of that?"

t w o

I was behind the bar in The Club, a music place where I had worked for a long, long time. I tried not to think about the exact number of years, but trust me, it was lots. The place was packed. All the seats were sold out as were all the standing-room tickets. People were six or seven deep at the bar, and the music was loud, so customers were screaming their drink orders into my face. An enormous biker yelled, "Whiskey sour!" and a drop of his spit landed on my upper lip.

"Did you forget my tequila sunrises?" another guy yelled. "I ordered three tequila sunrises half an hour ago!"

I nodded that I got that, and I wanted to say that it wasn't half an hour ago; it was more like three minutes. But right then a girl squeezed her way through the crowd up to the bar. She had blond hair, and a lot of her chest was exposed in the low-cut shirt she was wearing. On the upper portion of her left breast, a tattoo of something with wings—a butterfly, an angel, the tooth fairy?—was peeking out over her shirt.

"Bartender!" she yelled in a piercing voice. She had a twenty-dollar bill in her hand, and she was waving it at me. "Margarita, extra salt!"

I had a lot of money in my left hand from other customers, and I had to put it away before I could do anything about these orders that kept coming at me. I punched the buttons on the register, but nothing happened: dead. I got down on the floor to check the plug, but it was fine. Time was passing, and the orders were piling up in my head. My right hand got wet down on the floor, and I would have to wash it before I made these drinks. I stood up. I was still holding the money, and the register wouldn't open. Why was everybody ordering these fancy drinks tonight anyway? Didn't anybody want a plain old beer? I was pushing buttons again, but the register must have been jammed or something.

"Bartender!" someone yelled. "I ordered two white-wine spritzers! Like, an hour ago!"

"I ordered before you!" someone said.

Just then, the biker, who was wearing a leather vest and no shirt said, "Where's my whiskey sour?" And he lunged at me across the bar, grabbing my face with his enormous, scratchy hand. I heard something snap in my neck and everything was suddenly too bright.

"Oh, my God!" I yelled.

Then I was sitting up in bed in my own place, and my heart was pounding. The bartender dream. It was only the bartender dream, which I had at least a couple of times a month. I reached for my glasses and put them on. I looked around at my faded comforter, my yellowing lamp shade, my black-and-white TV with the coat hanger taped to where its rabbit ears should have been, a calendar on the wall from another year that had been over for a long time. "Phew. Everything's fine," I said out loud to no one. "Everything's normal."

In the bathroom, I turned on the water. While it was warming up, I took a look at my hair. A lot of guys my age had bald spots in back, like skin yamulkes. Or they had receding hairlines, ever narrowing peninsulas of hair in the middle of their oceanic foreheads. Not me. I had all my hair. It wasn't even thinning, and it was still dark brown. If I wanted to, I could grow it to my shoulders and make a substantial ponytail out of it, and it would be as thick and dark as it had ever been and not a bit stringy. But I didn't want long hair. I liked it medium, not too short and not too long, no sideburns, beard, or mustache.

My name is Tom Good, but since I was ten, which was also the year I started playing guitar, everyone, except my immediate family, has called me Good. I am forty-seven years old, but if you went to high school with me, even if you hadn't seen or thought about me since 1972, you would recognize me right away. I hadn't changed much. I still wore T-shirts and jeans, sneakers, and, when absolutely necessary, a denim jacket.

I took off my glasses and stepped over the side of the tub and into the stream of water. It was cold, causing me to shrivel and get goose bumps. Quickly, I soaped my pits and my crotch. I put a dab of shampoo in my hand, wiped it over my hair, lathered it up. I rinsed fast and turned off the water. I pulled back the shower curtain and grabbed for my towel.

I put on my glasses. It was as I was drying my leg, one foot up on the toilet seat, when I happened to glance down and see it: a gray pubic hair. I looked again. I pulled. It was attached. Clearly, it was an anomaly, I thought, a single albino among the dark masses. But I looked around and found two more. Three. I completed my tally at five. Had they been there a long time, and I hadn't noticed them? Or had they just sprouted suddenly? Once I'd heard a discussion on a talk radio program of people who had gone gray in a matter of moments. A sudden death in the family or a serious scare, and in a moment, their hair had all turned white. The hair on their heads, that was. But still. I guess it could be any hair. Same process, right? Maybe the dream about the biker, though not bad enough to make all the hair on my head turn white, had been just bad enough to zap the pigment from five pubic hairs. I looked again. Maybe I should see a doctor. Maybe I had a vitamin deficiency or too much stress.

I considered pulling the hairs out and tried one. The pain stopped me. And didn't people say that if you pulled out a gray hair, two more would grow in its place? Then I'd have *ten!* In the end, I didn't do anything about the hairs. Instead, I put on my clothes.

I was boiling water for coffee when there was a knock on my door.

After thinking about it a few seconds, I went to the door. I didn't get many visitors. My place was at the back of an old stucco two-story house. The old lady who owned the house lives on the second floor; a family lived on the first in front. My apartment was just one room for living and sleeping, plus a bathroom and a kitchen. I didn't get too many door-to-door salespeople, as they didn't realize there was another unit back there.

I opened the door and there was Kevin, a friend I hadn't seen in quite a while. We grew up on the same street. Later we worked together at The Club, where I was still a bartender.

"Oh!" I said, startled to see him. "Hey. What's up?" I smiled and slugged him on the shoulder before backing up to let him in. Kevin was one of the guys I was thinking of earlier with the hair peninsulas. He was married and had two kids and another one on the way. He met his wife at one of those software mills in Sorrento Valley, where they both still worked, as far as I knew. She was a little younger than we were. He had a first marriage that didn't work out. Whenever he wanted to remember what he had lost with the passing of his youth, he called me for comp tickets to a show. I hadn't seen him in six months or so, since the last time Steve Poltz played at The Club.

"What are you doing here?" I said. "This is a surprise!" I didn't think he'd ever been to my place before. But since I had been living in this house for as many years as I had worked at The Club, I was not hard to locate, if you were willing to put even a small amount of effort into it.

"I had to talk to you. Kind of important. Can I sit down? Do you have a minute?"

"Sure," I said. "Help yourself. Do you want some coffee or something? I was just about to—"

"No, thanks," he said. "I only drink it in the morning."

It was 12:30. He must have been on his lunch break.

"Listen," he said. And then he looked at me for a minute without saying anything. He exhaled and glanced at my row of guitars, my unmade bed. "Do you remember Diana?"

"Diana? Hmm. Diana?" This was a bluff. Of course I remembered her. I used to be in love with her. We were together for a few months. One minute she was asking me if I was ever going to get rid of my motorcycle and get a car so other people could ride with me without freezing and wrecking their hair, and the next minute she was gone. Untraceable.

"From The Club. You worked with her," Kevin explained. "Waitress?" he said.

"How long ago?"

"Come on, Good. I know you remember her. About ten, eleven years ago. Blond hair. Beautiful. Smart. She was in graduate school. Education." He clicked his fingers. "Snap out of it! You guys were together for two months! Maybe three."

"OK, anyway, what about her?" I was bracing myself. I could almost feel that something bad was coming. She was dead, and it was my fault. Or he and Diana wanted to use my place. No one knew him in this neighborhood, and he would promise it wouldn't be often—poor Cathy! Quickly, I made my decision: I would do the Nancy Reagan thing and just say no. I would say, "Kevin, it's none of my business, but why don't you and Cathy get some counseling? You've got a couple of great kids, another on the way—"

"Listen, we ran into her," Kevin said. "We saw Diana. Geneva started kindergarten this year, and Diana works at her school, Corona Vista Elementary. She's a speech therapist there. She and Cathy started talking, and it turns out Diana's a single mom who lives not too far from us. So anyway, Cathy invited her over for dinner."

"*Yeah?*" I said, trying to urge him to get to the point.

"So she shows up with her kid. Her son."

"OK," I said. Single mom. I didn't like the direction this conversation was going. I had an almost irrepressible urge to throw him out before he continued his story, to open my front door and point outside. This was a man I liked, a man I'd hung out with, a man whose wedding I'd ushered. I almost said, "Get out of here and don't come back!" But then I sort of watched myself not do this. In a way, I waited to see what was going to happen next.

"Good, listen to me." His voice got softer until he almost whispered. "The kid looks exactly like you."

All the blood evacuated from my head, and my armpits started to drip. "What?" I said.

"Yeah," Kevin went on. "Same dark hair with that cowlick right over here, same mouth. Good, he's even got glasses."

"What?" I said. Eloquent, I know.

"He looks exactly like you in the fifth grade! He's *in* fifth grade. Same school where she works, Corona Vista. So is this just some huge, weird coincidence? Should I back off and just never mention it again? Could it be a fluke to find a kid who looks just like you in the fifth grade and happens to be the child of one of your old girlfriends—"

"Diane, you said?"

"Dian*a,*" he said, shaking his head.

"Blond hair?" I said. I scratched my head. "Brown eyes. She wore a silver necklace with a tiny star on it?"

"I don't remember that. Maybe I wasn't—"

"She was trying to finish graduate school without borrowing any more money, so she had to live with her parents. It drove her nuts the way her mother would always ask her what time she was coming home and what she wanted for dinner. And her father was—"

"But you said you didn't—"

"But I do," I said. "I do." I lowered my head and looked longingly at the floor. I am not proud to say that there was nothing I wanted more than to crawl under my bed.

We sat there for a long time not saying anything. I swallowed and looked out the window. Kevin looked at his hands and then at his feet. Finally, after a long time, he said, "So what are you going to do?"

"I don't know," I said. "I seriously have no idea." I was thinking, *Do I have to* do *something?* I looked at my row of guitars. I wanted to pick one up so badly, just to play a few notes, a familiar chord or two. But this was exactly the kind of moment when it would seem heartless and unfeeling to pick up a guitar. Too bad that this was also the exact kind of moment when I needed one most.

"I know what I'd do," Kevin said. "I'd call her. I'd want to meet the kid. I'd definitely make contact. Right away. Immediately."

I didn't respond. I didn't say, "Easy for you to say, Mr. Suburbia!" I just sat there willing him to leave. I liked Kevin; I really did, but he really had no idea what my life was like. Right now I just wanted him to get the hell out of my house.

"I guess I'll go," he said. "I should get back to work." He stood up and moved to the door.

For once, my wish had come true. "Yeah," I said. "OK." I didn't even get up as he walked out. I just sat there.

three

After you find out for the first time that you have a kid, it is hard to know what to do with the rest of your day. First, I called a somewhat new bartender, who I knew was saving for a better car, and I asked him to work for me that night.

"Sure," he said easily, without even thinking about it.

" 'Preciate it," I said.

I hung up. Now I had given myself this whole load of free time, but I knew how to fill it up. I chose a guitar and went into my music room to play it.

When I first moved here, I built a miniature music studio in my place. It was off the main room in what used to be a closet. It was a walk-in closet, almost a small room. I saw the potential the first time I looked at the apartment. It may have been the reason I decided to move here. So I soundproofed it with some dense foam. I rigged it so that there were plenty of electrical outlets in there. The cracks in the door were covered with extra strips of foam. I had never had a complaint about the noise, and I played in there every day. I didn't think Jeanette, the old lady upstairs who owned the house, even knew I played guitar. I had all my recording equipment on shelves along one closet wall. It was old stuff that I got a long time ago, but it still worked. On a shelf above that were all the tapes I'd made.

I must have stayed in there for over two hours because when I came out, I could hear that the kids from next door were home from school.

I got my keys and went outside. The oldest of the neighbor kids, a skinny girl with hair the color of wet straw, was nine. I knew this because she had recently had a very noisy Saturday morning birthday party that woke me up at ten o'clock, hours before I was ready. Her name was Elise, pronounced "A Lease." Mike was a few years younger than Elise and stockier, with their father's brown hair and eyes. Then came Maddy, a girl who had curly brown hair, followed by Ray, who looked like Elise, long and thin with light hair. He was still in diapers. No, wait, checking him out now, as he scooped a shovelful of dirt into his empty shoe, I saw that he wasn't wearing a diaper. Maybe he hadn't been for a while. Their mother, Robin, must be inside, watching from a window. Their father used to live here, too, but he'd moved out some time ago.

Elise was loading Maddy and Mike into an orange plastic wagon, while Ray added more dirt into his shoe. The two passengers jerked backward and then forward as Elise took off too fast. There was a slight slope to the sidewalk and she started to trot down it, with the two of them screaming with joy. They were getting awfully close to the end of the sidewalk, I noticed, craning my neck and taking a deep breath. But just before she reached the stop sign and the traffic, Elise turned the wagon sharply to the left. Maddy and Mike tumbled out onto the sidewalk and started to cry.

Elise said, "You guys didn't hold on! I *told* you to hold on tight!" She dropped the wagon handle, crossed her arms, and started to walk back to the house. "Babies!" she snarled over her shoulder. Then she lifted her eyes and saw me.

Elise went back to Maddy. "Are you OK, honey?" she squeaked in the voice of a girl playing mother to her dolls. She patted Maddy's back. "I'll get you guys some juice." She hugged Mike hard, glancing over her shoulder to make sure that I was getting this.

I looked at the mailbox, walked to it, opened its door, and removed a pile of crap addressed to me. "I'm not the kind of adult who will get you in trouble," I wanted to tell Elise. "You're thinking of real grown-ups—parents and teachers, not me." I looked through the mail, put it back in my box, and closed the little door.

I put on my helmet, got on my motorcycle, and took off as though I had a destination.

I ended up at a shopping mall in a part of town that I hardly ever visited. Everywhere I looked today, there seemed to be children. Since the last time I came here, they'd put in a fountain, a thing that shot water up out of the pavement in unpredictable squirts that seemed to invite kids to get their clothes wet. And there were all these stores that specialized in cartoon characters and tiny clothes and toys.

I walked into the Discovery Channel Store and wandered around, picking things up and putting them down. There was music on, of course, the way there was music everywhere these days. I had a problem with this. The song playing in the store was Sinéad O'Connor's "Nothing Compares 2 U." And right there, in the middle of the store, I had what I called a music-induced flashback. It happened all the time. I had strong associations to most pop songs going all the way back to the sixties. I heard a song and everything that was going on at the time came pouring into my head.

Diana happened to love this song. She had blond hair that she washed every morning. Her conditioner smelled really excellent. Her parents lived in Encinitas. She didn't like mushrooms or any kind of nuts. She was extremely ticklish. Right before she left, we had a horrible fight. She cried. I remember what she said. I remember all of it, and now with this song playing, there wasn't any way in the world I was going to be able to get her words out of my brain. She said, "Are you ever going to buy a car? No, you are not. I don't believe you will ever, *ever* buy a car. Your whole life. You should get a better place to live and some different clothes. Why on earth do you have to buy your T-shirts, socks, underwear, jeans in quantity once a year at Kmart? Couldn't you just go shopping at a different store every now and then? A normal store? Does every single shirt have to be a pocket T from Kmart? And why would a talented person like you waste his life being a bartender? I really want to know. Really."

Here she waited for me to say something. She was crying. I didn't say anything, so she went on.

"Why can't you just be normal?" I think she asked me that. But maybe I just remember it from knowing what she meant. I didn't have any satisfactory answers to any of her questions. She left. I thought she was coming back. I really did, and I planned to explain myself to her. I was going to sit her down for a long talk. I would start from the beginning and not stop until I got up to the present day. I thought she would be gone a few hours at most. She left a turquoise sweatshirt that said GAP on it; a book she was reading, opened to page 261, her toothpaste, shampoo, and some of that conditioner I liked.

She didn't come back. I was wrong about that. I still had her stuff in a bag from Trader Joe's in an upper kitchen cupboard. The conditioner had probably completely solidified by now.

As I was looking at a small fountain suitable for use on a coffee table or desktop, "I'm a Believer" came on. With a song like that, I had a double-decker dose of memories. First came a flash of the

Monkees' version and the pin-striped bell-bottoms I had in seventh grade. Then came this new Smash Mouth version that I heard for the first time over at my sister's place. She was depressed about her job; we were eating minestrone. It's not necessarily a pleasant experience to continually rewind your own life and the history of rock and roll and watch it again and again in unrelated sections as you walk through grocery store aisles or wait in line at the bank or fill your tank with gas or watch a car commercial on television. I took earplugs with me wherever I went, and I wished they worked better. I wished they were 100 percent effective, because to be honest, there wasn't much about my life that I want to relive.

Just then in the store, I saw something that seemed to be exactly what I had been looking for. I picked it up. It was a lightning maker. Inside a glass bulb, flashes of purple lightning were happening over and over again. How did they do that? I wanted it. I put the sample back on the shelf, picked up one of the boxes, and walked to the counter with it. I pulled a wad of one-dollar bills out of my pocket—tips—and counted out the right number.

"Would you like to join our Discover Club?" the boy behind the register asked me.

"What? Oh. No," I said.

"It's a really good deal," he told me. "See every time you—"

"No," I said. "Really, no, thank you." I didn't plan to make a habit of this. Besides, I wanted to get out of the store before another song came on.

I walked out with my lightning ball. I was going to put it on a shelf next to my bed and watch it at night when I couldn't sleep. I was looking *forward* to not being able to sleep.

f o u r

By the time I got home, it was dark. I'd used a bungee cord to strap the lightning maker to the back of the seat for the ride home. Bags are a problem on a motorcycle. The trick is not to buy much. These days, I had a car too, but it was parked on the street. I didn't use it very often. It had surprisingly few miles on it for an old car. I parked my bike on one side of the garage next to Robin's car.

I was going to go inside, but at the last second, I decided not to. Instead, I walked down to the 7-Eleven to get some ice cream. There was music on, of course. This one had strong enough associations to require earplugs, but I decided to just grab something quick and hurry home as fast as possible. The song was "We Can Work It Out" by the Beatles. As ever, it brought an instant lump to my throat. First, there was the song itself, a guy trying to convince his girlfriend to stay, because life is short. Then there was the image of my brother and a new guitar that he had saved up for. He could play very well for a ninth-grader. There was no doubt in anybody's mind that he would one day be every bit as good on that guitar as George Harrison, his favorite Beatle. I defy you to get through even one day of normal life without hearing some version somewhere of some Beatle song. If you think you've done it, you probably were not paying attention. Whether you acknowledge it or not, those songs are in you, and even on the rare day when you don't hear one on a radio or a PA, you hear it in your head, your heart, your soul.

Now I had a pint of Heath Bar Crunch in one hand and a pint of Mud Pie Madness in the other, and I was telling myself, "Decide!" when a bright orange shape caught my eye. It was Jeanette, my elderly upstairs neighbor. Tonight she was wearing a ski parka, even though it was only slightly cool. The jacket was a castoff from some kid, judging from the look and size of it. She was leaning on her aluminum walker and staring intently at a can of nuts, concentrating so hard that she didn't notice me. I backed up and went around the magazines to the cashier so I wouldn't have to talk to Jeanette and could get away fast from the song.

I was just getting my change when her sharp voice zinged right through my eardrums. "Well, don't say hi or anything!" I nearly jumped out of my skin. Jeanette's voice was another reason for earplugs, which were lying unused in my pocket. I think the last time I heard that phrase was junior high.

I turned around and acted surprised. "Oh, hello, Jeanette! What are you doing here at this hour?"

She held up the can. "Have to have my peanuts! I was all out! Midnight snack! Had to make sure they're not low-salt! They're not!" She said everything loudly, as if every sentence were a surprising announcement, like "I won!" or "It's twins!" She hurt my ears. She smelled like a combination of fabric softener and green Life Savers. It wasn't a bad smell, just distinctive.

"Uh-huh," I said. "Well, good night!" You had to be abrupt with Jeanette or before you knew it, you were in the middle of a long, long story about something that had happened in the 1930s on the way to her piano lesson or about the trash the gardener found in the bushes this morning. Jeanette had a lot of material to draw on. I picked up my bag and started quickly for the door. I still had the lightning maker with me, and I was eager to get home and plug it in.

"Wait a second!" said the girl at the register. I turned around, expecting to find that I'd left my wallet on the counter. But there was nothing, just the cashier glaring at me.

"What?" I said. "Me?"

"You have to walk her home! God! It's *dark*. Don't you guys live, like, right *by* each other? Walk her home!"

"Thank you," Jeanette said, smiling at me, as if I'd offered.

I glared at the girl. She busied herself straightening the packages of beef jerky standing up in a jar and didn't look at me. Next time I was in here, I would make sure to tell that girl that Jeanette was more than capable of walking home or any number of other places with no help from anybody. And furthermore, the girl had no business inflicting neighbors on one another. She had no idea, none whatsoever, how many long, pointless, boring stories Jeanette had up her baggy old sleeve. In seventeen years, probably more years than the girl had spent on this planet, I had listened to way more than my share of them.

I waited for Jeanette at the door. I held it open for her with one foot. The Beatles were finishing up, reminding me again about life being short, but they obviously had never met Jeanette. As she was shuffling through the door with her walker, I glared back at the girl behind the counter, one more try at punishing her. She was busy looking through a magazine about hairstyles and refused to look up and take the wrath of my burning stare, even though she knew she had it coming. All the way home, Jeanette told me about the school she had worked in for thirty years. She had walked this very same way every morning and evening on her way to and from work. "This was before the fitness craze! We only had one car! My husband took it to work! Every day, rain or shine, I'd walk! I didn't mind it one bit! Some of those kids, even the itty-bitty ones, are grandparents now! Can you believe that? And here I am walking down the very same street. I'm lucky, that's what! Lucky to be healthy and living on my own all this time!"

Whenever she'd pause, I'd think I was supposed to say something. I'd say, "You sure are" or "That's right." And then she would go on. One time I didn't say anything, just to see if it had any effect on the conversation. It didn't. After about the same amount of pause time, she went on with her story anyway. So I didn't bother anymore with the filler comments. Jeanette didn't need me at all. If I had managed to escape from the store, she might have told these exact same stories without me. When I first moved in, I thought of Jeanette as an old, old lady. She would be outside in a giant straw hat, squatting in the dirt, planting flowers in front of the house. Back then, I used to think that she would die any minute because she looked so ancient. She was in her early seventies when I first moved in. Now she rarely came downstairs, let alone planted anything. Her *children* were in their sixties. As the kids in the neighborhood grew bigger, Jeanette seemed to shrink. Her dresses were baggy, loose things now that she had to fold and cinch with a belt. She didn't even have a cane when I first moved in, and now she had a walker.

She used to be the secretary of the public elementary school down the street. I think that was how she got so good at watching and listening to everything that was going on, staying informed without being told anything. If you bought anything new, Jeanette would call down from her door, "How much did you pay for that?" as you carried it in from the car. After you told her, she would let you know where you could have gotten it cheaper, if only you'd come to her first. If you brought anybody home, Jeanette would provide an uninvited assessment: "The prettiest ones don't stay, you know" or "She's going to starve to death if she doesn't eat something. And I mean today!" Often, she had instructed me, "Just pick one and marry her. One of these days, if you're lucky, you're going to be as old as I am. And believe me, you won't always have so many to choose from."

Finally, we reached the house. It seemed like hours since we'd left the store. "You've been awfully quiet," she said. "The strong silent type! Now, run up there with my walker, would you? Thank you, dear."

I did. I didn't actually run. I took the steps two at a time, though, as I wanted this to be over with as soon as possible, and it had been annoying to walk so slowly.

When I got back downstairs, Jeanette was only on the second step, grasping the banister with both hands.

"See you, Jeanette," I called without waiting to hear her answer.

By the time I got into my apartment, my ice cream was squishy.

Without turning on another light, I plugged in my lightning maker. I stood watching it, eating my ice cream out of the container.

f i v e

I was having dinner with my sister, Ellen, again. I had brought frosted brownies from the Vons bakery, which she wouldn't eat. She always asks me to bring dessert and then she tries not to eat it because of the calories.

"So how's work?" I asked her, dipping a fork into the brownie pan. My sister was a lawyer.

"Are you going to eat that whole thing?" Ellen asked me. "Don't you want to put it on a plate?"

"I might eat the whole thing. I've done it before, and nothing bad happened," I said.

"I hate to think how much fat is in that."

I got a knife out of a drawer and cut a corner piece. "So how's work?" I asked again. My sister hated her job, and usually we avoided this topic.

"Work is the same as ever, busy and complicated. Why?"

"I was just wondering what kind of stuff you're working on. What kind of cases do you have right now?"

"The usual stuff. You know, a little carpal tunnel, some back injuries. A neck thing. Why? Did you get injured at work? Do you need representation?"

"No, not that. I was just wondering if you ever had any of those cases where, like, a mother of a kid sues the father, even though they were never married and maybe he didn't even know about the kid."

My sister froze and looked at me. "Uh...," she said. "You know I don't do that kind of thing."

"Yeah," I said. "I guess I did know that."

"So...are you trying to tell me something? Is someone—did something happen?"

I didn't say anything. I swallowed because my throat suddenly felt thick and tight.

"Tom?" she said. "What's going on?"

I looked up at her and still didn't say anything.

"Is somebody suing you?" Her eyes narrowed. She was willing to go to battle for me; I knew that.

I shook my head. "No." The word came out as if someone had both hands around my throat.

She waited, just sitting there, not saying anything, just like a therapist would. There were all these dishes piled up all over the table, and I looked at them, as if I were taking inventory.

"I think I have a kid," I said. "Kevin told me. There was this girl. Woman. I was seeing her for a while. A long time ago. She left. She moved. Now she's, you know, back. In San Diego. And I think she had, you know, I think we—"

"OK, OK," Ellen said. "So she hasn't contacted you directly. It's just that Kevin said—what *did* Kevin say?"

"He said she had a ten-year-old boy who looks exactly the way I looked in fifth grade."

"Oh," she said, thinking. "OK. Well."

"Well, it's good that she hasn't asked me for anything," I said. "Don't you think that's a good sign?"

"I guess it is." She nodded slowly. "I guess it could be. Wait. What do you mean? A good sign of what?"

"I meant that if she hasn't contacted me, he's probably not my kid?" I was asking her, not telling her.

She sat there for a minute or two. "I guess it might mean that."

We both waited for one of us to talk again. I decided it wouldn't be me.

Ellen didn't speak for a long time. Then she took the knife from my side of the table and cut the opposite brownie corner from the one I had cut. She got up and got a plate and a fork. She sat down and started on her brownie. "Do you want to get in touch with her?" Ellen said.

"Me? What? Why would I . . . Not if, no—I—I honestly don't know what to do."

"Sounds like you have time to think it over, if she hasn't come to you to ask for anything."

I waited until Ellen put down her brownie fork before I stood up. I started clearing the dishes, my job. Ellen was taking stuff off the table, putting it into the fridge. I rinsed the dishes, put them into the dishwasher.

"What was she like?" Ellen wanted to know.

"Who?" I could be really annoying. Ellen must have wanted to slug me sometimes, but she never did. I knew I was being annoying, and I did nothing to stop myself.

"The *woman,*" Ellen said. "You *dated.*"

I let a glass fill up with water.

My sister let out a gust of frustration. Then she said, "The woman who might've had your child! Who do you *think* I'm talking about?"

"Diana. That's her name. She was, she was blond and small. She had freckles and—"

"Cut it out. *Personality.* What was her personality like?"

"Nice," I said. "She was nice."

She mimed tugging a rope out of my stomach, like it was a huge effort to haul any information out of me.

"Kind of, you know, independent. Smart. Stubborn. She liked to do things her way."

"How long were you together?"

"Not long. A few months. This was ages ago, so a lot of it is—"

"I understand. I think you should take some action. Right away."

I looked at her. My sister doesn't usually tell me what to do. She's more the whatever-feels-right-for-you type.

I finished the plates and glasses. I picked up a sponge and started wiping the counters. "What kind of action were you thinking? Just for example," I said. But now it had been so long since she said the thing about taking action that her thoughts had probably moved on to something else. "You said I should take some action. About the woman? Diana?"

"No—I know what you're talking about, Tom. I'm just thinking. Well, you know, nothing complicated. Get in touch. Call her," Ellen said. "Talk to her?"

"Just like that? Out of the blue? I don't want to freak her out."

"Fine. OK. Then ask Kevin to ask her if it's OK to give you her phone number. That way she can say no if she wants to. She gets some warning. And you get to test the waters."

"But if she's in the phone book, then it's OK to just call. I mean, anybody can call, right? It's, you know, public information if it's listed. It's not an invasion of anybody's privacy if you look up a number and dial it. Is it?"

"No," she said. "Of course not. But you just said you didn't want to freak her out."

"I don't."

"But OK, if she's listed, you could just call."

"If I go through Kevin, then I have to deal with him giving me his opinion and lectures and who knows what all."

"I see what you mean."

"I'll write her a note!" I said.

"Good idea."

"What should I say?"

"Tom!" She exhaled as though she were fed up with the questions, but I knew she could handle it. My sister had a lot of patience, and I gave her plenty of opportunities to put it to use. "Say you heard from Kevin that she had moved back here. Say you were wondering if she would please get in touch with you, that you'd like to talk to her."

I nodded. "What if she says no?"

"If she says no, we'll think up a Plan B."

I smiled at her. I knew Ellen would help me. I loved Ellen.

At home, I looked around for something to write the note on. I had a lined yellow pad that I wrote songs on. I found a pen. I wrote:

Dear Diana,
Kevin told me that you had moved back into the area. I was wondering if you could give me a call sometime. I'd like to talk to you.

Then I put my phone number. I signed my name. Under it, I wrote, "P.S. Please call!!" I looked at it. Wrong. The note was OK until the P.S., which ruined it. I tore off the page and started over. I thought I'd make it a little more informative.

You will not be surprised to hear that I am still working at The Club.

Wait. Why wouldn't she be surprised? Was I assuming that she thought I was in exactly the same place as when she left? Plenty of people had the same job. That was stability, which could be a good thing, a positive character trait. I guess it made a difference what the job was. If you taught high school for seventeen years, then you were a stable, contributing member of society, somebody making a difference. I pictured a small boy watching me work. I looked like a TV character somehow, wiping down the bar, making drinks, watching the band onstage. If he had been born the day I started the job, he would be almost finished with high school now. OK, I didn't have to mention the job. It wasn't the whole story about me. I did other things. Bartending didn't define me, after all. It was what I did, not who I was. I did not need to explain to Diana or anybody why I was still doing it.

I rewrote the note:

Dear Diana,
I hear you're back in the area. Please give me a call.
Good.

I looked it over. I flipped to a clean page.

Diana—
Call me.
Good

I put my phone number at the bottom. I found an envelope and wrote Diana's name on it. I looked up the address of the school Kevin's daughter went to and found a stamp. I walked down to the corner to put it in the mailbox so that I wouldn't chicken out after a good night's sleep.

When I got back from the mailbox, my place looked different, as if someone had tampered with it while I was out. It wasn't that anything was missing or had been added. It was just that it seemed to have shrunk. And the lamp shade over by my bed had a tear I hadn't seen before. The paint on the walls had gotten dingy. Wasn't it a lot whiter just a few minutes ago? I looked into the refrigerator and found no real food and some dried up brown spills on the shelves. My phone looked old-fashioned, like something an elderly person might cling to, insisting that it worked *fine*. My television was a black-and-white Kenmore that I'd grabbed off my parents' Salvation Army pile years ago. I really ought to throw that thing away. The antenna was broken off, and replaced with a straightened hanger. It was too much trouble to keep one hand on the hanger to improve its reception, so I never watched it. The clothes I'd left in a heap on a chair seemed like a random assortment of nondescript rags. The windows were dirty. An old flowered comforter, one of my mother's castoffs, lay in a jumbled mess on the bed. The place looked—I had a startling stab in my chest with this thought—like a crazy person lived here and had for a long time.

I brushed my teeth and got in bed quickly. I wrapped my funky old comforter all around myself as if I were making a cocoon. I pulled it over my head, a hood. Then I closed my eyes, and I was gone.

s i x

I had to go to work. At 5:15, I took a shower and washed my hair. I put on a pair of clean jeans and a black T-shirt with a button-down plaid shirt over it. I put on clean white socks and sneakers, Converse high-tops, black. My standard uniform. I was ready at 5:22. At 5:30, I walked through the front door of The Club. You had to be there at 5:30 to get dinner. I don't know why I bothered, but I ate here every work night. Tonight it was lasagna—vegetarian, luckily, because I have not eaten meat, at least not on purpose, since eighth grade when I read that George Harrison was a vegetarian.

"Good, how're you doing, man?" said the chef, James, who had worked here even longer than I had.

"I'm doing OK, James," I said, though now he was not listening to me anymore but sliding plates at other employees.

"No, you may not order something from the menu!" James shouted at a new waitress. "This ain't good enough for you, you eat at home tomorrow night!"

"God, *sorry,*" the girl said.

She was going to have a long night. She had on a striped T-shirt, and her hair was pulled back into a tight ponytail. She looked too young to be in here, but lately I thought that about every new hire. I went to the walk-in box and got a can of orange juice for my bar. Walking back through the kitchen, I could feel the greasy wooden boards through my shoes. For the most part, I did my best to stay out of the kitchen. The constant tension between the waitresses and the kitchen staff made for a stressful atmosphere.

I walked to the bar at the front of the club. Roxanne, a waitress, was setting up her station, wiping down her tables and straightening the chairs. "Hey, Good," she said.

"Hey, Roxanne."

Three more waitresses were eating dinner together. "Good," one of them called. "How many tickets are sold?"

"Twenty-seven. Almost nothing," I said. Everyone knew I always checked ticket sales on my way in. I liked to know what to expect.

"How much did you make last time these guys played?" another waitress, Mary, asked me.

"You don't want to know."

"I do. Tell me."

"Fourteen dollars." I always remembered the exact number of dollars I earned in tips for each band who played here. I didn't try to; the figure just attached itself to my brain and stayed there, another quirk of my annoying memory.

"Time before that?" Mary wanted to know.

"Time before that it was nineteen. Sorry, ladies. This is not going to be your best night."

"Oh, no!" Mary put her head down on the table. "How do you stand it? I'm going to have to ask my parents for money again!"

I set my dinner down on the bar and emptied the can of frozen orange juice into a pitcher, which I filled with hot water. When it was full, I turned off the water and ate my dinner. By the time I was finished eating, about three minutes later, the orange juice was melted enough to stir. I made some Tom Collins mix also, which I probably would end up pouring down the drain, and a pitcher of margarita mix. Weezer was playing on the sound system, and a roadie was on the stage taping down cords.

The roadie straightened up and looked at me. "Good!" he said. "You still here?"

After a while, you get tired of hearing the same question over and over. "Yeah, looks like it," I said. "How long you been working for these guys?"

"Few months." The roadie rolled his eyes and shook his head. "I'm too old for this," he said. "And so are you!"

"Apparently not," I said, "since we're both still doing it."

I got the cherries, lemons, limes, and oranges out of the small fridge under the bar.

The door to the front office opened, and Elvis stepped out. His name isn't really Elvis. Everyone just called him that because he started work at 3:00 in the box office and left at 11:00 every night, right after the second show started. If you looked for him during the late show or at closing time, he was always gone. "Elvis has left the building," everyone said.

Elvis said, "Good, somebody here to see you. A woman."

My stomach dropped. I took a deep breath. "Is it my sister?" I asked Elvis hopefully.

Elvis shook his head. "It's someone I've never seen." He went back into the office. He had worked here five years or so, still a new guy, compared to me.

I walked out the front door. I didn't see anybody for a minute. Nobody at all. Then she stepped out from around the corner. She had expected me to come out the kitchen door, so she had been waiting over there. She was wearing a pale blue T-shirt and denim shorts. She didn't have a purse, and she was holding her car keys, meaning she wasn't staying.

"Diana," I said.

"Good," she said. She didn't smile or throw her arms around my neck. Far from it. She pressed her lips together into a thin line. "What'd you want to talk to me about?" she said.

"Oh, I—I just wanted to—I thought we should—"

She nodded as if she knew what I was trying to say, even if I didn't. "Be in touch," she said. "Well. So. We are."

"Yeah, well," I said. "That's, that's good." My mouth was all dry. "Right? Isn't it?"

"I don't know," she said. "What exactly did you want to be in touch *about?*"

"Oh," I said. I put my hand on my hair. "I'm sorry if I—I sure didn't mean to—"

"Whatever," she said. "Anyway, what's up?"

"Kevin came over. To my house. The other day. He told me you had a kid, a boy."

"Yep." The mouth line again.

I lowered my voice to almost a whisper. "And he also said the boy looked just like me." There was traffic noise on the street and a little breeze, so it was possible that my words might not even reach her.

"What! No, he doesn't!" she snapped.

"I'm sorry—I thought—Kevin said—so your son is—" I could breathe a little now as relief started to spread through me.

"He has my eyebrows totally and my ears!"

"Oh. Right, I—"

"Yeah. People say all the time how much he looks like me! All the time. OK, not that often, but sometimes."

"Oh," I said. I was nodding, trying not to make her mad. "Sure. I'm sure they do, after all he's your—"

"OK, maybe he does look a little more like you than like me."

There was a thud inside The Club. A door slamming? An amplifier case being dropped from the stage?

Diana scowled. "But he has my personality! And he thinks like *me!*"

"Thank God for that," I managed to say. "That's a lucky break for everyone, isn't it? So, so he is, you're saying he's my—"

"He's *mine*, Good. Some of your DNA, maybe, but entirely my child. Understand? I know all these fathers sue for custody. It's like the fashion or something. I've heard about all that, but if you even think for one minute that I would—"

"No way," I said, moving my head quickly, almost violently, back and forth in short insistent no's. I put my hands up, open palms out, as if to show that I was not concealing any weapons. "I wouldn't even—"

"You better not!"

"I won't. I swear." I kept my hands up and backed up a couple of steps.

"So why did you call me, then?" she wanted to know. She folded her arms.

"I wanted to know," I said. "I just—wanted to know. About him. If he—you know if he was—not *mine*, of course, I know he's *yours*, but if my, um, genes had been, you know, involved. Way back. At the beginning." I sounded like a complete idiot.

"Well, now you know," she said.

"OK," I said.

"Fine."

"Fine," I said.

There was a long, miserable pause. She looked at me. I looked around as if searching for an exit sign, but we were outside.

Finally, she said, "I'm going to go now."

"OK," I said.

She turned around and started walking. "Bye," I said. "Bye, Diana."

She didn't answer.

I stayed outside for a few more minutes, and I saw her drive away. She had a little purple car, one of those updated Beetles. It was a nice purple, a tasteful purple. I kept standing there, even after the car was gone.

"Good, man, you OK?" Elvis was leaning out the front door.

"Me? Oh, yeah. Superb. You? How are you doing, Elvis?"

"Really, can I get you anything?"

"What do you mean?" I said. "I'm fine. Just enjoying the night air."

"I'm sure. You have no color in your face and this expression like you just witnessed an accident."

"Oh, that," I said. "That's just my—Are we ready to open?"

"Yeah," said Elvis, "all ready. All systems are go. Except there are no people here."

"I better get behind the bar then," I said, as if he had told me a crowd of customers were banging their fists against the bar, demanding to be served. I went inside.

All the kids were home next door, and it was a Wednesday. I was positive that it was a Wednesday. Pretty sure. Or Thursday, maybe. I woke up at 7:30 because of the racket over there. Somebody got all of something and didn't leave any for anybody else. But it was nothing to cry about. Their mother, Robin, would get some more; she promised. But today? Would it be *today* that she would get some more, or in a long, long, long time? It would be today. She promised that, too. Really.

It was some kind of cereal that they wanted, probably. Or gum. These kids had an irrational passion for gum. I had overheard a lot of these conversations. But you *said* you would *yesterday*, the complainer insisted, you promised. I said I would *try*, came the response, and I *did* try, but there wasn't enough time left and then I had to pick you guys up. It isn't *my* fault. I didn't *say* it was your fault. I said it was time for me to pick you up. And so on. Back when the husband was here—Vic, his name was—he would eventually explode, then there would be silence, followed by crying. I wasn't sure which was worse, the yelling and crying or the whining and promising.

At 8:05 exactly, they all started crashing out the side door to go to their car. Now it would be quiet, and I could go back to sleep.

Trouble was, I didn't. I lay there and surveyed my apartment again. Usually, my belongings were invisible to me, I was so used to them. Now that I had found out about Diana and her son, I was staring at everything as if I were about to file a detailed report.

From the survey of the shortcomings of my belongings, I moved on to a review of my scene with Diana the night before. I handled that wrong. I hadn't said what I wanted to at all. Now the two topics converged, and all I could think of was what Diana would see if she walked in here. She wouldn't like it at all, I knew that. She wouldn't like my *patterns,* if you know what I mean, and they were far too well established for Diana. I could just see the way she would count off my patterns on her fingers:

Clothes: I only wore certain clothes. In my early twenties, I developed a kind of uniform that didn't vary too often, the pocket T-shirts from Kmart and Levi's and cotton sweatshirts from Miller's Outpost. I did my clothes shopping in one day, once a year. I did not own a pair of shorts, pajamas, a bathing suit, or a raincoat. These were extra things that I did not need.

Food and drink: I drank flavored instant coffee that came in a can. You could get it in vanilla, hazelnut, and chocolate mint. I liked chocolate mint the best. For breakfast, I had frozen waffles with syrup. There were a lot of vitamins in those. They added that. For lunch, I bought sandwiches from different places. If I wasn't working, I ate a frozen dinner. There were spinach lasagna, tofu meat loaf. There's a lot of really good stuff out there these days. That was my diet. Oh, and orange juice with ice cubes. I thought it was varied enough. Occasionally, someone—my sister or a woman I was seeing—opened my fridge and had a fit about how little was in there. But what was I going to do—buy a whole bunch of stuff that was just going to go bad? Anyway, it didn't happen that often that someone opened my fridge, which brought us to...

People: My social circle was small. Tiny. Ellen may have been the one person I saw on purpose in those days.

At least I was aware of it. And when you're aware of something, you can change it, right? It's just a matter of deciding you want to.

Working in The Club wasn't all I did. Being a bartender was just a minor part of my existence. The rest of the time I played guitar. I wrote songs. That's the way I spent most of my time, as a matter of fact.

I used to be in a band. Not just *a* band, a band you've heard of, a band you know, a band almost everybody knows. It was possible that even Jeanette, my elderly landlady upstairs, had heard of my former band. It was Point Blank. I didn't usually talk about this. I avoided the topic as much as possible. Occasionally, a rock journalist or an avid Point Blank fan would hunt me down and feel convinced that they deserved answers to their questions about my life as a reward for their effort. But they were wrong. I didn't have to tell anybody anything. So they described me as "reclusive." Ha! The reclusive bartender.

You know the song "I'm Losing My Mind," right? Maybe you know all the words because at the time it was big, you were in love with your math teacher. Or you had just broken up with someone, and it fit so perfectly. Or maybe they played it at your wedding. Or you heard it last week on your parents' oldies station. Or you heard it in a couple of movies. Anyway, I wrote that song. And what about "Self-Destructive Tendencies"? You might be familiar with either Point Blank's version or maybe Aerosmith's. They were the first to cover it, and theirs was considered a "classic," if not an original. Then Sting did it, followed a few years later by Gloria Estefan, at which point the song reached a new audience, and so did Gloria. It was also in a bunch of movies that I'd never seen. And then there was "Worse Than Ever." As soon as you thought that the world had heard enough of that one, someone else covered it in some different musical genre. Last year, Clint Black did it. That one's mine too.

These songs and a few others had given me some income over the past twenty-odd years. I never added it up for a grand total, but you might be surprised at what a popular song can do for a person. I had a lot of the money still. I didn't do anything with it. What would I spend it on? I didn't need anything.

A long, long time ago, I left Point Blank, a band I had started myself. I quit. This was before they were famous, but things were just starting to come together. All the hard work was finally paying off. Their biggest gig at the time was playing The Club. Ironic, isn't it? I had gone no further.

Don't ask me what happened.

There had been lots of stories about it. I was a drug addict and/or a boozer, and the band threw me out. Or I was this egomaniac who insisted on having the band named after me. The Tom Good Experience, maybe, or The Good Band or something. Or there was a woman involved, and Adam Blackburn, the lead singer, and I were both in love with her. He won. He got the woman *and* the band. Or I got the woman, and he got the band. Wrong. Not true. None of the above. I didn't drink, and I'd never done drugs. I truly did not care what the band was called. Adam had been with the same woman since ninth grade, and I'd never settled on anyone in particular.

I had been asked why I left the band so many times that the faintest possibility of this question coming into a conversation caused me to grit my teeth and clench my fists. How could I give it all up? I just did, that's all. I quit. I didn't want to be in that band anymore. "So, why don't you write some more songs?" you proba-

bly want to ask. I did write songs, all the time. I wrote them and I
played them and I recorded them. I had all the tapes. I worked on
them every day of my life. In my music-studio closet.

"Why don't you start another band?" you probably want to
know too. And "Why don't you choose some of your songs and
play them all around the country and make a million dollars?"
Or, "Hey, you work in a club! Why don't you play *there?*" You
know, I'd been over this stuff with all kinds of people for years. I
didn't do those things. Period. I played every day. I practiced, and
I wrote songs. It wasn't a career; it was something I did. Alone in
my closet. With the door shut. I liked it that way.

I met Diana at The Club, and we were together for a couple of
months. I was crazy about Diana. Just hearing her move the water
in the bathtub in the next room was a thrill that could give me goose
bumps. I wrote about a thousand songs about Diana. OK, maybe
it was more like eight directly about her and another twelve or so
with portions she inspired. What can I tell you? I loved her. The
band sent me two tickets to the Grammy Awards that year.

After we had that big fight, I came back to the apartment after
work one night and there was a note, just like in a movie. It said,

Dear Good,
It won't be a big surprise to you to find out that I've decided
to go. This is not working for me, as I've told you many
times. I don't believe my future is here. Take care!

Diana

It was a surprise, of course. A more sensitive, less self-absorbed
individual than myself might have seen it coming. I did not. Sure,
we were arguing about my not having a "real" job or even ambi-
tion, my not having a "real" house, clothes, vehicle, etc. But that

wasn't at the center of what was happening with Diana and me. At the core was this: I could have been perfectly happy just looking at her every day for the rest of my life, watching her drink ginger ale through a straw or tuck her hair behind her ears. For that, to earn the right to look at her, smell her hair, and see her toes disappear as she put on her socks, I was willing to do just about anything. Anything. I would even have been willing to rake over my past and rethink some of those "patterns" that she found so offensive.

The night I got the note, I had looked in the two dresser drawers I'd cleared out for her to put clothes in—empty. I looked for her bike, which she kept locked and leaning against the side of the house—gone. I searched in the bathroom for her toothbrush—not there. I did find a few traces, which as I've mentioned, I put into a paper bag. She would have to come back for her things, I had told myself. I repeated these words many times for many weeks, finding them less and less convincing. As it turned out, conditioner was not a thing you come back for in a situation like this. Time passed, and I was glad that she left a few belongings, or I might have thought that I'd made her up. I didn't know where Diana went when she left, because she didn't get in touch with me again.

She left because she was pregnant. Ah. I saw that now. I did. All those discussions about whether I was ever going to do anything differently were about the baby she was going to have. Yeah. OK. It made sense now. She knew that being a father was not on my to-do list. She kept asking if I would ever buy a car. And here I was thinking those discussions were about, well, whether or not I wanted a car.

e i g h t

Apparently, I did fall asleep again, because I dreamed that Diana came to see me at The Club, but it went differently than it had in reality. She said, "I came back because I need help. I don't have any money, and Eddie needs a father." I woke up sweating from this dream. I didn't know what the kid's actual name was, though I was fairly certain that it wasn't Eddie.

The dream convinced me to get in touch with Diana again. The meeting we had was unsatisfactory. I hadn't said anything. I hadn't asked to see the kid's picture. I hadn't gotten his name. I could do better; I knew I could. And for some reason, now that I knew that Diana didn't want anything from me, I found that I was determined to give them something. I called information. "At the request of the customer," a machine told me, "that number is unpublished." I couldn't call her at work, of course.

Great. Just great. Now I would have to call Kevin. I really didn't want to talk to Kevin. "You'd better get a lawyer," he would tell me. Or, "She's not going to want to talk to *you.*" Or maybe he already knew that she had come to see me. "She wants you to leave her alone." Or, "She said she didn't want anything. What are you harassing her for? What do you want from her anyway?" Kevin would demand to know.

I wanted to see the kid. My kid. My son. I wanted to see my

son. He had my DNA; I was at least entitled to have a look at that cowlick.

Before I called Kevin, I rehearsed my possible responses to his comments and questions, explanations of my actions, excuses for my behavior. I got all sweaty thinking about it and put off calling. Then I realized that I could just say it was none of his business. I could say, "I'd prefer not to discuss it." Yeah. I didn't have to explain anything to Kevin. I braced myself and called him at work. He answered right away. "Hey," I said. "It's Good."

"Oh," he said. "Good."

I didn't know if he meant it was good that I called, or he was just confirming that it was me. This happened often. Without any preamble or small talk, I just said, "Could you give me Diana's phone number? Home number, if you have it?"

"I'll get it from Cathy and call you right back," he said. A minute later, the phone rang. He read me the number, complete with area code, which was the same as mine and the same as his.

"Thank you," I said.

"You're welcome," he said. "Take care." And he hung up without asking any questions or making any comments.

I put the phone number on the kitchen table next to my pile of unpaid bills I was planning to pay.

I went into my closet and closed the door. I practiced guitar solos from famous songs, "Day Tripper," "Born to Run," just whatever came to mind in no particular order. I like to think I can play anything if I listen carefully and practice a lot. There have been very few days since fourth grade that I have not picked up a guitar.

The only problem with my closet was that there was no ventilation. After two hours of playing, my hair was wet, my shirt was sticking to me, and I had to keep wiping my slick hands on my pants to keep them from slipping on the strings. I walked out, and the air felt cool, chilly almost, against my wet skin.

At 5:30, I dialed Diana's number. She answered right away.

"Hello, Diana?" I said.

"Yes," she said slowly, carefully. I hadn't thought about her voice, what it sounded like, when I saw her before. But now it did something to me. My legs felt watery, and my heart started thumping.

"This is Good."

There was a pause, a pretty long one.

"Oh...," she said. "I thought we were done."

"I, well, no, I guess I wasn't. Done."

"OK," she said. "What?"

"So, OK, so...how are you?"

"Fine." She didn't ask how I was.

"Glad to hear it. OK. Well, so anyhow, if you want to, you know, reach me, I'm at the same number as before. Maybe you don't still have it. Let me give it to you. It—"

"That's OK. I still have it."

"Oh, you do. Well, OK. So if you need anything, or you want to talk to me or anything, you can just—"

"Good?"

"Yes?"

"I don't. I'm sorry. That sounds mean, and I didn't mean it that way. It's just that I'm fine. I have a job I like and a nice place to live. I'm all set, and I don't want to mess it up now. And don't worry—I'm not going to come knocking on your door one day and ask for money or something. I'm not going to ask you for anything."

"Worry? I wasn't worried. I just thought—maybe you'd like to, you know, get together. For dinner or something. To talk."

This wasn't what I'd planned at all. It was going all wrong! I was supposed to ask her to mail me a picture of the kid. I was going to mail her back a check or something. But now I found I couldn't ask for a picture. I didn't know why.

"I don't think that would be a good idea," she said.

Instantly, I felt my whole body slump in disappointment. "You don't? Why not?"

"I didn't move back here to resume my old life. Really. I moved here because I thought it would be a great place for Jack to grow up. And there was a job, and—"

"Jack?" I said, as if two hands were squeezing my throat. "Who is Jack?"

"My son. Who did you think Jack was?"

Jack? She named him *Jack?* My mouth dried up. Now my legs felt shaky. They were actually trembling. Why had she named him Jack? I had to sit down.

"Oh," I said.

"Now, was there anything else?"

"Oh. No."

"I have to go. I wish you all the best, really I do," Diana said.

"Well, thanks. Same to you. Really."

"Good-bye."

"Bye."

n i n e

I dialed Ellen's work number.

"Are you busy? Are you right in the middle of something?"

She said, "I have a few minutes. What's happening?"

"I saw her," I said. "Diana. She came to The Club."

"How did that go?"

"Fine. She didn't want anything. She just wanted to tell me that she didn't even want to talk to me."

"Well, you're safe then. You have nothing to worry about."

"Safe, yeah," I said. "She kind of yelled at me. She thought I might sue her for custody or something."

"Oh, no. So you reassured her. You told her you had no such intention."

"I don't know. I guess. She sort of stomped off and I—I don't remember what I said, to be honest. But then, then later, the next day, which is today, I called her. Just now, I did."

"You did?"

"Yeah. See, I wanted to ask for a picture of the boy. I wanted to see what he looked like."

"How did that go?"

"Go?"

"Tom."

"Oh, sorry. Yeah, it went—well, she doesn't want anything from me, that's for sure. She keeps saying that."

"You must be incredibly relieved."

"Oh, yeah. Sure. Of course."

"What about the picture?"

"I sort of—I don't know—I sort of chickened out on that. I asked if she wanted to get together, though."

"You did?"

"She said no. So I won't have to do that. Either. So that's a relief. Too."

"Is it?"

"What?"

"*Tom.* A *relief!* Is it really a relief that you aren't going to have anything to do with Diana and her son?" She waited, gave me time to say something, but I didn't. "Or are you disappointed?"

"Disappointed? What—that I don't have child support payments draining my bank account? Am I disappointed I don't have to put up with a lot of recriminations about not taking responsibility?"

She didn't say anything. Then, "Are you?"

"Listen, I didn't even know about this! You can't blame me! I wasn't in on her little plan. She got pregnant and left. Without *telling* me! Therefore, *she* took full responsibility for it. Him. If you don't even tell someone that he has a kid, how can he do anything for that kid? Tell me that! She doesn't need me. Or *want* me. Why does everyone think that she's going to come after me and take me for everything I'm worth?"

"You don't feel you're missing out?"

"Missing *out?* On what?"

"On the kid's life?"

"Oh. Well. No. I mean I—no. I don't."

"OK, then. So...great. That settles that."

We didn't say anything for a couple of moments. Then I realized she was waiting for me to say the next thing. But my thoughts had moved on from our conversation. Still, it was my turn to talk. "I just called to let you know that everything is fine. Perfect. Nothing to worry about."

"Glad to hear it."

"Everything can go on as before. The same. Exactly as it was. No changes."

"Right. Sure," she said.

"*What?* It can."

Ellen said, "Good."

"What?"

"No, I mean, that's good. That everything is the same."

"Oh, yeah. I see. OK, I have to go."

"Fine," she said.

"Talk to you soon."

"OK, Tom."

We hung up. I got a Coke out of the fridge and popped it open. I sat down on my bed and took a sip.

t e n

I turned on the radio then, just to try to erase everything, and wouldn't you know? "Layla." That's the song that was playing on the radio at that moment.

My brother ruined the *Layla* album for me. I don't mean he scratched my record or left it in a hot car. I mean, every time I hear a song from it, all I can think about is the series of events that started the night I first heard that record. A lot of people my age love *Layla*. Many consider it brilliant: a flagship album that captures a whole era. For all I know it might have been one of my lifetime favorites. As it was, I switched stations as quickly as possible anytime it came on, which I did right now, and which didn't help, as a music-induced flashback was already in progress.

The first time I heard *Layla* was at a party. I was fifteen. My brother, Jack, was there too. He was two years older, a senior. Jack was my hero and had been since we were little. We were in a band together, but Jack was the one with real talent. I was just in the band because I was his brother. He could play anything he heard, and he could write original lyrics that, I believed, were better than anything we heard on the radio. The band was called Elements of Danger. He made that up, and I still thought it was a great name for a band.

At the party, I was sitting on the floor between two stereo speakers with the album cover resting on the knees of my new denim bell-bottoms. They didn't look new; that was the point. They were faded and soft, as if I had been wearing them for years. I loved those pants. I thought they elevated me to a level of cool that I could not have attained on my own. I was staring at the painting on the album cover and listening to the first song. Near the end of the first song, I saw my brother go outside. The song stopped, and I heard his car start.

At the time, I wondered why he hadn't taken me with him. I considered getting up, running out, saying, "Wait!" But I knew my brother had been drinking. He could be a jerk when he drank, and I didn't feel like a confrontation. Besides, I wanted to listen to the rest of the album, and then "Bell Bottom Blues" came on and I decided to get a ride with someone else. I turned my attention to the chords of the song and its lyrics' connection to my new pants.

I didn't know yet about Eric Clapton's own substance abuse problems. In those days, I hadn't even heard that term. It would be years until I learned about substance abuse and even longer before it occurred to me to apply this term to my brother. But when I did find out, it didn't make anything any easier; it didn't make me able to listen to the album or to forget any of what I didn't want to know.

A friend drove me home from the party. I was in bed asleep before midnight. I assumed that my brother was too.

Later, around three, our parents came into my room to tell me that my brother was dead. He'd taken a curve too fast and flipped his old Dodge Dart over the edge of a canyon. No one had been with him at the time.

My sister, Ellen, came home from college. There was a funeral and lots of visitors. Girls came out of the woodwork. Guys I'd never seen before stopped by to give our mother song lyrics Jack had scribbled on sheets of notebook paper, lunch bags, napkins from Denny's. Some of these kids had tapes of him singing either his own songs or other peoples'. Oceans of tears were shed over the loss of Jack Good, who lived only seventeen years.

Although I've spent much of the subsequent thirty years listening to music, I had never purposely listened to any part of *Layla*. And whenever a song from it came on somewhere unexpectedly, I tried to turn it off or move away as fast as I could. It's a shame, really, because I was exactly the kind of person who would have appreciated that album and all of its significant reverberations at the time and since.

I picked up the phone and dialed Ellen's work number again. My sister answered on the first ring. "Hi," she said. She knew it was going to be me.

"Ellie?" I said. "The boy? She named him Jack." My voice cracked on the last word.

"Oh, Tom," she said softly. *"God.* Why did she do that?"

I said, "She didn't know. I never told her about him."

"What do you mean you never told her? You guys were together for—"

"I don't talk about it. It's a rule I have. I don't discuss it."

"Tom, that's a very bad rule!" she said sharply. Other people in her office must have heard her, but she did not tone it down. I was annoying enough for even my levelheaded sister to blow up at me at work. "How do you expect people to know you or feel close to you unless you let them in on your life? You just can't ask people to—"

I didn't hear what else she had to say on the subject because I hung up.

e l e v e n

My sister was right, of course. Secrets can be toxic, but sometimes it was hard to know where to begin telling what you've been holding back, and once you did, how to stop.

I called Diana again. She didn't answer. I left a message. "This is Good?" I said, as though I were trying to guess who it might be. "Could you call me? Please?"

I waited around. I took the phone into my closet and tried to play songs I knew by heart but didn't make up myself, Bruce Springsteen songs or Steve Earle songs that were about situations way worse than anything in my life. I knew about a million songs, but that night I just couldn't think of the right one. I started a lot of songs, but I never got to the end of any of them.

I called again and left another message. "Diana? Are you there? It's Good. Again. I think I need to talk to you about some stuff." I waited. She didn't call.

It's a law of nature that if you want someone to call you, if you desperately need to hear from someone, you have to be away from your phone. I went out.

I was locking my door, and my neighbor Robin stepped through hers, which was right next to mine. Her keys were in one hand and Ray, her youngest, sat on her hip.

"Hi," she said, nodding. We didn't have much of a relation-

ship, so it was always awkward whenever I found myself face to face with her unexpectedly this way. She had a round face with pink cheeks and amazingly straight brown hair that was cut off in a sharp, even line about halfway down her neck. She had a cushiony, soft body, and she usually wore overalls or jeans with big, loose shirts. I didn't have anything against Robin, but we seemed to have nothing to say to each other. I had the feeling that I made her nervous, and I could understand her point of view on this. I worked weird hours and not many of them. The rest of the time I lurked around my small apartment, unoccupied, as far as she knew. We kept our distance from each other. In the several years she'd lived here, we probably hadn't exchanged more than ten sentences.

The three other kids were coming down the stairs from Jeanette's apartment. Robin said, "Did she like the magazines?"

"Yeah," Elise said. "She said to tell you you're 'an absolute angel.' "

The kids laughed about this.

"And she gave us gross candies!" Mike said.

"Shh," Robin said. "You don't want to hurt her feelings. Let's see."

Elise and Mike opened their hands to display butterscotches from grocery-store bins. Maddy spat something into the bushes.

"Yeah, well," Robin said. "She's just saying thank you." She turned to me. "Say hello to Mr. Good."

"Hello," we all said without looking at one another. Then I left for 7-Eleven.

I was waiting to pay for my sunflower seeds. I was fine with what they were playing on the radio. I could have stood there all night, listening to Sugar Ray singing "Fly," which didn't mean anything to me. But then my luck ran out. The woman ahead of me realized she had forgotten half-and-half, and while she was getting it, Sugar Ray faded out and another song came on. Just who

decides what songs to put with what? The song that came on was "Let It Be," for God's sake, which reminded me again of my brother's death and more specifically of my subsequent depression and hospitalization, because it happened to come out at about that time. It's just not a song that should be playing when you're waiting in line at a 7-Eleven.

Jack and I had gotten a lot of attention from Mr. Smeltzer, our music teacher at school. We hung out with him in the band room, and we even went over to his house sometimes. He always made us promise not to do drugs or drink. We promised. He cited famous people who didn't get to "fulfill their potential" (he was a teacher; he talked this way) because of their use of alcohol and/or drugs. Even before Jimi Hendrix, Jim Morrison, and the rest, there were already plenty of examples of excellent artists whose work had been cut short.

I kept my promise. Even now, I had never had so much as a beer in my life, though I often wondered about the benefits of my abstinence. I completely understood people's attraction to drugs. It was a protective coating, a shield between them and the world. What did I have? My closet and my choice of guitars to hold in front of me.

Mr. Smeltzer wasn't old, and he wasn't young. Now that I think about it, he was probably about my age, the age I was now, in his mid- to late forties. He was married to an elementary-school teacher, and they had no kids. He called me after Jack died. I wouldn't talk to him; I wouldn't even come to the phone. I didn't want him to hear me cry. I didn't want to cry at all. Mr. Smeltzer would have understood what it meant to lose Jack. At the time, I thought Mr. Smeltzer might have been the only one who did, and I just couldn't face that right away, his complete comprehension of the depth of my grief. I was pretty sure that he got that I adored Jack. Mr. Smeltzer would have understood, too, about Jack's drinking. He would when I explained it to him. He would understand how hard it was when my brother got drunk and acted like a jerk and wouldn't practice. He might even understand that our band had recently broken up and that I was angry about this. Any minute, I had expected my brother to return to normal, for things to improve between us. I was picturing us working on songs together. I was seeing Jack on lead guitar, playing a solo, with me backing him up on rhythm guitar. In my future image of us, Jack was singing lead vocals into a microphone, and I was stepping up to harmonize. We were sharing the same mike, the way John and Paul used to do.

Certainly, Mr. Smeltzer understood that it wasn't my fault that Jack was dead. And at the same time, he would know that I might have prevented Jack's death. I was there that night, after all. I could have grabbed his keys and run. I could have let the air out of his tires. I could have called our father. And Mr. Smeltzer would know that not one of these scenarios had occurred to me at the time Jack left the party, because I simply had no idea that anything that bad could happen to Jack. If I had known what was going to happen I would have tried anything to stop it. Anything. But I didn't. I should have known, which made my brother's death my fault. Sometimes, though I was furious with my brother for getting drunk and dying. He had ruined everything! Mr. Smeltzer got all that. I'm pretty sure he did.

I planned to visit Mr. Smeltzer when I felt better. I planned to try to straighten some of this out with him. Eventually. I planned to tell him a few things about my parents too. Mr. Smeltzer was at Jack's funeral. Several people told me. I didn't see this myself because I did not attend. I was at home, lying on my bed, holding a guitar across my stomach, looking at the ceiling, as I had been for most of a couple of days. A neighbor had to be called in to baby-sit me, in case I chose the moment of Jack's funeral to find some creative way to kill myself. All the obvious potential methods had been removed from the house—pills, razors, even my dad's radio had been taken out of my parents' bathroom. They really didn't get it. I was far too stunned, too inert, to take that kind of decisive action.

The neighbor, Francy, came in my room twice to check on me. I heard her feet approaching on the carpet, and I closed my eyes. She opened the door, stood there for a few seconds, went out. When my parents and Ellen came back, I heard Francy say, "He's fine. He's still napping." Can't you just imagine how eager she was to get away from there? I can. I was feeling it myself.

A few days later, I was even considering going back to school, just to be away from the house and my sad parents. They weren't asking me all those questions without answers anymore. But the quiet sobbing, staring into space, and drifting from room to room were even worse.

Then all of a sudden, Mr. Smeltzer had a heart attack and died. Just like that. It wasn't completely out of the blue, though, I learned. It turned out that he had a history of heart disease, and he smoked. All that talk about drug abuse, and he smoked. But again, in those days, people knew so little about addiction. I don't think it was more than ten days after Jack's death.

I wigged out. I crawled into my closet and slept almost constantly for two days, curled up on the floor. My parents couldn't get me to eat, drink, talk, bathe, or do anything else for several more days. Then they checked me into a nuthouse. A *nice* nuthouse, but it didn't seem that way to me at the time.

In the hospital, I spent a lot of time being "uncooperative." The way it seemed to me was that a bunch of assholes and dorks were sticking their faces into my face every other minute, asking me how I was feeling and inviting me to talk about my brother and Mr. Smeltzer, whom they had never even met. I couldn't stand to be around people. I couldn't be in a room with another human being for more than a minute or so. There was a therapist I had to see every day. For many days, I sat in the chair and stared at the Kleenex box. Once I shredded Kleenex for the full fifty minutes and then, at the end of my session, brushed it all off my pants and walked out. I was a lot of fun. When I came into his office one day, there was an album by, well, let's just say someone I didn't like on his desk. We'll call him Singer-Songwriter X. I blew up. How did anyone expect someone who liked Singer-Songwriter X to be able to help me? How was it possible that someone with that kind of hideous taste would even know what to say to me? He listened silently for a long time. Of course this was the most material I had given him to work with in all the days I had been coming to him.

When I finished ranting, he asked me what songs I liked. I said, "I like my brother's songs! My brother wrote good songs!" I yelled this at top volume. *"Anybody* could write better songs than Singer-Songwriter X. Even I could." Of course, I didn't realize what kind of a trap I was falling into. If I hadn't been nuts at the time, I would have seen this. But I was.

All he said was, "Really. Well, I'd like to hear one."

That was the end of the session. So before the next one came around, I had a song ready. I pretended it was one of hundreds. Really, it was all I had, and I had written it just for him. It was "Self-Destructive Tendencies," which, as you know, still gets played on the radio. It's all about being crazy, and it's sort of funny in a dark, serious way. You think of therapists as these reserved guys who don't react much. Not this one. He laughed and bounced his head during the song. When it was over, he jumped out of his chair and came over to pat me on the back. "That was great!" he said. "You wrote that? God, that was good!" He probably would have hugged me if I hadn't smelled so bad at the time, and if he weren't afraid he would set me way back on my so-called journey.

I didn't smile or anything. I couldn't give him that much.

I had another one ready for the next session. I saw right away that songs were my way out. How crazy could I be if I could write a song, complete with a bridge, a hook, and a chorus you could sing along with? It worked. After five songs, they let me out.

They weren't real songs. The therapist wouldn't know this, because, as I saw it, well, he didn't know anything. After all, he listened to Sing-Songwriter X and couldn't even see the obvious dull phoniness of that guy. My songs were exercises I had to perform to extricate myself from my prison, the hospital. I realized also that if I didn't start to act normal, I would never get out of this place, and people would never stop asking me how I was feeling and if I wanted to *talk*. I started to talk. I talked about my brother and Mr. Smeltzer.

I said that my brother got drunk sometimes, but even so he was the best person I knew in the world. I said that he had been just about to stop drinking forever. Our band was going to be famous, I told him, and we were good—really—and we had been planning to make it. Like the Beatles, I said. And now it was over, I said. (I didn't mention that the band had broken up before Jack died or that I was mad at him.) Now I said that I would miss him and Mr. Smeltzer for the rest of my life. Here, the therapist disagreed with me. He said that grief gets easier to handle over time. I thought, *As if you know anything! This will never change, ever. This will not even shrink to the slightest, tiniest degree!* I said, "OK. I sure hope that starts soon." I was faking everything.

Faking my recovery was a lot of work. I started eating and making my bed in the mornings. I took showers. Even though I could make myself do these things, there seemed to be a thick sheet of glass between me and the rest of the world. The front of my brain seemed to be packed with wadded, wet cotton that muffled and slowed my thinking. But I knew what to do to make myself appear to be recovering.

When he came to drive me home, my dad turned on the radio. He probably did this out of nervousness and because he couldn't think of what to say to me. And even now, waiting for my change in a 7-Eleven, I couldn't hear "Let It Be" without remembering the movie that went with it, the Beatles breaking up, the events that led to my hospital stay, and all the details of my time there. Sometimes I am amazed by how much emotional complexity you can load into a few rhyming verses, a melody, and a chorus.

When I got home, there were no messages.

I called Ellen again. By now she was home. I said, "Sorry I hung up before."

She said, "It's OK, I was pushing. Sorry."

"No you weren't. You were right."

"What are you going to do?"

"I left some messages for her. I'll get together with her again. I'll try to talk to her."

"I see," she said. "Well, take it easy, though. She might not want to. She might need some time to come around."

"Yeah," I said. "I will. I'm not going to be obnoxious or anything."

As soon as I hung up, though, I called Diana again.

This time, she answered. *"What?"* she said. "Am I going to have to have my number changed?"

I swallowed. "I just want to talk to you, that's all. In fact, I was just discussing this with my sister, and she suggested that maybe I should have been more communicative with you years ago. Maybe I should have, you know, talked more way back then. I wasn't, um, at my best then."

Diana said, "You have a sister? I didn't know that."

"I have an excellent sister," I said. "And I think we should get together. You and me. I think we should talk."

"No, I don't think so."

"Really. This is important. I can see why you wouldn't want to, but I would really appreciate it if you could do this for me. Please."

"Why didn't you ever tell me you had a sister?"

"I don't know," I said. "Could you just think about it?"

"I guess, but I'm pretty sure—"

"I know, I know. But this is really important. Just think about it."

"Fine."

"How long do you need to think about getting together? How about I call you tomorrow?"

She sighed. "No."

"The next day, then."

"Is she older or younger?"

"Older. I'll call you day after tomorrow."

It wasn't the first time my sister had saved me.

When I came home from the hospital, Ellen came home from college. She took a leave of absence. We went to a lot of movies. Our parents probably thought this was callous, but TV and movies were the only analgesics we had available, and we made liberal use of them.

I never returned to high school. But when we weren't watching movies, I did all my homework. Ellen looked it over for me. It was home school, but we didn't have that term then. My sister took the work in to my teachers and got more for me. (My mother was in some kind of nonfunctioning state of her own in those days.) The teachers talked to Ellen about what I was supposed to be learning. I took all my tests at home with a retired teacher sent over by the school district. I didn't see my friends

or even talk to them on the phone. When anyone called, I had Ellen say that I would call back, which I did not do.

Ellen transferred to UCSD, which hadn't been open all that long. She hadn't applied there originally. The whole point of college for Ellen had been to leave home. She had been looking forward to it since she was little. She wanted to live somewhere with snow. She came back for me, I knew, to provide a shield between our parents and me, between me and myself. When Ellen went to classes, I sat at my desk with my books open and a pen in my hand. What I was really doing was waiting for her to come back. If my mother came in, I'd hunch intently over my homework and not look up. Other than the time she spent at her classes, Ellen and I were together almost always. To pay her back, I took extra courses for the next two semesters and graduated half a year early. When I think about Ellen, I have very few memories of her when we were young kids. It was only after Jack died that Ellen came into focus for me.

Meanwhile, I had hardly picked up a guitar for a year. When I did, it was to move it to the garage and hang it on a nail by its strap. I remember just wanting it out of my room. It seemed to be watching me, refraining from comment. I didn't even put it in a case. Somehow I had come to think of this one guitar I had at the time as my enemy, my harshest critic. I'm not sure why. I hoped it would become covered with dust and cobwebs, like a chandelier in a haunted house. I hoped its strings would get rusty and the whole instrument would disintegrate into dust.

Ellen graduated and applied to law school. She was accepted and packed her things to move to Pennsylvania. Before she left, she asked me eight thousand times if I was going to be OK. Every single time, I said, yes, I was. Fine. Then she was gone, and I had nothing to do. I didn't go to the movies anymore. I didn't even watch TV.

I started to go crazy again. I could feel it coming, and I could see it reflected in the way other people looked at me. "How *are* you?" my father started to ask again. "Tom?" I would hear my mother ask, "Tom, are you feeling all right?" "Do you want to talk about it?" One night, I curled up in my closet to sleep. I felt a little better there. In the morning, I didn't feel like coming out. I pictured what was about to happen, the alarm bells that would go off in my parents' heads, the therapists I would have to endure, the long silences and endless debates with myself about what I should or shouldn't say to make them think I was fine so they would leave me alone.

When I crawled out of the closet the next day with a stiff neck and rug designs on my face, my brain was scrambling for an alternative to going nuts again. All I could think of was to get my guitar out of the garage. Now, I had an idea that the thing that had seemed to be my enemy was the very thing I should put my arms around and embrace. I needed something in my hands, and it was a bonus that I thought of something that made noise. People are less likely to ask you how you're feeling when loud chords are blasting out of your amp. In the unlikely event that they ask you anyway, you can easily, convincingly act as though you haven't heard the question.

I picked up the guitar again out of an overwhelming wish to avoid attention and concern. My playing wasn't from any innate talent or creative drive. Honestly, I had no desire to make music ever again. I was just using it as a smoke screen, a diversionary tactic. I started a band, the sole purpose of which was to make people think I was getting over Jack's and Mr. Smeltzer's deaths, that I was moving on with my life. I had to create the impression of emotional stability by appearing to be occupied.

It was a fake band. I made up a fake name for it, Point Blank, and wrote some fake songs. It worked. I held auditions at my parents' house. You could almost hear this collective sigh of relief in my family as guys (mostly guys; there were a few girls, but not many) I knew, sort of knew, and didn't know at all showed up by appointment to our garage to show me what they could do.

I picked a lead guitar player, a bass player, a drummer, and a keyboard player. I saved rhythm guitar for myself. I didn't want to play lead, didn't want to be in the spotlight. My musician selections were pretty random. I didn't pay much attention to the auditions. But I made sure that no one I picked had known either Jack or Mr. Smeltzer. The other guitar player and the keyboard player could both sing. We worked up the songs I'd written pretty quickly, which probably shouldn't have surprised me, as I was very demanding of everyone's time. Whenever someone had a time conflict, I would say, "Do you want to be in the band or not?" Instead of telling me to go to hell, they cancelled their other commitments, stopped seeing girlfriends who objected to their neglect, quit jobs they couldn't squeeze into nonpracticing hours. We started playing around town.

People fell for it. Before you knew it, we even had a little following, a group of kids who showed up everywhere we went and offered to help us set up and break down our equipment. Girls wanted to go out with us. Some of them even wanted to go out with *me*. I kept wanting to say, "Don't you people get it? This isn't a *real* band. I made all this up! It's a fake! Don't be so gullible!" But no one, not even the other band members, saw through it. Obviously they didn't, because, as you know, the band still exists and builds on its popularity, its universal respect, with every CD, every music video, every *Letterman* and *SNL* appearance, every annual music awards ceremony. But the band had served my purpose before all that started to happen, and I got out after the first three years.

When I made my announcement at the start of practice one day that I was quitting, that I was finished with Point Blank, the other guys just looked at me for several seconds. They were trying to figure out if I was joking. They didn't believe me. I had to repeat it a lot of times and a lot of different ways before I convinced them. As you know, the songs went on without me. Songs have lives of their own. I didn't know that then. Maybe it's a little like having children: you can never have complete control over them, even though you imagine that you will. As soon as you've performed a song for people, even once sometimes, it can be off doing its own thing, and you couldn't stop it if you tried.

Those songs have brought me an extra income that is very helpful for a bartender. I haven't used much of the money, though. I've bought sound equipment that I couldn't have afforded otherwise. I've had a couple of emergencies now and then, wisdom teeth and that kind of thing. Ellen made me open an account that's managed by someone at one of those big investment firms. If I ever need money, I guess I'll use it. If it's still there. I don't keep track as much as I should.

In addition to the money, those songs have brought me a lot of grief too. I can't tell you how many conversations about them have ended with someone saying, "You *wrote* those songs? *You?* So what are you doing here? Man, *what happened?*" This is the question I hate more than any other. A lot of potential friendships have ended with that question.

Now playing guitar and writing songs were my substitute life. I fully acknowledged that to myself. I worked on them compulsively every day. A song could focus on anything from a small emotion—say, embarrassment at saying the wrong thing—to a whole life of a made-up person. These life-story songs were done in series. I had one set called "Annie McCampbell" that consisted of twenty-five songs, written over a period of two years. (I pictured it as a double-album set.) Annie McCampbell was a waitress I invented. The story started as a daydream I had on a slow night at The Club. Annie grew up in Las Vegas. She wanted to be a singer/actress/comedian. The story started off with a song about her tap-dance lessons and recitals. There were a couple of songs about her school years. And then there was a song about her relationship with an older blackjack dealer who dumped her. The next song picks up with her in Los Angeles, waitressing and auditioning. It goes on; she makes it big on a TV sitcom. Anyway, you get the idea. A big story in songs that work both independently and as a group. I have another series about a guy named Ricky who wanted to be an astronaut and ended up a math teacher. You can see my recurring themes, just from these short descriptions: dreams of a larger life, either realized or unrealized; disappointment; death. I could make myself cry, almost, but as I've mentioned, I have a shortage of tears.

Not all my songs were installments in epic sagas. Some were just fictionalized versions of things that happened to me, an annoying encounter at the post office, or deciding to change my life because I was worried about some life-threatening illness, then reverting back to my old ways after the problem cleared up. I thought of the songwriting as occupational therapy, like weaving lanyards or making jewelry boxes out of Popsicle sticks. It was something to do. I mean, you have to do something with your time, right? And, as you've seen, there was not a whole lot going on in my life that took up a lot of my time.

thirteen

On our mother's birthday, a Saturday, Ellen was picking me up for the visit. It was a ritual we acted out for every family occasion. We preferred to drive up to Alpine together to visit the parents. This year she was seventy-four. That sounded pretty old. I had this very same thought every year.

While I was waiting for Ellen, I called Diana. I left a message. "Hello, this is Good. Give me a call. Thanks."

Ellen had bought the present. I gave her half the money, another tradition.

Now I said to Ellen, "Tell me again why we're giving her walkie-talkies."

"For the mall," Ellen said, as if this were the most obvious thing in the world. "And you know, the gardening."

I looked at her.

"OK, they go to the mall and lose each other all the time. So this way, they can stay in touch as they walk around, arrange a time to meet. You know?"

"Do you think she'll be able to work them?" Our mother still had trouble with some of the trappings of the modern world. So did I, for that matter.

"I don't know, Tom. Maybe this wasn't a good idea. Let's see— what was your idea again?"

"No, I didn't mean—I wasn't criticizing or anything. I'm just saying that she's not very technical. It takes a lot of concentration for her to switch channels with the remote."

"Trouble is, they have pretty much everything they really want. Let's just hope for the best, OK?"

"We're not going to stay long, right?"

"Tom, do we have to go over this every single time?"

"Maybe," I said. "Yeah, we do. How long are we staying?"

"We will stay an hour."

"Promise?" I had to torture her; there were certain rituals we both found comforting.

We pulled into the driveway, and there was this sour, squeezing feeling in my stomach. Another tradition.

Before I could even open my door, Mom was on the front walk, waving as if greeting an ocean liner docking after a dangerous passage.

We got out.

"Good to see you, dear." She kissed Ellen on the cheek and hugged her.

Then it was my turn. Fumes from her hairspray and Vaseline Intensive Care Lotion enveloped me. "How's my boy?" she said, squeezing me. It was one of those questions not requiring an answer, my favorite kind. She stepped back and squinted up at me in the bright sun. Our mother is small and appears to be growing smaller. She is very proud of the fact that she buys most of her clothes in Nordstrom's children's department during one of their annual sales. "This sweater," she'll say, as if she's gotten away with something, "was only twelve dollars!" Right now, she was wearing a purple T-shirt with a pair of those pants women are wearing lately that appear way too short, white socks, and a pair of purple sneakers. Sometimes it is all too apparent that our mother buys her clothes in a children's department.

Our dad lumbered outside. Dad is as large as Mom is small. He favors plaid shirts, gray chinos (the kind a high-school janitor might wear), and work boots. He always looks as if he is about to go chop something down or weld something together. The top of our mother's head reaches the top of his shirt pocket. He nodded and shook my hand, hugged my sister briefly.

We went inside and followed Dad into the living room, while our mother made a side trip to the kitchen. It's one of those living rooms that people hardly ever sit in. You couldn't relax in there because everything looked too nice. There was a couch and matching love seat covered in white fabric with occasional pale flowers scattered across it. I never sat there. I worried that I would leave some kind of stain on it, a big dark smudge that would ruin it forever. There was a pale pinkish orange chair. That one was covered in velvet. Its fabric had a "memory," my mother once commented. She meant that your butt leaves a print. Also not for me. I got a ladder-back chair from the dining room, the way I always did.

"Tom, you got about fourteen places to sit in here. What are you bringing that in for?" our father said.

"My back," I said. I didn't say there was anything wrong with it; I just said, "My back," and then I sat down on the unupholstered chair that I was less likely to wreck. Conceivably, it could splinter into small pieces, or I could rip out the wicker seat, but these were unlikely possibilities.

This wasn't the house we grew up in. The parents sold that one quite a few years ago, and I was glad I would never have to go there ever again. Our parents had lived in five or more houses since then. I had lost track. Each successive house felt as remote and unrelated to me as the previous one.

Our mother brought in a tray. "No coffee for me, Mom," I said, before she had a chance to ask.

"Oh, all right," she said, a little pouty, as if I didn't decline the coffee every single time I came. She offered me a plate of cookies, homemade.

"No, thanks," I said. "Just had lunch."

Ellen took a cookie and a cup of coffee.

"So what have you two been up to?"

Ellen groaned softly. "Just work."

"Now, dear," said our mother, "you're doing a wonderful job. Think how many people you've helped, all those lives you've improved!"

Ellen nodded. She took a bite of her cookie. "Ooh!" she said. "Coconut!"

"Like it?" Our mother smiled. "And, Tom, what's new in your life?"

I didn't look at Ellen. "Just, you know, same old stuff, Mom," I said.

My mom couldn't say much about the people I'd helped by handing them Heinekens and tequila sunrises and taking their money. So she said, "Well, as long as you're enjoying yourself!"

I know Ellen was thinking the same thing I was. When confronted with her two mildly miserable adult children, our mother said something upbeat. Our father didn't talk. He just took a cookie.

Ellen said, "So happy birthday, Mom." She handed Mom the present.

"Well, now, isn't this nice? What could this be?" She opened the flowery pink paper. "Oh, heavens, what's this?"

"Walkie-talkies, Mom. So you and Dad can find each other in the mall."

"Oh, now, isn't that something? How thoughtful. Look, Chuck. One for each of us. That's a lovely gift, kids." She took them out of the Styrofoam form inside the box. "Now, do they—hmm— do they need batteries? Or what?"

I looked at Ellen. *See?* "They need batteries," I said.

"But I already put some in!" Ellen said. "So they're all set to go. Tom and I will demonstrate." Ellen grabbed one of the little radios out of our mother's hand. "Tom, go out in the driveway."

I looked at her: *Do I have to?*

"Go!" she said, handing me the walkie-talkie.

I got up and walked out of the house. I switched on the walkie-talkie.

"Come in, Tom. Tom, do you read me?"

Oh, God.

"Hi," I said.

"See that, Mom, it works!" Ellen was saying. "Tom, what is your location?"

"What? I'm out in the driveway, like you told me!"

An older man walked by with a dog on a leash. I didn't want him to see me talking into the radio in my parents' driveway. So I turned the thing off and went inside.

Into the radio, Ellen was saying, "Go all the way to the corner and then say something!"

"I'm right here," I said. Ellen looked up, disappointed. You'd think she'd never seen a walkie-talkie before. "Here." I gave the radio back to my mother.

She put it back into its place. Then she put the box on the table and stared at it as if the box might explode.

My mother was thinking about Jack. I was sure of it. He and I used to have a pair of walkie-talkies. They were kind of frustrating because you had to hold down a button to talk, but while you were holding down the button you couldn't hear the other person. We spent most of our time talking simultaneously, missing what the other said, and yelling at each other for doing it wrong. I loved those things. There was nothing better than hearing from my brother from the other side of the house or upstairs, even if I never quite got what he was saying. It seemed miraculous. That was about forty years ago. But our mother was thinking about it now, I could tell. I folded my hands across my knees and looked at them, guiltily, as if I were personally responsible for not keeping track of and maintaining those walkie-talkies in perfect working condition.

"That was just so thoughtful," said our mother softly.

I wanted to go.

"Tom, you've only been here fifteen minutes," my mother said suddenly.

"What?" Had I accidentally said out loud that I wanted to get out of here?

"Stop looking at your watch!"

"Oh," I said. "Sorry."

There was an ugly little pause.

Then our father said, "Let me show you what we've been doing in the yard!" Another ritual.

"Great!" Ellen said, as if this were not the most boring part of the whole visit.

We followed our parents outside for a tour of their plants. Their yard was an ever-changing project. Frankly, it always looked about the same to me: bushes, flowers, patio. But they worked on it; every week they did a lot of hard labor to get it the way they wanted it, digging up plants, eradicating pests, weeding, building structures to hold in dirt or elevate flower beds.

Our father was talking about compost, and I wasn't listening. I tried not to be rude, but honestly, I had heard far more about compost and mulch than any one person should ever be subjected to.

"All right, Tom," my mother said. "You can go! You've put in your time."

"What?" I said. "I wasn't—"

"You just looked at your watch again! I understand. You're busy. And you should be!"

"I did not. Did I?" I turned to Ellen.

Ellen said, "Dad, could I have a couple of lemons?" Always the diplomat.

"Sure, honey!" Our dad walked briskly to the corner of the yard to pick a couple of lemons. Nothing pleased him more than giving away his produce.

"Oh, Mom," Ellen said. "Look at that rose! It's perfect."

"Let me go get my clippers, and I'll give you that for your desk."

"No, don't you want it? I mean, I love it, but you might want it for the dining room or something."

"I've got plenty!" Mom bustled inside the house and got her clippers for the rose. "There you are, dear. Now, do you have something pretty to put it in?"

"I'm sure I'll find something, Mom."

"Oh, you're very resourceful."

"I'm going to have to get back. I have these two cases I have to review before tomorrow."

"Do you? On a weekend? Poor you! Well, you know, I have some wonderful soup to give you both. It's all packed up. It won't take me a minute." She hurried off to the kitchen and came out with two containers of soup. She handed them to me because Ellen was driving.

We climbed back into the car, with me in charge of balancing the soup and the flower.

I waited. She was going to say, "Why do you do that? It's just for an hour. A lousy hour, Tom. Why do you have to make it so clear to them that you don't want to be there?"

We passed the grocery store. We got on the freeway. She didn't say it yet. She was waiting to get her stride, and then she would let me have it.

"What kind of soup is it?" she said.

"Lentil."

"Oh, good."

We drove some more. "Do you have to work tonight?"

"Yeah," I said.

"Who's playing?"

I thought. Nothing. "I can't remember. Want me to find out and call you? Want to come?"

"No," she said. "Thanks, though."

When we got all the way down the 8 and she hadn't said anything about my bad behavior, I knew she wasn't going to. She didn't have to. Not necessary. I should have been more patient, let them tell their news, thought up something to tell them. I should have just settled in for a visit. In an hour, hour and a half, I'd be free to go. Was it so hard to do that for them? Yes, it was. Clearly. I was a selfish person.

At work that night, when I started cutting lemon wedges, they reminded me briefly of my dad. A small burst of guilt fired off in the back of my neck and then faded, a mere aftershock.

I went to the pay phone. "Diana?" I said when she answered. "It's Good again." There was a pause. For some reason, it sounded as though I were talking about some situation or condition or maybe even relationship. "As in Tom Good?"

She said, "I got that. And I got all your messages."

"So I was wondering if you'd had a chance to think about things...if you'd maybe decided to see me, after all."

"No," she said. "I haven't. I've been busy."

She sighed, and somehow I knew there was hope.

"OK," I said. "Take your time." I would keep calling until she said yes.

fourteen

I was sitting in a restaurant with Diana. I had finally talked her into it. OK, I made a complete nuisance of myself, wearing her down until she caved. While I was pleased to get my way, we were starting out the dinner with her already irritated from all the pestering.

She looked the same, only, I guess, older, though I couldn't see exactly where this showed up. Her hair was about the same, straight and multishaded blond, to her shoulders. Her eyes were the same, a sort of yellowy brown. True, she did have little crinkles at the sides when she smiled, which she was not doing now. But did she have these before? I wasn't sure. The crinkles looked as though they belonged there.

"Does he ask about me?" I wanted to know.

She looked at me, pressed her lips together, head tilting to one side. She wore lip gloss, no color.

"Jack," I reminded her. "Your son, Jack," I said. He was my son too, but I didn't want to push it.

"Sometimes. Not often."

"What do you tell him?"

She sighed. She didn't want to get into this. "I just tell him that you were someone I used to know, that we had different plans about our lives. Having a baby was part of my plan, but it was not part of yours. I tell him that I really, really wanted him, and that nothing was going to stop me from having him."

"Oh. That—that's excellent. I mean, that's what you *should* say, really. That probably makes him feel very—" She cut me off with a glare, meaning she hadn't asked for my opinion about what she should or shouldn't tell her kid. Who was my kid too. Biologically.

"That's it," she said. "That's what I've said. When he asks. Which he doesn't very often."

"Did you tell him that I play guitar?"

"No, Good. I haven't. I really haven't gotten into any personal details."

"Why?"

"What would that accomplish? Think about it. I just want him to know that you exist, but that we're not in touch anymore."

"But now we are."

"This minute we are. Only because you wouldn't leave me alone. Only because you kept calling and calling. But I don't want to be in touch, Good. I think I've made that extremely clear. So ask your questions now, and then we're done."

I looked at her, swallowed. "Sure," I said. "Fine."

She bit her lip and looked out into the room. Was she going to cry? Was she conflicted about this? Was she thinking maybe she did want to be in touch with me after all, now that she saw me? Maybe she was having doubts. Were those doubts I saw crossing her face?

"I'm sorry," I said. "I didn't mean to make you feel bad. I just wanted to—"

"It just stirs up a lot of old..."

I waited, but she didn't finish. "Old what?" I said. Feelings, maybe? Longing? Desire?

"Old crap," she said. *"Painful* old crap." The dam burst. She wiped her hand across her face, but there were enough tears to get both her face and her hands wet. She picked up her napkin, but then she put it down again. It was cloth. Maybe she was too polite to mop up her tears and snot with a cloth napkin that someone else would have to wash.

Oh, God, what have I done now? I was thinking. And, *This is bad.* I didn't cry myself, and I hated it when other people cried. I did not do well with crying. "Diana?" I said. "Diana? Do you want to get out of here? Should we go?" I wanted to go. Personally, I wanted to get up and run.

She nodded. I took some money out of my wallet and tossed it onto the table without even counting it, just like in a movie. I took Diana's hand and walked her out. She didn't pull her hand away, but then maybe she was just trying not to make a scene.

Outside, she said, "I didn't want to do this, remember? I didn't want to get together. I said it was a bad idea, and I was right!"

"You were right," I said. "You were right, and I was wrong." I find it's a good idea to say this, maybe more than once when someone is crying. Sometimes it really does rescue the situation and pull things back from the direction they were going, which is toward crying *and* yelling, which I enjoy even less than plain crying. I repeated the phrase once more for good measure, softly this time, "You were right and I was wrong." Then I added, "I'm sorry. OK?" in a whisper. I swear I didn't know this was going to happen next. She sort of leaned into me, and I could smell her shampoo, or no, I guessed it was the conditioner, a different kind now. We were standing next to a planter at the entrance to the restaurant. The planter contained a geranium with red flowers. You know that kind of sharp dirt smell that geraniums have? I discovered then that the geranium smell combined with the conditioner smell is an aphrodisiac. I put my arms around her and didn't dare move.

"Let's go, OK?" she said. She twisted away and started into the parking lot.

"Sure," I said. "Should I drive you home?"

As we walked toward my car, she brushed a few tears away. Mascara was now smeared across her face, giving her a wrecked look that, unfortunately, just made me want to touch her as gently as possible.

"I'll get you home," I said. "This was a bad idea. You need a tissue, and I don't have any, of course. Here, use my shirt." I pulled my shirt out of my pants.

She looked at me sideways, and I worried for a second that I had just done something really disgusting. But next to my car, she actually wiped tears on my sleeve, dabbing carefully under her eyes to get the mascara. She looked up at me for half a second before she dried her dripping nose. "I'll get you home, OK?"

"Thanks," she said. "Sorry, that's going to be kind of wet—"

"Not a problem," I said. "Least I can do. Don't give it a thought. OK." I unlocked her door, and she got in. I went around to my side. "Let's take you home." It was the third time I'd said it. I knew that. But now instead of wanting to get her there as fast as possible, I was hoping that she would say she didn't want to go home, after all.

"Could we just drive around for a while? I don't want Jack to see that I was crying."

"He would—you think he'd be able to tell? He must be really, God, *attuned.*"

"Well, yeah, he would. And he'd worry about what was wrong."

"Did you tell him it was me you were meeting? I wouldn't want him to think that his father—"

"Of course I didn't!" she snapped. "Why would I?"

I had just ruined a nice, soft moment. "No, of course not. You wouldn't want him to—"

"He doesn't even know you live here or anything. That just wouldn't be helpful for him to know. Why do you—why do you *always* have to . . ." She couldn't find the words to describe the stupid thing I did, had always done, every single time, even though it was more than ten years ago, the last time I did whatever it was.

"Because I don't know any better," I said. "Because I'm an idiot." She hadn't named the thing, but I was sure she was right about whatever it was.

"No, you're not." Now she felt guilty. "You're not, Good."

"I am. Really," I insisted. "Don't feel bad about it. I *know*. I'm fully aware of my many flaws."

"I'm sorry. I should know better. Really. What's wrong with me? I'm thirty-nine years old!"

I was getting on the freeway now, going north. I had no destination in mind. We passed the Family Fun Center and its miniature golf course on the right. The place always depressed me. Whenever you see "fun" in the name of something, you can bet it won't be. The excessive use of lights made it look even sadder than it was, with families trying to enjoy themselves, despite the nasty frustration of trying to get a little ball into a tiny, distant hole on the other side of many complex obstacles. The Ferris wheel turned with no passengers.

"Jack adores that place," Diana said.

"What? Oh! Right! I bet he does! It sure looks like a lot of— well, *fun!*" Now I pictured myself on the Ferris wheel beside a small boy with glasses. We were never going to do that. I knew that. I probably didn't even want to do that. It was just one of those thoughts that comes to you.

"He had his last birthday party there."

"Really?" I said. "Oh, wow. How fun!"

We didn't talk anymore. The sun was going down in that slow, drawn out way it has getting toward summer, rinsing half the sky in orange. This always happens to me. I see something really beautiful when I'm in an ugly situation. Then I don't know what all that beauty is trying to tell me. Maybe it's saying, "You could do better. Check this out." Maybe it's saying, "If you were more in touch with life and love, this is what the world could look like all the time." I don't know. Whatever it is, I never get it.

"What a sky!" Diana said next to me. And then she started crying again. Why? Do you see why I keep myself isolated? I can't decipher what happens with people.

Now we would have to wait even longer before I took her home because of her fresh tears and her even redder eyes. Again, I started longing to drop her off somewhere. This was too hard for me. It had too many layers. I wanted to rewind the whole evening, and start over more simply. Maybe I could find the place where I'd lost track of what was going on. Or maybe I could put in a different tape altogether.

"Should I—do you want to eat or drink something?" I said. "Would that help?"

"No," she snuffled.

"Do you want to drive by the beach or something?"

"No thanks."

I mean, this was *hard*. And I had asked for this, practically pleaded. What was I thinking when I kept calling her and asking her to get together with me? What had I wanted? I tried to remember. I wanted two things:

I wanted her not to be mad at me.

I wanted to see the boy.

Now here I was with this crying woman beside me and I wasn't any closer to what I wanted.

"Why did we do this anyway? Why did you want to see me?" She was thinking the same way I was; maybe we had a common ground after all.

"I wanted to know about Jack," I said. "I wanted to ask you about him."

"What did you want to ask me?"

"Oh. Well, what he likes, what he's like," I said. "I mean, I just wanted to know what—"

"It's hard to sum up a person like that," she said.

One minute she was being accommodating, and the next she snapped. Now she leaned her head back on the headrest, and I sensed that she was going to try to give me a little something. "He's smart, he's funny. He likes maps. He's kind of messy."

"What's he good at in school? What's his best subject?"

"He doesn't like school very much."

"Oh."

"He's good at video games."

"Music? Does he like music?"

"Not much."

"Oh."

"Why do you want to know all this?" she said. She turned her head to the side to look at me. "All of a sudden, you appear out of the blue and ask all these questions! You didn't get in touch with me for ten years! I just want to know what you're planning."

"I'm not *planning* anything. I didn't know I was the father of a kid before, or I'm sure I would have gotten in touch with you." That didn't sound right. "I mean, it's not as though I forgot about you or anything. I thought you—I mean, we broke up. You moved, and I..." I gave up. I was making her cry again. "You didn't like me, remember? You got really fed up, and you left."

I sat there looking through the windshield at the truck in front of me. I looked into the left mirror, even though I wasn't going to change lanes.

"Well, you were wrong," she said quietly.

I nodded. "Of course. Wrong. Sure I was. I admit it." I thought a minute, to review what I was so wrong about. "Wait. Which part?"

"You were completely, totally wrong. I did like you. I was in love with you." She looked at me. "If you say you didn't get that, then I will know that you're lying. I just wanted you to say, 'Diana, let's stay together. Let's get a bigger place, where you can have a closet to put your clothes away.' Don't even try to tell me you didn't know, because I won't believe you."

I didn't say anything. To be perfectly honest, I was having enough trouble just breathing out and breathing in and keeping the car on the road.

Finally, after several miles, when Diana had composed herself, she said, "I knew I shouldn't have done this. I told you this was not a good idea, didn't I? So, was there anything else you wanted to know? Any other reason you wanted to get together?"

Then I said, "I was just hoping to, you know, meet him, and maybe, like, hang out with him, or something. I thought maybe I could take some kind of a role in his life."

"No," she said quickly. "And can you take me home now?"

"Sure," I said. "What did I say? Why are you getting so upset all of a sudden?"

"I'm not upset all of a sudden. I've been upset for a while now, but I guess you haven't noticed that!"

"I noticed! Of course I did. I let you wipe your nose on my—"

"Just take me home! This was a mistake!"

"I'm sorry. God, I didn't mean for this to turn into—" I got off the freeway at the next exit. I crossed the overpass and waited for the left turn arrow to get back on the freeway going the other way. "I thought, I just, I was trying to—you know, maybe you might need some money sometime, and I could—"

"Money?" she said. "He's in fifth grade!"

"They don't need money in fifth grade?"

"I mean, I've been managing fine on my own for some time. I didn't ask you for any help."

"No. You haven't asked me for anything. I'm just offering."

"No, thank you." She folded her arms.

"You don't have to talk about it right now if you don't want to—"

"Now is fine. I took full responsibility for having him. And now you just decide one day to get in touch, and *poof!* There you are! You knew I wouldn't want this. If I'd wanted you to participate, I would have contacted you, wouldn't I?"

"I guess you would. But how can you refuse—"

"Easy. Look. I have a good job. We live in a nice neighborhood. He's fine. He doesn't need—he's fine!"

I glanced sideways at her. She was looking straight ahead with her chin tipped up a little bit. She exhaled upward, and her bangs lifted for a second, then came to rest on her forehead again. I looked back at the road.

I suddenly had a flashback of the way she looked at The Club and the way she squeezed her eyes shut to memorize her drink orders. This wasn't right at all. Here she was, yelling at me about serious, weighty matters, and I was thinking about how cute she looked more than ten years ago. She still did that thing with her eyes when she tried to remember something.

"I didn't think you'd react this way," I said. "If I'd known, I—"

"How did you *think* I'd react?"

"I thought, I don't know, that you might be, um, glad?"

"You really have some kind of, I don't know, learning disability."

"I do? Well, maybe I do."

Now I couldn't get to her house quickly enough, but I had driven a long time in the opposite direction, so it would take a while. I figured I could just drive and not talk. *Hang on. You'll make it. Soon this will be over,* I told myself. I passed an In-N-Out Burger we had gone to together long ago in ancient times. I didn't say, "Remember that time we—" But I saw her looking at it too. In those days she had been living with her parents, saving money. I met them. They weren't bad. She looked a lot like her mother. I would hate to run into them again, though, now that, well, now.

"Why did we do this anyway?" Diana wanted to know again. "This is torture. What were you trying to do? I mean, really."

As I'd already answered this question, I didn't say anything.

"I see you finally got a car," she said. She looked around herself, not at all impressed. It was an unimpressive vehicle, to be sure. It was used when I bought it. "When did you get it?" she wanted to know.

"Almost eleven years ago."

"Really? Oh. Well." She seemed a little startled. "So—I don't understand. You bought the car because I wanted you to?"

"Yeah."

"But you didn't tell me. So how could I—"

"You never called. I thought you would come back for the stuff you left, but you didn't."

"Did you really think—" She brushed away a thought with her hand. She looked out the window. "So do you play guitar for people now? Or is it still just you and your closet?"

"Closet," I said. "Still just the closet."

"Do you still get your shirts at Kmart and your jeans at—"

"Still. Yeah. The same."

"I see, well. Good, why don't you get some therapy? It might really help."

As you might imagine, this wasn't my favorite topic of conversation. So I went in another direction. I said, "Listen. Now, don't get mad. I'm trying to be helpful. I may not be the most conventional father, you know. I may not be exactly normal in a lot of areas. But about money—if there's anything you need for Jack, just tell me, OK? I'd be happy to give you something every month if you want, or just help out whenever you feel you—"

Out of the corner of my eye, I could see her turn her head toward me in this curious way. "You're kidding."

"No."

"What money do you have? Since when do bartenders make—well, I guess your expenses are pretty low, but I don't think you have any idea how expensive a kid can be."

"Probably not. I'm just saying I'm willing to contribute—I'd *like* to contribute—and—"

"What money are we talking about? Are you suggesting twenty-five bucks a month, something like that, or—"

"No, sorry, I meant more than that. I mean, if you're OK for the regular expenses, then let's say for college or if he—"

"So where do you get all this money to give away all of a sudden?"

"I've had money for a long time. Years and years. So if later on, maybe, or if all of a sudden you need—"

"Really, where did *you* get money? I want to know."

"Oh, just—it's—" I started stammering and scrambling in my head about what to say. "You know, my songs. The songs I wrote for Point Blank. They still earn royalties, and as you've noted, my expenses are pretty low."

"What songs? You wrote songs for Point Blank? Royalties? Seriously? What songs?" She looked at me. When I didn't say anything, she said, "You told me you used to be in a band. *A band,* you said. Half the male population used to be in *a band.* You never said anything about Point Blank. How could you possibly not mention that?" For a minute she looked straight ahead. Then she turned to me again. "OK, Good. What songs are we talking about here? I want to know."

I exhaled. Here we go. I really didn't like talking about this, as I've mentioned, but I named the songs. Then I said, "I started the band."

She gasped and said, "Oh. My. God. Are you telling the truth?"

I focused on the road ahead of me.

"Good," she said.

"Yeah."

She was quiet for a minute, processing. I picked up our speed a little. I was almost to her place.

"Really?" she said, turning sideways in her seat to face me. *"Really?"*

"Uh-huh," I said. "It was a long time ago. I was pretty young, and I—"

"How come you never told me? I mean, why would you keep a huge piece of information like that from me."

"Oh, I—I don't know." I tried to think of an answer. "I—I don't know. I guess it never really came up?"

"You're the Tom Good who left Point Blank way back when?"

"Well," I said, "yeah."

"All these years, and I didn't even know who I—I can't believe this!"

Any second, she might start crying again or maybe yelling at me. I got off at the next exit.

Diana was shaking her head, stunned by the information that I had written famous songs. "God, well, that's just—gee, so *that's* why you called me. You wanted to finally tell me that?"

"No, I, well, there were a lot of things I wanted to go over actually. And I just wanted to ask about—Jack." It didn't really matter now what my original plan was. This had all gotten away from me a long time ago. My original plan seemed remote.

I drove into Diana's condo parking lot. I got a space right near her unit. She had her car door open before I'd turned off the engine. She hopped out pretty fast, but I could be fast too, if I wanted to. I hurried around the car and walked her to the front door, even though, clearly, she would have preferred it if I'd screeched out of the parking lot before she got inside; it would have gone better with her image of me. Too bad though, because I wasn't going along with it. She had the key out already and opened the door.

"Good night," she said, as she stepped through the door. Then she closed it.

"Good night," I said to the closed door. It was blue, and there was a tiny nail at about nose level where she would probably hang a Christmas wreath in a few months.

fifteen

At home, the house was dark. Not just my side, but both sides. Upstairs was bright. Jeanette was probably logging me in right now. I managed to find the keyhole and get in the front door. My answering machine light was blinking. Blink blink. Pause. Blink blink. Pause. Two calls. I closed the door, locked it, and flicked on the light. I didn't listen to the messages yet. I went into the kitchen and boiled water. I hadn't eaten dinner. I got out a little can of that flavored instant coffee. *They ought to sell this stuff in bigger containers,* I was thinking, *jumbo drums of it, the way they did with laundry detergent. This would be great for people like me who could never get enough of the stuff.* I put a couple of tablespoons into a cup.

The problem with seeing old girlfriends was that the things that initially attracted you to them are always still there. You didn't expect that, for some reason. You thought it was going to be all neutral, and it just wasn't. You could still picture them happy or wet or surprised or asleep, and just what were you supposed to do with all that stuff? Then the reasons you were not still with them were there too, right on top, and what were you supposed to do with *that?*

The phone started ringing, but I didn't answer it. It was probably The Club, saying that it was unexpectedly busy and would I come down and work the front bar? Well, no, I wouldn't. I let it ring.

The answering machine went on. It wasn't The Club. It was Diana. "Good? It's me," she said. "I'm sorry. I shouldn't have been so—well, see, the thing is, I—you know, I should have been more appreciative of your offer. So thank you for offering. And, well, that's all, I guess. Bye."

Another confusing thing. People should be one way or the other, not several ways at once, and I'm including myself when I say this. They should hate your guts or love you. They shouldn't have both feelings at the same time. The water boiled. I poured it into the powder and stirred. Then I played the other messages. They were both from Diana. First, could I call her back? Then, she guessed I wasn't home yet, but when I got home, could I call her back?

I turned on the TV. Then I turned it off again. I sipped from my cup. She hadn't shown me a picture of Jack. I really wanted to see what he looked like. She probably had a picture of him in her wallet, if I'd just asked to see one. Or maybe she wouldn't have wanted me to see him. I sipped again. I put the cup down on the floor and took the phone off the desk. I dialed. I had the number memorized from calling it so many times over the last several days. She answered right away.

"Diana?" I said.

"I'm sorry, Good. Really. I shouldn't have been so—"

"You weren't. It was me. I shouldn't have expected you to—"

"It was just kind of a lot to deal with all at once. I didn't really expect to hear from you and then there you were, and it brought back all my—God, the whole thing. It was so hard, trying to figure everything out. I was pregnant, and you were so—I don't know. I just didn't think you were ever going to . . ."

She stopped here. "Amount to anything?" I suggested. "Change? Get a real job? Get a real house? Get real clothes? Get a car?"

"No, no," she said quickly. "I wasn't going to say that. I was going to say, I didn't think you were ever going to want to have a family. That was what I was going to say."

"Oh," I said, "that."

"And at first, I didn't think it was a good idea to get together, but now, I'm really glad we did."

"You are?"

"Yes, and I was thinking, would you want to do it again some-time? Maybe now that I'm used to the idea, I won't be so—so emotional."

"OK," I said. "Sure."

I had just spent the past half hour getting used to the fact that I would not see her or my kid. Now I might after all. "Take your time," I said. My heart was pounding, and my hands were sweaty. Hope flooded in, and I absorbed it, like a paper towel sucking up a cupful of grape juice in one of those old TV commercials.

"Yeah," she said. "I'll call you."

Words started rushing out of me. "You will? OK, because I didn't want you to be mad at me. I was really trying to, to, uh, you know..."

"Help. I know that. Thanks." She wanted to hang up. She had called me three times, and now she wanted to get off the phone. More conflict.

"I'll let you go now," I said, taking her lead. By the time I hung up, I was feeling pretty good. I would have to be very care-ful, though. I saw that now. I'd be following her one way, and any little change in the wind could send her off in a whole different direction. But I was up to the challenge.

sixteen

I dreamed about the band, my old band, Point Blank. I saw Diana sitting in a theater lit to be taped for TV. She was dressed in a shimmering silver gown, her hair arranged in a complicated twist, earrings dangling. I was sitting beside her wearing a tux. "And the winner is Tom Good!" said a voice. Diana screamed with happiness and threw her arms around me. I had tears in my eyes as I held her tight, kissed her, then let her go and walked to the stage.

OK, I didn't dream it. I thought it. I daydreamed it. I wanted that, not the TV part, necessarily, but the part where I was a winner at something and she loved me for it. I used to have a chance at that. I hadn't always been a bartender who had once, accidentally, had something to do with some hit songs a long time ago.

I remembered the band's disbelieving stares when I told them I was quitting. What had done it for me was the interviews, people asking about my life. I couldn't say, "My brother died. My teacher died. Everyone was looking at me, so I had to act busy. My brother was the talented one, not me. I have nothing. It's not a real band; it's just something I made up to get me out of a bad situation!" I couldn't tell them that, because it would just lead to more questions. Besides, all I wanted to do was hide. So I quit.

I couldn't know then that once you started something like this, once you made a band and wrote some songs, it could go on forever without you, whether you wanted it to or not. Nobody told me that. How would I know?

Looking back on it, I could see why everybody was so shocked when I left the band. From here at the other end of a couple of decades, I supposed that band might have seemed to people as real as any other band. At the time, however, this idea had not occurred to me.

Now I got out a cassette of some songs I'd been working on. I put the tape in the machine and pressed play. The songs seemed to have melodies, singable lyrics, and even, well, meaning. People might accept these as the real thing. If I could just get in touch with the guys in Point Blank and let them know I was available again, they could use some of these. I pictured Diana singing along with one of my songs as it played on the radio, my son bragging to his friends. It was my band, after all. I started it. I picked those guys out of everyone who auditioned. I'd listened to their last CD. Some fresh energy couldn't hurt. They *needed* me. And once I got going writing songs for the band again, well, anything could happen.

I made a new tape of fifteen songs. It took me a whole day. I'd pick a song, put it on the tape, listen to it, think about the ones that led up to it, choose one to come after it. Twice I had to change the order completely, starting over at the beginning. It had to be right. I thought fifteen was the right number to start with. I didn't want to overwhelm them with too many, but still I had to let them know I had plenty. I looked at my tapes shelved by date. Lots and lots of songs. There were certainly plenty to choose from.

I thought about the life I could have been having. I pictured Diana and Jack in a house with a pool. I heard one of my songs floating through the air. "This is my house," I sang. "And this is my family..." There was a whole song there, I could tell, but I didn't have time to write it down now. I was focused on another project: I was creating my real life. I looked in the phone book for the number of Point Blank's management company. I dialed, and a receptionist answered. I said, "Bill Gladstone, please."

"Mr. Gladstone is no longer with the company. Is there someone else who could help you?"

"Oh, well, who represents Point Blank these days?"

"Point Blank, the band? Oh, I don't know. I love *Point Blank*! Do you work with them?"

"What? They don't—no," I said. "Never mind. Well, thanks anyway," I said. I hung up.

I must have one of their CDs around here somewhere, I thought. I dug around for a long time until I came up with one. Luckily, they thanked their manager and everyone at their management company, which was in New York, of all places. Well, fine, whatever. I called information and got the phone number.

I got another receptionist. "Hi, my name is Tom Good, and I need to get in touch with the band Point Blank."

"Could you hold, please?"

"Sure."

"Thank you."

Very polite, I thought. They *ask* you if you can hold, they don't just force it on you. I waited a long time. A song played in my ear. It was new, thank goodness, a girl singer whose name I couldn't remember. It started with a *P*. It was a seemingly simple melody that stuck in your head and lyrics that also seemed straightforward but had resonant meaning that twisted back on itself a couple of times.

"Hello?" It was the receptionist again. "May I help you?"

"Oh, I'm waiting for you to connect me with Point Blank's manager."

"I'm sorry, sir. I can't do that. You can contact him by e-mail or by traditional mail through this office. The address is—"

"No, you don't understand. This is Tom Good. I wrote 'I'm Losing My Mind,' 'Self-Destructive Tendencies,' and 'Worse Than Ever.' "

She didn't say anything for a second. Then she said, "So did you want the address or not?"

"No," I said. "I want to speak to—"

"Sir, I can't—hold on," she said, because another line was ringing. Now I was listening to another song, a hip-hop song about sex.

She was back. "Sir, let me put you through to one of the secretaries."

"Good idea, you know, I'm not just some—"

"Mr. Frank's office?" said a different voice.

"Oh. Hi. This is Tom Good. I wrote Point Blank's early songs, on the first album, I actually started the band, and I was wondering if I could get a message to them. To the band."

"Sure."

"Sure? Oh, great, because I was expecting you to put up a fight! The woman who answered first—"

"What's the message?"

"I mean, look, I know it's part of your job to protect these guys from weirdos and obsessive fans and so on, but isn't another part of it getting people through when they need to get through?"

"Absolutely," she said. "What's the message?"

"OK, um. OK, it's for Adam Blackburn. This is Tom Good. Tell Adam that I would like him to call me." I gave her my number.

"I'll give him the message."

"When?"

"As soon as possible."

"Like, today?"

"As soon as possible. They're recording right now, so I'm not sure they're going to be available."

"They're recording? Perfect. If you could try to get that to them right away then, I would really appreciate it." Of course, I realized that she had no incentive to do this. *"They* will too," I added. "The band will. Appreciate it. They will." I was becoming less convincing with each word I uttered.

"I'll do my best."

"I know you will. You sound really—"

I was going to say "reliable," "sincere," something to inspire her to rise to that level, but she interrupted me.

"I'm sorry. I've got another call."

"Well, thank you for doing this for me. Really. I appreciate it. So much."

"Sure thing."

She hung up. I hung up. I tried to calculate how long it would take to hear back from them. The trouble was, I had no idea where they would be recording, so I couldn't figure out the time zone. I pictured Adam waking up to the blinking red light of a hotel phone. I saw him get the message, smile, and call the other guys in the band. I smiled myself.

seventeen

As soon as I woke up in the morning, while I was making some of that sweet coffee, I looked in my empty refrigerator. Pathetic! I really did need to get some real food. Come to think of it, I better get some pretty good stuff. Diana might call and want to come over. Or she might just drop by without warning me. What if she brought Jack? I'd need—what?—chips and cookies and healthy stuff like apples and celery.

I made a long list of groceries. I re-recorded the outgoing message on my answering machine. "You have reached Good. I'll be right back."

Wait! Better put some music in the background. I got a guitar, pushed the button, played a little greeting riff.

"This is Good. I'll be right back."

Hold on. Did that mean they shouldn't leave a message? OK, I played the greeting riff again, making sure it was a happy, welcoming one, then I said, "This is Good. Please leave a message." On second thought, music on an answering machine was cheesy. With no music, I said, "This is Good. I'm out right now. Please leave a message," which was exactly what I had in the first place.

I went to the store. I tried not to take too long, although I knew it was really too soon to expect any calls.

. . .

Adam had begged me to stay in the band. It was painful remembering it, embarrassing. The poor guy was panic-stricken when I told him I wasn't going to stay. He kept asking me to get together with him over the next three months, meeting with me at various coffee shops, a club, a park even, to try to get me to change my mind. He said. *"Don't* do this. Don't *do* this! You're going to regret it for the rest of your life. And what about *us?* Don't you feel any loyalty to us? The band? We were counting on you! You told us this band was forever, and we believed you! What happened? Really. What happened to you, man?"

God, I hated that question. Even that long ago I hated it.

I kept telling him, "You'll be fine. You don't need me. Really. You can write your own songs." Of course, he had never written a single song in his life. He came into the band as a good-looking lead singer. He really had no other marketable talents. I just wanted to get out, and I was willing to say anything to make that happen. I wanted to be away from the interviewers and the fans who thought they knew you from listening to your songs. They thought they could read your whole life story in a lyric sheet. "The songs are fake!" I wanted to say. "I made all that up. The songs are just a brick wall for me to hide behind!"

Adam finally gave up. Sure, I felt guilty for sending the band out into the world with their limited abilities and no leadership. Of course I did. But what choice did I have? It was too awful having everybody try to see inside me all over again. I mean, it was bad when it was just my parents and a couple of therapists. But it was unbearable when it was a whole audience full of people who didn't know me at all. It was way too much like when Jack died, when everyone was checking my facial expressions all the time and trying to figure out what I *really* meant by everything I said. I didn't mean anything, of course, just like in my songs.

I cleaned my apartment while I waited for the phone to ring. If Diana dropped by unexpectedly, just on the spur of the moment, to, oh, visit for a few minutes, I'd wanted the place to be clean.

I had to work at The Club that night, and I wasn't looking forward to it. Probably as soon as I walked out the door, someone would call. Wasn't that the way it always happened?

The Club was nearly empty all night. The guy who was playing had had a hit song about twenty years before, but nothing of his had taken off since then. I tried not to look at him too much or listen to the songs he played. It depressed me. Was he a version of me? I tried not to think about it. Out at the front bar, though, you couldn't do much on a slow night. You could hardly pull out a novel and start reading or launch into a massive bar-scouring session in full view of the performer who had not drawn a crowd. You had to stand there and look interested. It was part of the job. Half of the waitresses were sent home early that night because there wasn't enough for them to do. The hours stretched out. By the last song, it seemed as though I'd been there a week. I was exhausted, completely wrecked, from standing around and doing nothing.

When I got home, I was stunned not to find the light on my answering machine blinking. I had not even considered this possibility. I pushed the button anyway, just to make sure. The fake woman's voice came on: "You. Have. No. Messages."

"That's OK," I told her. "It's way too soon anyway." I mixed up some of that coffee and went into my closet with my guitar.

The next afternoon, I was still waiting. I was playing my guitar, but really I was waiting. I had the phone in the closet with me.

Eventually, I told myself, Diana would call. She would say that she had thought it over and that she wanted Jack and me to get to know each other. They would come over, and I would give them cookies and coffee. I wouldn't give Jack coffee, of course. I would give him orange juice or lemonade or soda. If she let him drink soda. She might not. But anyway, I had all those drinks at my house now. I had cleaned. Again. All my guitars were lined up on their stands, ready to go. Jack would say, "Cool!" when he saw all the guitars. He would eat cookies and ask me if he could play a guitar. I would let him choose the one he liked the best. It was fine with me. I had bought real coffee for Diana, not that artificial, sugary crap that I drank myself. In fact, I had even put that little tin way in the back of the cupboard so that she wouldn't see it when she came, if she happened to open up the cupboard to get something for herself. She might feel comfortable enough to do that. She really might.

I was trying to work on a song I'd been writing. I was sweating in my closet. My shirt was starting to stick to me. I opened the door and went out, getting a drink of water from the fridge. I stepped outside my door for a minute to stand in the fresh air.

I went back inside to get an acoustic, the sunburst again. Some people in the neighborhood might not appreciate hearing an electric guitar outside. I took a stool and the guitar out behind the house. There was a patch of crabgrass there in back that gave way to the cracked asphalt in front of the garage. My neighbor Robin had most of the garage for her car, an old station wagon. I parked my bike between her car and her boxes of stuff. I left my car parked on the street. Anyway, I sat there in back on the stool. *What?* I was thinking. So maybe I hadn't played anywhere but a closet in a really long time. That didn't mean I couldn't do it today. All I had to do was pretend that I was exactly the kind of person who didn't mind playing my guitar outside. I could work on the chord progression for the song I was writing. Maybe some lyrics would come to me out here.

I hadn't looked at my watch. When I heard all the noise of the four kids next door, I realized that being outside wasn't going to work. They were arguing about who got the biggest and why it was no fair. I pictured brownies. One of them got a little extra and that was what was causing all the trouble.

I was still tuning the guitar when I heard their door slam. I heard them coming but did not move. Maybe if I didn't talk to them they'd go away. Elise was on a skateboard, I saw out of the corner of my eye. She was pretty good too. She was flipping it around 180 degrees over and over. Mike was licking an ice-cream cone and looking at me. That was what it was. I could see how ice-cream cones would be hard to make exactly the same. Even if they were equal in size, they might not appear to be equal.

"Hey, cool, Mr. Good. You got a guitar!" said Mike.

"Well, duh," Elise put in. "He had that before."

Mike said, "Is it hard to do that? It looks hard. It sounds good, though. Get it? Good, like your name. Do you know how to play any songs, or do you just know how to play like that?"

"I know a few songs," I said.

"Can you play a song?"

Elise said, "He's trying to, if you'd just shut up."

"I'm telling Mom you said 'shut up'!"

"So? You just said it."

"What song would you like to hear?" I asked, hoping to keep them from getting violent.

"Do you know how to play 'Kryptonite'?"

"I think so." I played the intro. Their mouths dropped open.

Naturally, they thought I was going to say, "Never heard of it," and ask if they wanted to hear "If You're Happy and You Know It."

Mike took three steps back in absolute wonder at my genius. "That is so amazing. Elise, go get Mom."

"I'm not getting Mom. You get Mom, you big fat baby."

"MOM!" Mike bellowed, his face going red with urgency.

Elise took a swipe at him before she covered both ears with her hands.

Their mother came surging around the side of the house. *"What?* What happened? Who's hurt?"

"No, I just wanted you to hear something. He can play 'Kryptonite.' "

She just looked at him. She didn't see me sitting there, as there was a bush between us, and she didn't know what he was talking about. "What? My God." She put her hand to her heart. "I thought you were injured. You scared me half to death, Michael Gunther."

"Mr. Good knows how to play 'Kryptonite'!" Mike said quietly, pointing at me.

I pulled down the branch of the bush.

"Oh!" I had startled her. "I didn't know you were there. I'm sorry. Were they bothering you?"

"He knows how to play 'Kryptonite,' Mom."

"Well, he's very talented, then," she said and smiled at him. "Wow, you know Mike's favorite song! That's great! Wonderful." She smiled at me too. "But, Mike, next time, just walk over and get me, OK? You scared me."

"He played it for me. It was so good. Do you know any other songs, Mr. Good?"

"A few," I said.

"Can you give me guitar lessons?" Mike said.

"What?" I said. This caught me off guard. "Lessons? Oh, I—no, I don't give lessons. I don't do that."

"Just one then? One lesson?" Mike held up a small index finger.

I shook my head. "You're not—old enough. Your hands are too small to fit around the neck of the guitar, and—" I looked at his mother for help.

"You'll have to excuse Mike," Robin said. "He's a music fanatic."

"Maybe he knows how to play one of your songs, Mom."

"Honey, I don't want to bother him. And I don't want you to, either. Why don't you come inside, Mike, and let Mr. Good play his guitar in peace."

"No way," Mike said. "He *wants* me to hear him play. Don't you, Mr. Good? I want to hear him. Play 'Babylon,' Mr. Good. You can play that, can't you? It's by David Gray. It's my mom's favorite. Listen, Mom. He's going to play it right now."

"How do you know all these songs?" I asked Mike. "You're only, what, eleven?"

"I'm seven." He looked hurt. It was supposed to be a compliment.

"Oh," I said. "Sorry. My mistake. So how do you know all these songs?"

"Me and my mom listen to the radio together at night."

I looked at Robin.

"Insomnia." She sighed.

"*Both* of you? Do kids get insomnia?" I said.

"Unfortunately," she said.

I played a little of "Babylon" for them.

"That's really good, Mr. Good," Mike said in a hoarse whisper, moving closer.

My phone was ringing! It would be either Diana or Adam. I was ready for both! For either. For anything. I jumped up and took several giant steps to my door. "Excuse me!" I called over my shoulder to the kids and Robin. "Phone call!"

Inside, I grabbed the receiver. "Hello?"

"Is this Tom Good?" said a woman's voice.

"Yes," I said.

"This is Angela. I work for the band Point Blank."

"Yes?" I said.

"Our New York office said you were trying to get in touch with us."

"I was trying to reach Adam," I said.

"OK, well, that's why I'm calling you back," Angela said.

"He can't return his own phone calls?"

"Not at the moment. They're recording."

"Right. And?"

"And they don't see or talk to anyone when they're recording. It's distracting."

"Ah. I see," I said. *Asshole,* I thought.

"So, what was it that you—"

"Wanted to talk to him about?" I filled in for her. "Just—well, I have some songs I wanted him to listen to."

"Sure. Right. I see. I'll tell Adam for you and call you back."

"Fine," I said. "Whatever."

I hung up. To hell with Adam. Fury flared up in me so quickly that I almost threw something. Can't even make a phone call he's concentrating so hard. My God. What *happens* to people when they get famous? It just confirmed, once again, that I had made the right decision in the first place.

I went in the kitchen and turned on the radio. "Kryptonite." Now I would never hear that song again—or "Babylon," for that matter—without thinking of Robin and Mike sitting up with insomnia, the boy in pajamas with cars or dinosaurs on them, and

Robin with—Great! Just great! That was not an image I needed lingering in my head forever.

The phone rang again. Diana! I jumped for it.

"Hi. This is Angela again. From Point Blank. I gave Adam the message."

I was about to say, "Angela? Could you do me a favor? Please tell Adam to go to hell."

But Angela spoke first. She said, "Adam said to tell you that it's great to hear from you. He's really happy you got in touch, and he would like to invite you to come to a show they have coming up."

"Oh, he would? Where are they playing?"

"In Los Angeles. On the tenth. Tickets will be waiting for you at Will Call."

"I'll think about it," I said. "Thanks for calling." I hung up.

I wasn't going to go. Why would I? What did I need those guys for? I got out of that years ago. And for good reason.

I closed my eyes standing right where I was, and I could see myself unlocking the door to a new house. The door was white, and there was a circular window in the top. Behind it was a brand-new place with clean carpets and new furniture. It had different rooms, not just one general, all-purpose, messy area. People were talking there. Music was playing, and—

I opened my eyes, turned around, and looked at my bed. I started to get sweaty and hot. Was it stuffy in here? I opened a window. That didn't help. It wasn't the air; it was the things I was looking at, the stained carpet, the old blinds that I'd never changed, my accumulated crap. It was my own life, making me feel choked and suffocated.

All right, I'd go to the concert. I didn't have to enjoy it. I just had to behave as if I were the kind of person who enjoyed this kind of thing. No one had to know.

eighteen

For the next few days, I worked on a song about waiting, finished it, and recorded it. I put some synthesizer tracks on it and used a drum machine. I recorded a couple of harmonizing vocal tracks. It had been a long time since I had gotten so elaborate on a song.

Diana still hadn't called. I thought of calling her. Should I? Maybe she just needed a little encouragement. Maybe she needed to know I was sincere, that I meant it when I said that I wanted to be involved with her and Jack, that I would be consistent in wanting this, that it wasn't just some kind of a phase.

I could call her, and we could go to the movies, something easy, something neutral, where we didn't have to talk too much or deal with each other. Why not? She still liked me; I could tell. She called all those times after we got together, didn't she? I would just show her that I had always cared about her, that I had been thinking about her all these years. I could make a whole CD with the songs I'd written about her. It would be like *Layla*.

Something told me that I shouldn't call her, so I went to see Ellen.

"You just have to give her some time to think, Tom," she said. "You're sure there was chemistry?"

"I'm sure there was," I said. "Pretty sure. *I* felt it anyway."

"It usually goes both ways," she said, nodding, reassuring me.

I looked at Ellen, sturdy, emotionally stable Ellen. "Sometimes

I am so sick of being myself that I just don't think I can take another minute," I said. "Do you know what I mean?"

She closed her eyes, blew out a stream of air. "Yes. I do. God, yes."

Ellen used to be married. I went to the wedding. It was in Pennsylvania, where they were living. The guy worked in her law firm, and they stayed married five years. He left her for someone else in the same firm. Ellen quit the firm and moved back out here. She said she would never get married again. She wanted a kid, though. I think she missed the possibility of a child way more than she missed having the husband. She checked into the various options—domestic adoption, international adoption, in vitro fertilization with donated sperm. None of these things worked out for her, for one reason or another. Eventually, she stopped talking about it. I don't believe that she stopped wanting a child, but she seemed to have decided that it hurt too much to talk about it.

"Do you think it's possible to change things about yourself? I mean, on purpose. Let's say there was something seriously wrong with your personality. Could you change and be a different way, if you wanted to badly enough?" I asked her.

"Oh, Tom," she said. "I really, really would like to believe that." She sighed this heavy, sad sigh that had years of heartbreak in it.

I wanted to fix this for her, to repair the things in her life that had disappointed her. A little frantically, I looked around her place. "Ellen?" I said.

"What?"

"You know that TV you've got in your bedroom?"

"Yes."

"I could put that up on one of those suspended shelves. Then you'd have more floor space *and* a better view of the TV."

She said, "I guess. But you don't have to."

"No problem. I *want* to. I'll go to Home Depot tomorrow."

n i n e t e e n

The phone was ringing when I got home. I got to it on the fourth ring, just before the answering machine came on.

"Hi," she said. "It's me. Diana."

"Hi," I said. My heart was pounding, partly from the run to catch the phone and partly from the thrill of hearing her voice.

"I decided you should meet Jack. I talked to him about it."

"You did?" I said it too fast. "What did he say?" This was happening way sooner than I expected. I was settled in for a long, long wait.

"First he said he didn't want to. Then, about five minutes later, he said he'd think about it. He disappeared into his room for a while, and I didn't hear anything. But, anyhow, he came back out a while later and said he'd do it."

"He'd do it? Does that mean he *wants* to or just that he'll go along with it?"

"I can't speak for him, but I *think* what he feels is curious about you, but also a little angry that you haven't come forward sooner."

"Angry?" I said. "Come forward? How could I? I hope you told him that I didn't know he existed! He's angry? Already? Before I've even met him?"

"Well, yeah, of course," she said.

"Of *course?* Are *you* angry?"

"Well, yeah. You didn't try to find me. You didn't try to find out why I left, even. Wouldn't you be angry?"

"I thought you left because of the car thing! That's what you said. And I got a car. You just never gave me a chance to—"

"You've missed his whole life up to now is how it seems to him."

"It wasn't my fault! *You* did that. Have you mentioned to him that this was all *your* decision?" My voice sounded harsh. This was not going well.

She didn't say anything for a minute. "I mean, look at it from his point of view. You've missed a lot: birthdays, Christmases, school projects, sports events—"

"But *you* left *me!*" I said, incredulous. "You moved! You left town! You didn't contact me! *I* got in touch with *you!*"

"You didn't want a kid!" If it's possible to yell in a whisper, this is what she did.

"You're right! I didn't!"

"If you had known, would you have participated? Would you have stayed with me and been his father?"

"What? You left! You took off! I didn't get a chance! You didn't give me a chance to even consider it!"

"But *would* you? You didn't contact me! You didn't even try to find out where I was!"

I didn't answer right away. "How do you know what I tried to do?"

"My parents are listed in the phone book. You didn't call them. In more than ten years, you didn't call."

"OK, OK, fine. You're right, I didn't. But now I have. As soon as I found out about the kid, *I* called *you.* Now we're in touch. And I want you to know that I thought about you. I thought about you a lot. You never left my—you never left my heart."

She didn't speak for a few really long, heavy seconds. Then she said, "You know what, Good? That's a really great line. You might want to write it down so you don't forget it. You might want to use it again sometime. But you know something? Spoken live over the phone to me just now, it sounded like crap."

I didn't have to write it down, I had already used it in a song, which was about Diana, not that I'd tell her about it now.

"I'm sorry you feel that way," I said. "I meant it sincerely."

I heard a soft, moist sigh coming through the pause at the other end of the phone. Was she going to cry again? Oh, God.

"Well," she said. But she left it there, the word floating in space between us.

"Well?" I prompted.

"How do you want to arrange this meeting?"

"I guess you could come over here," I said.

"You don't sound like you mean that. If you don't want to do this, we don't have to, you know. You're the one who asked for it!"

"What? I *want* it. I just invited you over. Come right now, if you want."

"We'll come tomorrow. Afternoon. After school. About four."

"Great. Perfect. Can't wait."

"We'll see you then. Good-bye."

She said it in that way that is good-bye but also *go to hell*. People don't really say the whole word *good-bye* unless they mean *go to hell*. At least that's been my experience. *I'll change her mind*, I was thinking. *I'll make her see how nice I can be, how caring, and how sincere. I'll practice every day.*

The next day, I got up early and went shopping. I had to make my place look better. Right now it looked like the scene of a crime or something. Or like some weird person with a lot of odd pets might live there. I wanted it to look like a real person lived there. A nice person with real furniture and a real TV and matching towels. I didn't want to scare the kid with my ugly comforter the very first time he saw me.

I went to a department store, the kind that sells everything. First I bought towels, six blue bath towels, matching hand towels and washcloths, a bath mat, and even a matching dispenser for liquid soap. The saleswoman put it all into a giant bag for me. Then I went to the kitchen department and picked out a new kettle for boiling water. It was very shiny and would make all my pots and pans look dingy and banged-up. So I bought a whole new set of those too. I took all this stuff out to the car, and then I came back in for more.

I picked out a bed, a desk with a bookshelf that matched, an entertainment center, a new kitchen table and chairs, and a lamp with a white shade. I was thinking, *This is great. I can just buy the stuff as if I were the kind of person who had nice stuff all the time.*

The salesperson was a young guy named Chris. "Wow," he said as he typed the order into a computer. "Starting a new life?"

"Yeah," I said. "Kind of." He probably thought I was getting divorced or something. "I just needed a change," I said.

"Change is good," he said. "Change is a good thing."

"Right," I agreed.

"Last name?"

"Good," I said.

"Oh—like, G-O-O-D?"

"Exactly."

There was more typing involved in the transaction than I had expected. I was eager to get the new stuff home and set it all up. I would have to call the Salvation Army to pick up the old stuff. Temporarily, I could store it in the garage. The sales guy seemed to take a long time. I sat on a couch while I was waiting. If I had any space, I would get one of these too.

"OK, sir," said Chris. A printer started grinding out forms. "Your pieces should ship in about four to six weeks."

"What?" I said.

"Yeah, that's the soonest they can—"

"But I needed them right away!" I said. "I was hoping for, maybe, later this week?" I didn't want to say today, which was what I had really been hoping, because he would think I was a complete idiot.

"Sorry, see, your items are in all these different warehouses in different parts of the country. We don't actually have any of this stuff here."

"You don't?" Of course they didn't. What was I thinking?

"No, but you can track your order with this number here." He tore a pink form out of the printer and pointed to some numbers on the bottom. "You call this, and punch in this, and they'll tell you when to expect it. You can call as often as you want for updates."

"Oh," I said. "I see."

"So . . . do you still want to get it?"

I thought about it. "Yeah," I said. "I do. Thanks." I took the pink form, folded it, and put it in the pocket of my T-shirt. It really didn't seem like much to go home with. But I still had my bathroom and kitchen stuff. At least I could use that right away.

At home, I hung up the towels in the bathroom and filled the soap dispenser. I piled the old towels into a box. I got my old pots and pans and put them in the box too. I took all this out to the garage.

Then I went to work on my main living space. I tried to throw stuff away that looked messy or made me seem immature. I had been saving that calendar from a couple of years ago, because it had pictures of famous guitar players. Actually, it was more than a couple

of years, it was 1987. Not the decorating theme I was going for at all. I took it off the wall, meaning to get rid of it, but I had grown attached to those guys after all this time. I stuffed it into a drawer, which now didn't quite close.

I dusted, arranged, and dumped a bunch of old stuff into a garbage bag. Then I went out back and put the bag in the trash. I wanted to come back to this great surprise, a transformed apartment. No such luck. What I saw was a run-down bunch of old furniture that looked like rejects from the Salvation Army. I needed something to perk the place up. *A plant!* I thought. *A plant will help, something fresh and green and alive!*

I drove down to the grocery store to get one. My neighbor Robin was there. I had forgotten that she worked at the store. If there was one thing I did not enjoy, it was unexpectedly running into people I knew. It happened that Robin was working in Produce today, which was right next to Floral. She was unloading apples from a cardboard box. She looked up. "Hi! Can I help you find anything?" she said, then she saw it was me and got embarrassed. They're supposed to greet the customers. It's a rule that the employees have to be friendly.

"Oh, hi," I said. "I'm getting a plant." I bent to stare at a bunch of plants on a stand.

Robin nodded. "Gift?"

"No, I just—I thought my place needed one."

Robin nodded.

I looked at all the plants. Which one? They all looked fine together, but separately each one looked kind of pathetic. I straightened up and stepped back. I had no idea which to take. I wiped my hands on my pants, making wet finger tracks along the denim. I was sweaty all of a sudden, just from the strain of trying to choose the right houseplant. Free-floating anxiety, it's called. I knew all

about it because I'd had it before, and I'd researched it. I had done too much changing for one day. My heart started to pound, and I wanted to walk out of the store and forget about the stupid plant. But Robin was there, and I had already told her I was going to buy one. I just stood there, the plant decision far beyond my capabilities now.

Then Robin was standing next to me. What was she going to say? What's the matter with you? Choose one, would you? Just pick one up!

Robin bent down. "These are nice. If you forget to water them, they don't die right away. They kind of wait for you to remember them again. You could put it near your kitchen window. They get little purple flowers on them, if you're really lucky."

"Oh," I said, barely choking the word out of my sticky throat. I took the pot from her. "Yeah. Good idea." Now start walking, I told myself, before you have to talk again.

"Good luck with it!" she called after me.

I didn't say anything back. It wasn't absolutely required in this situation, I decided. I tried to convince myself that she had already turned back to the apples—or maybe she was helping another customer—and didn't notice that I hadn't answered.

I took the plant home. It had one of those plastic hooks on it, so you could hang it up. I gently tapped the nail into the plaster above my kitchen window. The nail went in. I hung up the plant. There. Easy. No big deal. Then a whole chunk of plaster fell right off with the nail in it. The plant crashed to the floor, spilling dirt and breaking off two major branches. I swept up the mess and set the plant down on the counter next to the sink. To hell with it.

twenty

It was almost four o'clock, and my place looked shabbier than ever. I thought cleaning it up had made it look worse. There were more bare spots from the things I'd removed so the dinginess of the paint and furniture was more evident. I didn't want to sit down because I didn't want to move a chair or wrinkle my cheesy bed-cover.

Now they were late. I was starting to get nervous about this when they pulled up at 4:08. Diana parked right out front. She had that purple Beetle. Very clean and new, of course. Perfect.

When they stepped out, my heart was pounding. I was seeing my son for the first time. He was tall, at least I thought he was tall. Of course, I had no idea what the normal height for his age was. He was slouching. Was he slouching? Did I slouch? Maybe he got that from me. He wasn't looking at the house. Maybe he was shy. Did he look like me? I couldn't tell. Diana knew the way, of course, as she had been here before.

They were getting closer, but still they didn't look at the house. Diana knocked in a way that was sort of gentle but strong at the same time.

I opened the door. "Hello," I said.

"Hi," Diana said.

The boy wasn't looking at me. *Give him time,* I was thinking.

He's shy. Nothing wrong with that. Perfectly normal. I said, "Hi, Jack. It's nice to meet you. I'm Good. I mean, that's my name. Last name. And people call me that. I'm your—Well, come in!" My voice made this phlegmy, croaky sound.

They walked in. He had on a big T-shirt that said VOLCOM and a pair of baggy shorts. Sneakers, of course. And he had glasses, very stylish, nice glasses, I was happy to see. They didn't make him look geeky or anything.

Jack looked around my place, at the walls, the ceiling, the bed. He peered around the kitchen door.

"OK." I clapped my hands together. It was a goofy thing to do. I don't know what came over me. Anyway, they both jumped at the sudden sound. "Sorry," I said softly. "Hey, can I get you something to eat?" I took three steps, and I was in the kitchen. "I have Oreos, ice cream, juice, milk, hot chocolate." I looked at them and waited. I wanted them to come in the kitchen and see that I at least had shiny new pots and pans.

Silently, they were consulting each other. He raised his eyebrows at her. She pressed her lips together. They were using a language that I didn't speak. What were they saying?

"No, thank you," Diana said. "We're fine. Jack just had a snack after school."

"Oh," I said. "Right. I see. Of course. So, OK, why don't you sit down?" I had exactly three chairs. The thing about the chairs was that they didn't match. I wished for, I longed for those matching chairs I had chosen today. I was tempted to explain that new, better, matching chairs were coming. I wanted them to know that these were not my *real* chairs.

We sat down. Diana was next to me.

"What do you think?" I said, gesturing around the place. I don't know why I asked them this. I was just setting myself up for criticism.

Diana said, "It looks exactly the same as I remember it." An indictment.

"Yeah," I said. "Well."

Jack was looking at the guitars, which I had carefully lined up along one wall. "Jack," I said, "do you play an instrument?"

"No," he said quietly.

"Oh. Well, when I was your age, I started playing the guitar. I had lessons." I waited for a reply. When there wasn't one, I said, "I loved it! The second I had the thing in my hands, I knew it was for me. The Beatles were a very big deal then. I don't know if you know about them, but I was a big fan. That's why I wanted to take guitar lessons. Hey! Maybe *you'd* like to learn!" I jumped up too fast and bumped into the table. Diana steadied it with her hand. I took an acoustic guitar off its stand and held it out to Jack. "Want to try?"

He shook his head.

"Oh, well. Just hold it. Here. It will feel so good!"

He shook his head again.

"Come on," I said. "You don't have to play anything. Just hold the guitar." Diana was giving me this look, like, *Take it easy, would you?* And the things I was saying, the sound of my voice, made it seem like I was trying to make him do something bad, something he really shouldn't. I knew I was pushing, but suddenly it was really important to me that he take the guitar from me at least and just hold it.

He took it, making it very clear that he didn't want to. He set it across his lap and leaned his elbows on the strings. I didn't say, "Don't do that! You'll get it out of tune!" I had *some* self-restraint. A tiny little scrap of judgment.

"I'll play you one of the first songs I ever learned," I said. I got another guitar, an electric one. I plugged it into a small amp and played "Gloria." I didn't sing. Frankly, it sounded lame without words. As I played, I heard the neighbors' door open and shut. When I was finished, I looked up to see Mike trying to peek through my window while appearing to make some minute adjustment to the wheels of his skateboard.

Jack was leaning on his hand, waiting for me to be finished.

"OK," I said. "Well, it's pretty simple. I could teach you to play that, if you want."

For the first time, he looked me straight in the face. He said, "No." He looked at his mother. "Thank you." It was then that I realized he didn't look that much like me; he looked more like my brother, Jack. His mouth had the same shape, and his eyes were the same gray blue. It was unnerving being stared at with those cool eyes again.

I put my guitar down. I nodded. "Got it." I took the one he was holding and put it back. "So, tell me. What are some of the things you like to do? Are you a skateboarder? Do you surf?"

He wasn't going to answer. For maybe the first time in my life, I was conscious of what it meant to be regarded as an adult, and not in a good way, either. I searched for something to say that might redeem me. "Do you listen to music? Who do you like? What radio station do you listen to? How about that new blink-182 CD. Do you like that?"

Silence. Then, "That CD has a parental warning label. I'm not allowed—"

Quickly, I said, "Of course, and you shouldn't—"

Then Diana said, "He doesn't care for music much. I mean, it's not a big passion with him the way it is with some kids. He doesn't listen to music at all, actually. We have a radio in the car that we never turn on. And we don't use the one in the house." She shrugged, apologizing.

I could allow for differences in taste. I knew there were plenty of people who didn't like what I liked or follow popular music with my particular zeal. But how could he not *care* about it at all when he was so obviously my kid? *Could there have been some mistake about that?* I found myself wondering. He had the Good nose, the hair, the eyes, that was for sure. But how was it possible that he could get my family genes for physical features and not the passion for music?

I looked at Diana. She shrugged again. "He likes video games," she said hopefully. "There's this one he's been working on lately. It's called 'Escape from the Nanolobe.' There's this main character named Parsifal, and he—"

Jack interrupted, suddenly coming to life. "He's locked into this tower at the beginning of the game. There's these evil guys who took over when Parsifal's father died. They each have special powers, but you don't know what they are at the beginning. You have to find out what they are and how to get around them. 'Cause, see, the whole place really belongs to him. To Parsifal. He has to get out of there and go to this other land, get all these powers, and then come back and get control of the castle."

"He's really good at it," said Diana. "He works so hard! You should see how he concentrates. He's beaten two levels already!" She patted his back.

"That's not that good. I'd be further if I could play it every day, instead of just on weekends." Jack shot her a look.

"I don't let him play on school nights," Diana said.

"Everybody else gets to play anytime they want," Jack whined.

"What if he has all his homework done?" I wanted to know.

Diana sat up straight and pressed her lips together. "Weekends only. That's the rule."

It dawned on me kind of late that she had expected me to

back her up on this. "Right," I said. "Exactly right. School nights are for, well, school stuff and, uh, and reading. Books. And all that."

"It's not fair!" Jack mumbled. "I'm the only one who has that rule."

"I bet you're way smarter than those other kids, though," I said, trying to score points with both of them. "I bet you read really well, and I bet you're great in all your other subjects."

"No, I'm not. The kids who play video games all the time are way better than me."

"Oh. Are you sure?" I looked from Jack to his mother. "But it's not *because* they play video games all the time, is it?"

"What *is* it because of then? They were just born smarter?" Jack said.

"No, of course—what? Are you kidding me? I'd bet anything you're the smartest kid in your school. Seriously, you seem extremely smart to me. I'll bet you're great in school. I'll bet your teacher thanks her lucky stars every day that she has you in her class."

"Yeah, right," Jack muttered.

"So listen," I said, desperate to change the subject, "was there anything you wanted to ask me? You probably have some questions, too, right?"

"Well, yeah," Jack said.

"OK, shoot."

I was leaving myself wide open here. He could ask, "Why didn't you marry my mom?" or "Why haven't you ever sent me a birthday present?" or "Why have you lived in this tiny apartment for all these years?" He might want to know, "What *happened* to you that you just sit in here and make up songs that no one ever hears?" I braced myself.

Jack took a breath. "What kind of car do you drive?"

"Oh," I said. "Uh, car? Oh, I mostly drive a motorcycle. I do have a car though." I looked at Diana. "My car is a Honda wagon."

He curled his lip a little bit. "I've never even *heard* of a Honda wagon."

"Yeah. Oh, sure. They made them for quite a few years. It's not their most popular model, for sure. I bought it used. I got a very good deal." What did he want to know about my car for?

"He's into cars," Diana said. "It's another one of his interests. *Loves* cars and everything about them! One of the first things he learned to name, right after colors, was models of cars! Before some animals. Really. He was two when he started pointing and saying, 'Toyota!' 'Ford!' "

"Oh. Well. That's—amazing. I guess he gets that from you."

"By the time he was three, he had all the makes memorized. *I* can't tell a Lexus from a Mercedes, frankly, but Jack's really good at it."

"Hmm," I said. If there was one thing that left me cold, it was cars. But I guess I could see the appeal. Sort of. Maybe I could get interested, if I worked at it a little.

"Listen," Diana said, standing up. "We have to go. Jack has homework." She gave Jack a visual nudge, sort of narrowing her eyes and pushing her head forward a little.

Jack stood up. "It was nice meeting you," he said to the floor.

"It was a pleasure meeting *you,* Jack."

They walked to the door.

"OK," said Diana. "So, I'll call you, OK?"

"Sure."

I followed them out the door and walked them to their car. After Jack got in, I closed the door for him, first making sure that his hands and feet were out of the way. I waved as they drove off. After they were gone, I stood next to where their car had been, looking at the For Sale sign that had recently gone up in front of the house across the street.

Shoot, I was thinking. *They didn't even go in the kitchen or the bathroom!* I bought all that new stuff and they hadn't even seen it.

twenty-one

I turned around to go inside. Mike was standing there. "Who was that boy?"

"Believe it or not," I said, "he's my son."

"Oh," he said. "Are you giving him guitar lessons? I wanted guitar lessons, and you said no."

"Well I—" I stammered. "Remember your hands are still too small."

Mike looked at his hands. "What should I do?"

"Wait," I said. "Until they get bigger."

"I want to do it now. I want to play 'Kryptonite.'"

"I know you do. I understand completely. I know exactly how you feel. You just have to wait a little longer, that's all."

"Can you play it for me again?"

Actually, I wanted to sit down and stare into space for a minute, to think about what just happened. But this kid was so urgent about everything, it was hard to keep telling him no. "Is your mom home?"

"Yeah," Mike said.

"Then go ask her if it's OK if you hear me play 'Kryptonite' again. Tell her we'll be right outside here."

Mike took off at a run. I went inside. I could hear their conversation through the kitchen wall.

Mike: "Mr. Good is going to play 'Kryptonite' again for me. Is that OK?"

Robin: "Was it his idea or yours?"

Mike: "Mine, but he said yes if you say yes. We'll be right outside here. He said to tell you."

Pause.

Mike: "Can I?"

Robin: "See, I don't want you to bug him. He's not used to kids. He doesn't have any and—"

Mike: "Yes, he does. One was just over there. Bigger than Elise. No, *really*. He's giving him guitar lessons, and he said when my hands are bigger—"

Robin: "Did he *say* it was his kid? Are you *sure?*"

Mike: "Yeah. So can I go?"

Robin: "For a few minutes. And be polite. Make sure you say thank you after he plays the song for you, OK? Don't keep asking him to play songs. Just the one is enough, OK? He might have to go somewhere and—"

Mike: "I'll be so polite!"

He was already knocking on my door by the time he finished the sentence.

"Well, what a surprise!" I said, opening the door.

"Are you joking?" he asked, tipping his head to one side.

"Yes."

"Oh. What are you doing?"

"I'm taking these chairs outside, one for you and one for me."

Outside, Mike looked over his shoulder toward his own door. "Thank you for inviting me," he said.

"You're welcome. Wait right here a sec, OK?"

I went back inside and took down the same guitar I had been using when Jack was here. "OK, buddy. Let's go." I played some of "Kryptonite." The kid's face lit up like a little beacon. It was hard not to feel good about your performance with that kind of audience response.

"OK, now I'm going to let you play it."

"What?" he said. Shock flooded his little freckled face.

"Yeah," I said. "I'll tell you what string to play. OK, now this one right here. See, I'm pressing it down up here with this hand. Perfect. Now that one. Right. This one. Wow, you're good." I got him through the chorus. I never saw such a small face concentrate so hard. It took a long time. I had to restrain myself from smiling, he was so serious. "You're great, bud. A real natural. Want to do that again a little faster?"

"OK," he said, getting ready to concentrate.

"Wait," I said. "You need a little break, I think. Am I right?"

"Yeah," he said. "It's hard."

"Sure is, but you've got talent. Hey, you want a cookie, while we're having our break?"

"Yeah!" he said. "I mean, yes, please."

"OK," I said. "Do you like Oreos?"

He nodded.

"Wait a second. I'll get you a couple." Since I had them, I might as well use them. Mike stood at the door watching me get the cookies from the kitchen. I left them out on the counter, in case he wanted more.

"Thank you," he said, taking two Oreos. "We don't have cookies."

Uh-oh, I thought. "You mean, your mother doesn't let you eat sweets?"

"No," he said. "I mean, we eat them so fast we always run out."

"Oh, yeah," I said. "Well, I have plenty."

We played the chorus again, very, very slowly. He was standing in front of me, while I told him what to do. His tongue was sticking out a little, and he was holding his breath.

When the chorus was finished, he said, "Wait! I have to go get my mom!" Halfway to his door, he turned around. "Can you please do it again with me for my mom?"

"Sure," I said. "Of course."

Robin came. "I'm sorry," she said. "Is he bothering you?"

"Not at all. We're having fun, aren't we?"

"Yeah," Mike said. "Hey, Mom, he has cookies. You want a cookie?" He opened my door to go get her one.

"Mike!" she said. "You're a guest!"

Quickly, I said, "Please get your mother a cookie, Mike. Get her two. They're on the kitchen counter."

"OK," Mike said, hurrying inside. "Do you want one, Mr. Good?" he called from the kitchen.

"No, thanks. I'm not really a cookie person."

"How come you got 'em, then?" he said, returning to hand the cookies from his sweaty little hand to his mother's smooth, white one.

"I got them for the little boy you saw earlier. My, uh, son. He didn't want any, though. Shall we play?"

"Yup," he said. He looked at his mother and smiled.

"OK, scout," I said. "That one." I pointed; he plucked. "Now that. That."

We played. They both smiled at me. "Thank you," Robin said. "That was really nice of you." There was a long pause. She ran her hand over Mike's hair. "I didn't know you had a son."

I nodded. I was so pleased with myself for not blurting out, "Neither did I!" or "You could have knocked me over with a feather!" I didn't say anything.

"No wonder you're so good with Mike."

"No, I—well, to be honest, I just met him today. This afternoon." So much for my tact.

"Oh!" she said, as if she'd stepped on a bee. "I'm sorry. It's none of my business. Thanks for letting Mike play your guitar. And thanks for the cookies."

She hurried him to their door.

twenty-two

The Point Blank show was at Staples Center in Los Angeles. I had been there once before, at the opening a couple of years earlier when Bruce Springsteen played. That was the last concert I'd been to—besides the ones at The Club, I mean.

The show was sold out, though a comp ticket was waiting for me at the box office, as promised. Inside, I looked around at the sea of milling people. With a jolt, I realized that I had started this. Me, of all people, Mr. Inertia. But now all that seemed to have happened to another person. There were lots of old people like me in the crowd but plenty of teenagers too. Broad appeal was the key to Point Blank's longevity. I found my seat, a good one in the center, close to the stage but not so close that saliva and sweat could possibly land on me or that the stage rushers would step on me or block my view.

As soon as I'd sat down, a young guy, about nineteen or so, started making his way down my row. He was looking at me. I checked the number on my ticket, checked my seat number. They matched. Did I know this guy? Had I waited on him at The Club? What did he want?

"Hey!" he said to me.

"Yes?" I said, feeling old again, the way I had with Jack, a grown-up in the children's department.

"Are you Tom Good?' "

Buckets of sweat gathered to spill out of my armpits. "Yes, I am. How did you know that? Who are you?"

"I'm Spike. I'm a fanatic fan. I've met all the guys in the band. Except you. Until now." He smiled, proud of himself. "And there was a *Behind the Music* about Point Blank. They had your picture. I taped it, and I've watched it like a hundred times."

I looked for Exit signs, which all seemed way too far away.

"Besides, every serious Point Blank fan knows about you. If they don't, they're not real fans. You're famous, dude."

I managed a small smile, forcing my face muscles to pull my lips up. It wasn't easy, but I did it.

"Really," he said. "You're like the Pete Best of Point Blank."

The fake smile was gone instantly. I looked at the empty stage. Could I just go back to my car right now? I didn't know this kid. It didn't make any difference what he thought. The band didn't have to know I had ever been here. In two hours, I could be home.

"Pete Best was the Beatles' drummer before Ringo," the guy explained to me, as if I might be slow-witted. "I did a paper on him for a history of rock 'n' roll class."

I said, "There's one major difference between me and Pete Best."

The boy thought about this. "OK. Wait now. I'll get this." He looked up, thinking. "Oh!" he said and clicked his fingers. "I know! He played drums and you played guitar?"

"*Play* guitar. I still play. Every day." He didn't have to know this. Did I think I had to prove myself to some Point Blank fan? Of course not. It didn't matter to me one bit what he thought about me. I said, "The difference is, Pete Best got fired. I left."

The guy just stood there looking at me, not saying anything. "*Why?*" he said. "What happened?"

"I didn't want to be in the band. I was done. I had other plans," I said.

He shook his head, uncomprehending. "OK," he said. "Can I have your autograph?" He handed me an open black Sharpie and turned around. He had on a Point Blank T-shirt autographed by all the band members. Except me. He was all prepared. "Right down here under Adam's would be excellent."

I could see that the only way to end this exchange was to write my name on this shirt. The guy leaned over, and the man next to me held the shirt taut for me. I signed beneath the autographs of the current members. You could tell I hadn't signed as many autographs as they had. I wrote "GOOD," and you could read it fine.

"Thanks, dude," the kid said. He shook my hand. "You're cool," and then as if I had strongly objected to this characterization of myself, he added, "No, really."

The lights went down then, so I didn't have to think of how to reply.

As the band came onstage, I stood up and worked my way past many sets of knees to exit my row. I went up concrete stairs and through a side door labeled EXIT, thinking how much I loved that word and that sign. The music started. Even out in the hall, it was about as loud as a jet taking off.

In the cement hallway, I saw the familiar boy/girl sign and walked toward it. I opened the door to the men's room. Fortunately for everybody in there, I found a free stall. I closed the door, locked it, and vomited repeatedly into the bowl, flushing several times. When I was finished, I wiped my face with toilet paper, which shredded in my sweaty hand.

When I came out, the men's room was almost as empty as my gut. There were small pieces of toilet paper clinging to my greenish-gray face. My shirt was soaked, as though I'd been caught on a lawn when the sprinklers came on. I turned on the sink and rinsed my face, which I dried with brown paper towels. I leaned on the sink a minute, getting my bearings.

I can leave anytime, I told myself. *I can get out of here in a matter of a few minutes.* I filled my cupped hand with cold water and slurped it up. *I can just go home, if I want to.*

I found my way back to my seat. I put my earplugs in. You might think this is funny, going to a concert and wearing earplugs. But let me tell you, if I hadn't been wearing earplugs for the last twenty-five years, I would not be able to hear conversations in crowded restaurants, let alone a dripping faucet in my own kitchen.

The show was long, three hours, including a little break before the encore. They played my songs during the encore, as I guess they had a thousand times before. Like everyone else in this gigantic room, I had heard those songs in grocery stores, on commercials, in movies, and on the radio. Still, after all that, they made me think of the summer I was trying to act not crazy, a music-induced flashback from my own songs.

Afterward, I went backstage. I had a pass. I told myself that if anyone questioned me in the slightest, I would go straight home. I did not have to prove anything to anyone. But no one questioned me. I had to wait a long time with a bunch of music journalists, friends of theirs I'd never seen before, and excited fans who had somehow finagled passes.

Finally, a door opened and a beautiful, young Asian woman walked out. She had on a skimpy black shirt that didn't reach the top of her skimpy black pants. Her navel was pierced. Angela, I guessed. She looked around the room. Her eyes landed on me. She crooked her finger, telling me to come with her. Everyone looked to see who I was, what made me so special. As if on cue, I began to sweat again. I went through the door with her, down a hall, to a room. There was the band. They'd taken showers. This seemed rude to me, to make all those people wait while they washed and dried their hair, put on different clothes.

"Good!" Adam called. He ran across the room and hugged me. The rest of the band gathered around, shaking my hand and patting my back. I was hoping I didn't feel as sweaty to them as I felt to myself.

"Did you like the show? What'd you think of the new stuff?"

"It was great," I said, smiling. "Really excellent." I have to say, it was nice to have someone care about my opinion for a change; it felt good to get all this attention.

"I'm glad you liked it. We were so nervous!"

"This guy puked right before we went on," said Colby, the bass player, pointing to Adam.

"You puked? For me?" I said. "That's very flattering. Thank you." I chose not to share my own experience.

"So tell us what you're doing," Adam said.

"Um, I write songs?" I said. I decided not to mention the bartending. "I . . . I write songs. Every day. And that's it."

"Cool," Adam said. "I bet they're great!"

"I don't know about that," I said, reaching into the back pocket of my jeans, "but I brought a tape."

"All right!" Adam said. "That is so cool. I'll listen to it as soon as I get back to the hotel. *Unbelievable."* He held the tape reverently. "New Good!"

I said, "Thanks for the ticket, by the way, and, uh, great show guys. My number's on there. So get in touch, OK?"

"Really? You mean it? After all these years, you'll let us call you?" He lowered his voice, and though I listened hard for sarcasm, irony, and sneering, there wasn't any. "That means a lot," he said. "It really does. Hey, thanks for coming! It was great to see you. Drive carefully!"

I left. It was a long way home, but I listened to a Springsteen tape and drank an enormous Coke. I was fine. Perfect.

At home, though, I couldn't sleep. Maybe it was the Coke. I lay in bed in the dark, listening to Robin's radio. It wasn't very loud, but as I said, earplugs have served me well over the years. It was a song from the Wallflowers' first CD. *What was worse,* I wondered, *being a musician who was known as the son of another, more famous musician, or being known as the Pete Best of Point Blank?* I had heard that part of Jakob Dylan's rider was that no one at any show at any time should mention his father. It must be brutal to have people forever comparing you to someone else. Every interview, every relationship, every interaction of any kind, must have all that nasty stuff lurking at its base at all times. John Lennon's sons must have the same problem. Horrible, and they were stuck with it their *entire lives.* Yeah, that would be bad. To my disappointment, however, I found that any way I looked at it, being Point Blank's Pete Best was worse.

I got up. I went to the fridge to get some water. Then I stood at the far wall of the kitchen so I could hear the song better. I pulled up a chair and leaned my head back against the wall. I heard Robin sigh and roll over. She was awake. I considered tapping on the wall to let her know I was there, just to say hello, a here-we-both-are-in-the-middle-of-the-night sort of thing. But right away, I could see complications that might result. She might think I was trying to tell her to turn the music down. Next time I saw her she would apologize. Or act peeved. I would have to explain what I meant by the knock. Or she might think my knocking meant that I needed to speak to her. She might make herself get up, get dressed, and come over.

So I didn't tap. I just sat there with my head against the wall, listening to the songs for a long time. I tried to pick up, from some subtle change in the atmosphere, some minute vibrational shift, when she fell asleep. I started to think about not being onstage, not being able to sleep, and listening to a wall. It all just sort of congealed into a song. I even had the bridge, the chorus, and a melody before I stood up to get a pen and put it in my trusty little notebook. I wrote it all out. It was called "The Things I Don't Do." It was kind of a rhyming list about being isolated and disconnected, one of my favorite topics.

I made up a nice lonely-sounding guitar solo with hardly any effort at all. Songs don't usually come in a big glob like that. Sometimes it's serious labor getting the right melody, or the words don't say quite what they're supposed to mean. This time it worked, though, maybe because I'd just been to the concert. I planned to play it for Mike in the afternoon until I realized that the subject matter was all wrong. Maybe I could write him his own song. About what? Something. Eventually, it started getting light and then the kids next door got up. Before I knew it, they had all left for school, and Robin had left for work. It was quiet again. I drank a cup of coffee, took a shower, and got dressed. Then I fell asleep facedown on my bed.

twenty-three

Diana didn't call. Was I surprised? No. Certainly not. I'm just saying what wasn't happening. I didn't call her either. Not getting or making phone calls was one of the verses of my new song.

Another thing I could have added was a verse about how I wasn't going to work. I hadn't gone to The Club in a few weeks. Every week, I called in for my schedule and then called other bartenders to cover for me. I had only two shifts a week anyway these days. After three weeks, Jeremy, the manager, called me.

"Good," he said, "are you OK?"

"Me? Yeah," I said. "I'm great."

"The reason I'm asking is because we haven't seen much of you for the last month or so."

"Right, well, I've had some things that, you know, came up. So, yeah, you're right. I haven't been in. That's why you . . . haven't seen me."

"So, Good?"

"Yeah?"

"Do you want me to take you off the schedule?"

"You mean, like, not work at The Club anymore? Like, you're firing me?"

"We could just say you're, um, taking time off or you're on a leave of absence or something."

"Uh . . . sure, OK, if that's what . . . yeah, sure," I said.

"I think it would be for the best, don't you?" Jeremy said. "Now, if you want to come back, just say so and it's done. OK? Everybody would be happy to have you. You'd have to, you know, show up a couple of times a week when your name was on the schedule. But really, you'd be welcome anytime. You've been practically a permanent fixture here for—how long? It's just that I want a little more staff stability. Are you OK with that?"

"Absolutely. I'm—yeah, I'm OK with that," I said.

"Fine," he said. "Be well, Good."

After I hung up, I had this shaky, dislocated feeling. *Maybe prisoners who have done a lot of years locked up feel this way when they're finally released,* I thought. I was happy to be free of that place, I supposed, as I had been there far too long. But now what? There was nowhere I was supposed to be for anything, nothing I was expected to do. I was just kind of rattling around loose. I called the store about my furniture. It wasn't the first time. A recording asked me what I wanted and instructed me to choose from a list of options. Then it asked me to enter my order number. Finally, it told me that my stuff would be delivered in one to three weeks. Well, great.

I went outside to throw away the trash. I got my mail and I picked up a gum wrapper I saw near the sidewalk. I watched as a young couple got out of a car across the street in front of the house that was for sale. Then a woman got out of the car, a real estate agent. They all went inside. I went back inside my apartment to get a guitar. I was out in the front yard strumming away when Robin and her kids got home. I was actually out there on a stool, playing my new song, as if this were the most natural thing in the world for me to sit around, playing songs in public for all the world to hear.

"Hi," she said, curious about seeing me there in the middle of the yard with my guitar. *What are you doing there?* her face was asking. She had her head tipped to one side, and she kept looking at me.

Just then, I realized what I was doing. I was waiting for them. I was sitting here outside, strumming my guitar, watching for their car, waiting for them to get home. I was practicing, not just guitar, but kids too. I needed kid practice way more than I needed guitar practice. I would hang around these kids for a while, get to know their likes and dislikes. Then when Diana did call again, I'd be ready; I'd have experience with kids. Kids can tell right away if you're clueless about what they eat and drink and like to do. I knew that much. And here I had a whole set of kids right next door to get started on until I could spend time with my real one.

"Hi, guys," I said. I smiled at them.

Robin looked a little confused, as if I might have mistaken her for someone else.

I felt my face go red as if they had caught me stealing.

"Hi," she said. "You look . . . Are you OK? Did something happen?"

"I got fired." I had to explain my aberrant behavior somehow, but as soon as I said it, I regretted it. Poor Mike. His face went pale, as if he might pass out or throw up, as if all the air had been sucked out of the atmosphere and he was left with nothing to inhale.

"Uh-oh!" Mike said.

"Oh, no!" Robin said with concern. "I'm so sorry. Is there anything we can—"

"No!" I shook my head. "It's not bad. Really! I'm glad. Relieved. It's a little change for me, that's all. You know, I didn't realize how much I didn't want to work there until I found out I didn't have to anymore!"

"Oh. OK," she said uncertainly. "Do you want me to find out if they need anybody down at—"

"No, thanks. But thanks. Really. I'm fine. I am."

Mike was biting his lip. Apparently, they'd had a previous experience with unemployment. How was I supposed to know that? Now I would have to prove somehow that I was OK. "Hey!" I said suddenly. "Are you guys free tonight? You want to go out to dinner?"

What was I doing? Didn't I have to wait around for Diana not to call? Didn't I have to eat my little frozen dinner?

I had an answering machine. I could save my frozen dinner for tomorrow night.

"Well..." Robin said. "Kids, go inside and get some cookies."

"We don't have any cookies," Mike said.

"We do! I got some more. *Go,*" she said.

The kids went in slowly, looking suspiciously over their shoulders at me and their mother.

"What?" I said to Robin as her gaze bore down on me. "*What?*"

"Are you sure? There are so *many* of us. Five. And some of us are noisy and hard to please."

I nodded. "We won't all fit in one car, you mean? So I'll drive myself. We'll get pizza someplace and after we'll go to an arcade." I was making this up as I went along, improvising.

She was shaking her head, looking at the door the kids had just gone through.

"No?"

"It's just—I mean—" Now she was biting her lip.

"Or something else," I said. "Mexican food and a movie?" How would I know what kids liked?

"Pizza is fine. Perfect, but—"

"My treat!"

She looked up. She opened her mouth but hesitated. Then she whispered, "Their dad was supposed to have them tonight, but he just cancelled. This would be a nice distraction for them, if you mean it."

"Of course I mean it!" What did she think, that I was some kind of a flake or something? Come to think of it, she might. "I mean it!" I repeated.

"I'm . . . well, I'm going to say yes! Yes! Thank you. We'd love to go with you."

"It will be my pleasure." And after I said it, I did this little bow. Honestly, sometimes I wonder what I'm going to do next.

There was a certain pizza place they liked in Mission Beach, which was good because I knew nothing about pizza places. And this new knowledge would come in handy very soon, I felt sure.

As we were eating, the kids gazed out the window at the roller coaster at Belmont Park, which was a block away. "You guys like roller coasters?" I said, making conversation. I saw Robin stiffen. *What?*

"Yeah!" Mike yelled.

"Don't talk with your mouth full," Robin said sharply.

"Do *you?*" Mike wanted to know.

"No," I said.

Mike looked crushed. What?

"Do you want to go on the roller coaster?" I asked him. Robin snapped her head toward me. "I mean, after we finish eating."

I was doing something wrong. Robin was shaking her head. Maybe she hated roller coasters, like I did.

"They're all too small, except Elise."

"Oh. Yeah," I said. "Got it." Height restrictions. This was just the kind of thing you didn't think about when you didn't have kids.

"I'm bigger now, Mom. You *said,*" Mike insisted. "Remember? My bathing suit didn't fit?"

I said, "Maybe there's something else they can—"

"And it's really *expensive,*" Robin interrupted, putting up her hand.

"I have plenty of money," I said and smiled. She didn't look happy. "We'll find something they can do over there. Let's go!"

Robin pressed her lips together. What? What had I done? Was I setting a bad example in some way? I was just trying to do what other people do. It was harder than it looked, believe me.

I paid the check.

At Belmont Park, there was a ride where you sat strapped into chairs. An elevator-type thing zoomed you up really fast and then dropped you down just as fast almost to ground level again. Everybody was tall enough for this, except for Ray, who didn't want to go anyway. Robin and I watched as the kids strapped themselves in. Then we watched them take off toward the sky at an alarmingly fast rate. I closed my eyes. It gave me a stomachache to watch them. When I opened my eyes, they were down again. They screamed as the thing started to rise. Robin was laughing, watching them.

"Oh, God," I said.

"What?" said Robin.

"I can't—I could never do that!"

"Go on that ride? Oh, it's not so bad, it's just—"

"I couldn't go on the ride either. No, I meant *watch* them go on that ride."

She laughed; I wasn't joking.

The kids did everything they were tall enough to do. Three times. Ray didn't seem to mind missing some of the rides. When he complained, Robin asked if he wanted a gum ball.

Ray was as excited to get to put a quarter in the gum ball machine as the others were to go on the rides. He took the task of putting the quarter in the slot very seriously. It required tremendous concentration, and by the time he was finished, the others were finished with their ride.

I rode home on my motorcycle behind Robin's car. I parked in the garage next to it.

Mike got out of the car, followed by Elise and Maddy. Ray had fallen asleep in his car seat, and Robin went to the back to get him out.

"Thank you, Mr. Good," Mike said, looking up at me.

"I keep telling you," I said as we started toward the house, "it's Good, man, just plain Good."

"OK, Good Man," he said in a whisper. The park had been noisy, and Mike was losing his voice. Or maybe it was all the screaming he had done on the rides.

We had almost reached our doors when I felt Mike's sweaty little hand tuck into mine. *Uh-oh,* I thought. Simultaneously, and inexplicably, a little spark shot through my crusty old, calcified heart.

I stood by the house with them as they waited for their mother to come with her keys and open their door. I did not let go of Mike's hand. Even I knew better than to let go now.

twenty-four

The next day when I woke up, there was something I had to do. What was it? It was important, and I had to do it right away. Then I remembered. I called the number on the sign across the street and asked how much the house was. A lot. Of course. What did I expect?

I looked at my most recent financial statement. I had some stock and some mutual funds. I checked the paper. My stock wasn't worth as much as it had been a while ago. But real estate prices had not come down at all, as far as I could tell. If I sold everything, I'd have enough for a solid down payment.

Why did I want a house anyway? I guess there were a few good reasons. I could rent out the rooms or maybe even the whole thing to get some income. I'd be a landlord then, and that seemed like a pain in the neck. I'd have to deal with tenants' complaints about leaky sinks, pilot lights going out, each other. No, it wasn't to be a landlord. I wanted a real house. To live in. This apartment wasn't a real house. It had only one room. I had just been waiting around in this one. The next time my son came to see me, I'd be living in a real house with a yard, bedrooms, bathrooms, new furniture, and my own washer and dryer.

I called the real estate agent back. "Hi. I just called about the house on Olivera. I was wondering if I could take a look at that house."

"Sure," she said. "Is this afternoon OK? I have a three o'clock opening."

"Fine," I said. "I'll meet you there."

At 2:58, I walked casually across the street, as if I were on my way to buy a newspaper. The real estate agent pulled up in a gold Mercedes, which did not help my plan to be inconspicuous.

"Hi, there," she said, getting out. "I've got the combination here somewhere." She had a huge bunch of papers in her hand that she was shuffling through. "Oh, yeah, here we go."

At the front door, my heart started to race as she fumbled with the combination of the lock hanging on the doorknob. "Got it!" she said as the door finally opened.

Inside, it smelled like paint. "It's been vacant for a month or so. Freshly painted, as you can see. This is the living room, which is nice and bright, and back here is a little study. Then you've got a powder room and the kitchen here. Do you have a family?" She looked at me.

"Uh," I said. "Well, I have a sister and some—but you mean a wife and kids? No. No family."

"Uh-huh," she said. "It will be very spacious for you then. And let me show you upstairs."

I followed her up the carpeted steps. There were four small bedrooms and one bathroom upstairs.

"Would it be just for yourself then?" she wanted to know.

"Yeah, it's kind of—I don't know, maybe it's too big, but I was..."

"Well, it's a great investment property. You'd be sure to make money if you just held on to it for even a few years."

"I guess," I said.

"All the bedrooms get a lot of light," the Realtor said. "You could trim that tree out front and make it even brighter. Do you want to see the backyard?"

"Sure," I said.

"It's not enormous, but you could put a barbecue on the patio there, and there's room for a table. These houses all have the separate garage. Some people take out the driveway and park on the street. That gives you a little extra yard space. Then you can either tear down the garage or maybe make it into a workroom or a guest house, or even a little rental unit for some extra income. There are lots of possibilities there. That play structure there would be easy enough to remove. You might even make that one of your contingencies."

I stood there looking around.

"So how do you like it?"

"It's nice," I said. "I'll have to think about it."

"I have plenty of other properties you can look at. Would you like to go right now? I have one that's an excellent value right off—"

"No, thanks," I said. "I was just going to look at this one. I'll just—have to think about it."

"These sellers are very anxious to find a buyer. As you can see, they've already moved out. So I wouldn't wait too long. At this price, it won't last."

I wanted to get back to my place. "Right," I said. "Thanks for showing it to me."

I hurried back across the street. I was just opening my door when Jeanette called down to me, "How much?"

"Too much!" I called back over my shoulder. Wouldn't you know Jeanette would be watching the whole thing?

twenty-five

I hadn't expected to hear from Adam right away about the songs.
A week would be too soon. Two weeks was reasonable. But three
had gone by and then a fourth. If you want your life to move forward,
I told myself, you're going to have to take action. Do something!

I decided to call Adam.

It took a few tries, but finally he called me back. I think they
were in New York or someplace at the time.

"Good!" he said. "So soon! First, years go by with nothing from
you, and now it's—what—like twice in two months? What's up,
man? What can I do for you?"

"The tape? Remember I gave you a tape? Did you listen to it?"

"Yeah, sure. Of course I did. Right away that night in the hotel.
I loved it. You're doing some great stuff. Thanks. It was really
inspiring."

"Right," I said. "So—"

"So, yeah, I liked it. The other guys liked it too. You have a lot
of layers to you, dude, complexity."

"Yeah, sure. So—maybe you didn't understand my—didn't
realize why—see, I wasn't just giving it to you for entertainment
purposes. I was submitting those songs for your consideration. I
was thinking maybe you might want to, you know, *use* some of
those songs. For Point Blank."

"Oh." There was a long pause. Then Adam cleared his throat. "I was—I'm sorry. I misunderstood. If you've been following us for the last fifteen years or so, and I'm not assuming that you would or anything, but if you've listened to our CDs, you know that all the songs we record are our own compositions."

"Well, yeah, I—"

"And, see, they follow a certain, um, progression. There are themes that we continue with each new work, so I don't—"

"Well, I do keep—"

"Listen. Of everybody I've ever worked with, you gave me the best advice, the best training."

"Training? Advice?"

"Yeah. Don't you remember? When you left? When you were yelling at me?"

"I guess I do remember a little yelling. I—"

Adam went on, "You were saying, 'You need to do it yourself! It's not enough to just play the music, you have to *create* the music! You have to *be* the music! It comes out of *you!* It has to be your guts, your brains, the raw insides of your heart that they hear!' And you threw a pen and a notebook at me. You said, 'It's in there right now, and no one can get it out but you!' "

"*I* said that?"

"Come on. You know you did. You don't remember? God, it was one of the most important moments of my life, I think. At first, I was completely freaked out. I thought the band and, well, my life were over! I had never written a song before, and I never wanted to write one. I had absolutely no desire or interest before you threw that pen at me. But I thought, OK, I'll try it once. One time. So I wrote one song. It was about you and what a self-centered tyrant you were."

"God. Really. I guess I was—"

"No, it's OK. I'm completely grateful. Are you kidding? Yeah, because if you remember, that was our first single off the next record. 'You Who Know Everything.' That was our first original hit. I'm still proud of that one. For a long time now, we've used only our own compositions. I'd consider using something from you, of course, because you're the founding member. But those songs weren't, they're just not, well, ours, for *us*. You know what I mean? We— they're just not the direction we're going. They're really *good* and everything. Everything you do is good. Hence, the name, I guess!" I didn't laugh. "I really appreciate the work you're doing, and I think if you'd like to get back into it, you really should. Audition some other players, start a band. Play some clubs. You'd be great!"

"Thanks for your input," I said.

"But if you don't want to, it's your choice. I mean, I have deep respect for you. You are the only person I know in this world who does music his own way, without compromise."

"Compromise isn't such a terrible thing, either, though," I said.

"I hold your individuality in the highest regard," he said.

"Thanks. Hey, listen, I've got to go. Good luck with, well, good luck with whatever it is you're working on!"

"Wait. Hold on. I meant what I said before, Good. What you told me when you were leaving the band? That changed my life. You *gave* me a life. It made all the difference in the world. It was like this, well, defining moment for me. If you hadn't said that, I think the band would have broken up when you left. Really. I credit *you* with my development as a songwriter."

"Well, thanks. But I don't deserve any credit. I was just saying that to say something. Because I wanted to get out. I don't even remember saying that stuff. I just needed to dump the whole thing on someone else because I couldn't handle it myself, and you happened to be the guy."

"Your motives don't matter at all. It's *what* you said. It was the exact right thing to say, and I'll be grateful to you forever."

"Well, don't be. I didn't mean any of it. I was completely confused at the time, and I didn't know what I was saying."

"I'm trying to tell you, none of that matters. Whether you care to recognize it or not, you gave me a life."

"OK, gotta go. So long."

I hung up.

I sat there for a minute, thinking. No need to panic. There are other things I can do to start my real life. What about the house? What if I did buy it? *My house. This is my house,* I could say, or *Meet me at my house in fifteen minutes.* I pictured myself mowing the lawn, barbecuing in the backyard. My new furniture belonged in that house. It would look great. When it finally got here. That house was exactly the thing I needed. It would be the beginning of my real life. Finally.

I called my account manager, Sherry. "If you liquidate your entire portfolio and cash in your IRA, you'll have the full purchase price," she said.

"So that means selling all my stock and bailing early on my IRA."

"Right," Sherry said.

"But then, of course, I would have no dividends to count on every month."

"That's right, but you'd have a house. And you'd still have your royalties."

"But the place I have is good, though. I mean, it's a rental, but it's worked for more than fifteen years. There's really no reason it shouldn't be perfect for another fifteen," I said. I looked out the window across the street.

"Your decision," she said.

"Yeah, go ahead," I said. "Sell everything." My heart was pounding, and I was sweating through my shirt again. What the hell, I'd been sweaty before. *I can do whatever I want,* I repeated to myself. *It's my money.* I wiped my wet left palm on my pants. Then I moved the phone to my left hand and wiped my right palm. "Liquidate everything. I'm going to buy the house."

"All right," she said calmly. Of course she was calm. It wasn't her life. "We'll have your check tomorrow. Would you like to pick it up, or shall I put it in the mail for you?"

"I'll pick it up," I said.

Before I had a chance to change my mind, I called the Realtor. "This is Tom Good. I'd like to make an offer on that house."

"What house was this now?"

"Oh, sorry. It was 16658 Olivera."

"Are you the single gentleman I showed it to the other day?"

"Yes."

"How exciting!"

This was easy. If I'd known how easy it was, I might have done it a lot sooner. You just say what you want to pay and the ball is rolling. Getting a real house, starting a real life, was going to be a breeze. I just needed a little toehold to get me started. I should have done this twenty years ago. Think of where I could have been now!

Nothing happened for a while. I hung around for two hours in my apartment before she called back. "I'm sorry," she said. "Another offer has just been accepted."

"What?" I said. "They can't do that! That was going to be my house!"

"It's disappointing," she said. "But you can put in a backup offer, in case this doesn't go through. Statistically one in every—"

"Thanks for letting me know." I didn't want to hear whatever it was she was going to say about other people's offers.

"I have other wonderful properties that I think you would—"

I hung up and called back Sherry at the brokerage firm. "Did you do it yet? The house was sold. I can't buy it!"

"Yes, I already liquidated everything," she said, instantly defensive. "Our policy is to act as soon as we're instructed by the client."

"I see. Well. Well, OK, then."

"I can put it in a CD until you know what you want to do with it."

I didn't say anything.

"Mr. Good?" Sherry said.

"That's fine, I guess. A CD is—yeah, fine."

I guess I hadn't realized how much I wanted that house until I didn't get it. It hadn't occurred to me that it wouldn't work for some reason completely separate from me.

I called Diana. I know I should have waited. I was not in the best mood, now that Adam hadn't wanted my songs and I lost my house. I knew I should have let her call me, but I had already waited a long, long time. I was tired of it. Besides, ever since I wrote that song, I kept noticing how many things I was *not* doing, and I was sick of not doing things.

"It's Good!" I said briskly and with a lot of fake energy.

"Oh, hi," she said, as if I wasn't at all what she had been hoping for.

"So, what's happening?"

"Jack is at a friend's, and I'm cleaning the kitchen. Why?"

"I just wondered if you'd thought about what I said."

"About money?" she said quickly. "Well, yeah. There's this computer camp that Jack wants to do, and it's really expensive. I was hoping you could—"

"Oh. That's not what I was—but sure," I said. "Be happy to. How much?"

"A thousand dollars."

"Wow," I said. "OK. I'll send you a check."

"And he'd really like a Playstation 2."

"I see. Sure," I said. "But what I meant was, I was wondering if you'd given some consideration to the idea of my spending some time with you and Jack."

"Oh, that," she said. "OK, we did talk about it, and he's thought about it."

"OK. And?"

"See," she said, thinking of how to put it, how best to tell me this, "he, well, he doesn't want to. I mean, right now. I'm not saying that couldn't change. At some point. He just, well, he—I guess because he's a kid and there's been all this time, he just doesn't feel, you know, any, any..."

"Connection to me? But I am his *father.*" These words sounded weird coming out of my mouth.

"Biologically," she said. "But not, you know, emotionally—"

"What? Like he has a whole bunch of other choices?"

She didn't answer.

"I mean, it's not as if he has someone else who can—"

"He does, though."

My stomach dropped. "Who?" I said. I sat down on a chair and closed my eyes. Of course, I should have thought of this. Now I would have to add some lines about not being Jack's dad to my growing list of verses.

"I've been seeing someone for a couple of years now. I moved here so we could all be together. When you got in touch with me, he had just asked me to marry him. That's why I got so emotional and everything. I mean, for so long I had really hoped that you were going to come and find us. I really did. I know it was this unrealistic fantasy that I was just holding on to. I've been in therapy about all this. I worked really hard to let that go. Bruce wanted us to move out here a long time ago, but I wouldn't because you were here, and I didn't want to get all confused again. And finally, after years of working on it, I was able to let go of my little dream about you growing up and coming through. I mean, I had to pray and do workshops, keep a journal, and all kinds of stuff. But it finally worked." She took a deep breath and let it out: relief and exhaustion. "We moved here, and everything's been going great. Bruce asked me to marry him, and then you showed up!"

"But Diana, you're not—"

"Stop. Hold it. Let me go on. I said yes. I love him. I do. Your appearance was just a little test. I passed. Bruce and I are getting married. He and Jack get along really well. They're just great together. You should see how—"

"I don't want to see that! He can't possibly—you don't mean he—but he's not Jack's *father!* I am!"

"Good, listen. You said yourself that you're the one who got in touch with *us,* not the other way around. I didn't ask for this. Now, if it makes you feel better to give him presents, pay for things, then I'm willing to let you do that. But I do not plan to give you visitation rights or anything like that, so don't even suggest it."

Would now be the time to tell her about the songs I'd written about her? Should I mention the house I just tried to buy? Why hadn't she just told me about her dream? Wouldn't that have been easier? If two people are simultaneously pining for each other, doesn't that mean they're supposed to be together? I always thought so. For a split second, I pictured screeching over there on my bike to change her mind. I saw myself and Jack facing her down. We were holding hands. In our other hands, we held guitars. Then I saw myself in front of a judge, explaining that I was the boy's biological *father.* I had *rights.* Some hot thing bubbled up in my

throat—maybe it *was* indignation and self-righteousness—but it was quickly replaced by doubts and questions.

If a kid is happy, is it right to set his life on a different path just because you're an adult and might be able to achieve it? If the kid didn't want to have anything to do with me, would it be fair to insist on it? I don't mean legally. I just mean as one human to another. And if he had someone else whom he preferred to think of as his father—someone, say, with a real house and real job— wasn't it more in the boy's best interests to stay out of the way of the life he wanted to make for himself? I had a feeling it was. I wasn't used to the father thing at all: even the word *father* sounded weird coming out of my mouth. And I knew that I didn't want to wreck anything for him.

"Well," I said into the phone before I had come up with anything else.

Diana waited for me to say more. When I didn't, she sighed, frustrated with me again. Then she said, "Good, I want to know something. You're smart. You have a lot of, well, natural abilities. Why are you sitting there doing nothing with your life? You know what I'm saying. You wrote these great songs. Big hits that still get played after all these years. What happened?"

Maybe I had realized before that particular moment that Diana wasn't what I had hoped for. Maybe I had seen the afternoon she came over with Jack or in the restaurant that night or even way back when we were together that she was not the woman I was supposed to be with forever. But now, with that question, she had just wiped away any lingering wisps of hope or desire I still had for her.

I should have thanked her then and there for popping the dreaded question and letting me drop her from my list of things that might have made my life work. I should have felt relieved and grateful to her for showing me the truth. But I didn't feel that at all. Instead, I felt as though I'd just lost a lover and a child.

I chose to disregard the question. I said. "So, if Jack wants to get in touch with me, hang out, or whatever, you know where to find me. And I hope your marriage works out perfectly. For everybody. I hope you're all really happy." Then I added, "You deserve it."

"Thanks," she said with a lighthearted lilt to her voice. "Thanks, Good. I feel so much better. Really, thank you."

"You're welcome." My own voice sounded different now from the way it had been in the beginning of the conversation; I could have been a different person altogether.

"And I hope you get what you need too," she said.

"Sure. I'll be fine. Thanks. OK, well, so long."

"Bye, Good."

"Good-bye." You might remember what I said earlier about using that whole word.

I reached for a guitar. I sat there holding it for a long time, feeling the empty space that was left inside myself where my pretend version of Diana used to be. I couldn't feel sad about missing her and Jack, because I hardly knew them. What I missed, of course, what I always missed was myself and the life I could have had.

There was a knock on my door. I opened it. Wouldn't you know? All the brand-new furnishings for my real life had finally arrived. The kitchen table and chairs, the desk, the entertainment unit and TV, the bed, all of it, finally showing up at exactly the moment that I no longer needed them.

twenty-six

Ellen was sautéing mushrooms. "So you felt that if you could make yourself available to Jack, maybe you could have him around, in your life."

"I thought he might, you know, need me, I don't know, like, as a father. I thought I might be able to figure out how to do that. But it turns out that they have someone for that already. They're all set."

She said, "Are you devastated?"

"I don't know what I am. I mean, first, I was all panicked that I might have to do something for them, that they might *want* something from me. But I came around. I kind of worked on myself, you know, tried to improve."

Ellen didn't stir for a second. She didn't want to turn and look at me and make me get all self-conscious. But she was listening hard, willing me to say more.

"I went to a Point Blank concert in L.A. I offered to sell them some songs. I thought I could sort of pick up where I left off, give myself a real job."

Now she opened her eyes wide, afraid to move, in case I clammed up again.

"Yeah. I gave them a tape." I drummed my fingers on the kitchen table. "They didn't want the songs."

"Oh," she groaned. "You're kidding? You must have felt awful. But, Tom!" Ellen almost yelled. "This is important progress! Do you know how long it's been since you—"

"Yeah, I know. It wasn't so great. I sweated buckets and threw up in the bathroom."

"But *still!* You did it! That's—oh, my God!—that's—"

"Right. But what I was saying was that in the beginning I was worried that Diana and Jack would want something from me, that I would have to protect myself from them trying to get at me. But I've come to this other place. I puffed myself into a whole new shape so that I could be, you know, more, for them! And *now* I'm all deflated because they don't want anything. Well, she did get a little excited about the money. She asked me to pay for a camp and a Playstation 2. I saw a little spark of desire when I told her about the royalties. They can have it all, if they want. I sure don't care about it."

Ellen went back to stirring.

I sat there a minute. "I thought I was in love with her. All this time. Then once I got close to her again, come to find out I'm not. I probably knew that before, I just forgot. I liked the fantasy better than I liked her. Isn't the human mind just the most interesting thing?" I smirked.

"So maybe your initial motivation was Diana and Jack, but now that you've gotten to this other place, the reason you went there doesn't matter so much? Now you can just keep going from where you are. This is a good thing, Tom."

"Do you think he took a look at me and kind of shook his head and walked away?" Even before she answered, I was thinking of using the phrase "shook his head and walked away" in a song.

"Oh, no," Ellen said. "No! Is that what you think? Kids don't—"

"I mean, it's not like I'm some, you know, orthodontist, or software engineer, or anything normal."

"Tom, no one is normal."

"Some are closer to the bulge in the old bell curve than others. I mean some people *are*, well, orthodontists."

"But I hope you're at least acknowledging that just knowing about Jack motivated you to move forward in your life. You do see that, right? And you have to at least feel a little bit grateful that, now that you know about the kid, he's well taken care of. Aren't you happy that you found this boy in great shape with all of his needs met?"

I hung my head even lower than it already was. "I know it's selfish of me, but I was hoping that I was the only one who could do certain things. I was hoping that only his biological father would do for birthdays and Christmas and, I don't know, guitar lessons. Do you know what the weirdest thing is?"

"What?"

"He doesn't like music. He has no interest in guitar lessons."

Ellen looked at me. "Ah," she said.

"Yeah." For some reason, I wanted to go then. She wasn't even finished making my dinner, and I was ready to head for the door. *I should have brought a guitar*, I thought, *something to hold and make noise with.*

Ellen looked at the mushrooms and took the pan off the burner. "I think it's a good thing that Diana has this man in her life who's willing to be Jack's father."

All of a sudden, I couldn't breathe for a minute, and my throat felt closed. I put my hands over my face to try to block everything out.

"Tom?" Ellen said. "Are you OK?"

"No," I said. "I've done a lot of things wrong, and I don't know how to fix them."

Ellen had a metal grater in one hand and a piece of cheese in the other. There was a long pause while she thought about what to say. "I was reading a column on how to get organized. This woman wrote in to say that she had all these pictures of her family that she hadn't put in albums, something like fifteen years' worth of snapshots. She kept taking pictures and not putting them in the books. They were all in shopping bags in her closet. So the columnist told her not to go back to day one but to start from her most recent roll of pictures."

"Huh?" I said.

"Yeah. So do you get it?"

"What?" I said.

"What I'm saying?"

"About pictures?"

"I'm saying, starting now, be whatever you want."

I looked at her.

"Starting now, if you want to do something else with your music, do it. If you want to, I don't know, move to a new place, do that. Don't worry so much about where you've been, what you've done, what you've missed, all that. Think about what you're going to do next."

I said, "See, I just tried that. It didn't work."

She poured eggs into the pan. There was a big hiss. She waited a minute. The eggs started to get firm, and she sprinkled in the grated cheese and mushrooms. Some people are good at everything.

twenty-seven

I heard Vic's truck pull up before I was awake. Its sound was as distinctive as the UPS truck's and at least as loud. He and Robin had had only two kids when they bought it. That seemed like a hundred years ago now. The door slammed. Vic must be picking up the kids for the weekend. I got out of bed.

"Elise isn't ready." It was Mike's voice. "Her hair is getting fixed. Mom said could you throw our stuff in the back." I could hear stuff hitting the bed of the truck. Why didn't Vic say hi to Mike?

"Dad?" Mike said. "Are we going to the beach?"

"We'll see. I have to stop by work for a couple of minutes."

"No," Mike whined. "I don't want to. We did that last time, and it was all day."

"You guys can play on the computers!" Vic said with feigned enthusiasm.

"We don't want to."

"You want to go back to the apartment and stay with Sandy?"

There was a long pause. "Can't we just stay here with Mom until you're done with work?"

"Nope."

"No fair."

Maddy and Ray were outside now. "I want to sit in front!" Maddy said.

"No, me!" said Ray

"You're not old enough," Mike explained. "Elise isn't even old enough, but Dad lets her. If he didn't, we wouldn't get to go."

Ray said, "I don't want to go!"

"Don't say that, Ray," Maddy said. "You'll hurt Dad's feelings."

"Get in." Vic opened the door. "Where's Elise? *Elise!*"

"She's almost ready!" Robin called back.

A few seconds later, two doors slammed, first the house, then the truck.

"Mommy!" Ray yelled at Robin. "I don't want to *go!*"

Then there was a minute or so of stuff I couldn't hear, except that Ray was crying.

"Make sure they're back by five tomorrow!" Robin said sharply. "They need to get their hair washed and their—"

"Fine," Vic said.

"Have fun, guys! See you tomorrow! I love you!" Robin was yelling in a cheerful, upbeat voice as the truck backed up.

"Bye, Mommy!" two of the kids called. Ray was crying, probably leaning out the window as the truck backed up.

I didn't look out the window, but I pictured her standing there, waving in her bathrobe. How could she let them go with him? They'd be gone for two whole days, and she'd be miserable. Robin and Vic had been saving for a house, she told me. They were going to buy a new place in one of the northern suburbs when Vic suddenly lost sight of the master plan. He got involved with someone from his office and left Robin with the kids so he could move in with the other woman.

I heard the sound of the truck engine fade into the general traffic noises. The crying would start any second now. As if I had stepped on a nail, I sprang into action. I was going to stop the crying before it started. At that moment, I was willing to do just about anything not to hear that sound. In three giant steps I was in the kitchen filling my new coffeepot. I dumped water in the tank and grabbed a filter. I scooped some coffee out of the bag and pressed the button. I pulled on some pants and a T-shirt, raked my fingers through my hair, and went next door.

She was just starting to tear up when I got there. It wasn't the bathrobe today. She was wearing an old pair of jeans and a work shirt over a white T-shirt. "Hi!" I said a little too loudly. "I just— I don't know what I was thinking! I measured out too much coffee. Do you want a cup? Just to, so I don't waste it?"

She wiped her face on her sleeve. "Uh, coffee?" she said.

"Yeah, coffee," I said. "That hot brown stuff people drink in the mornings?"

"Uh. Yeah. OK. Sure."

"Two minutes!" I said.

I went outside and grabbed two plastic chairs from the garage. Former tenants had left them here. There was a square of uneven bricks with grass growing between them that joined the entrances of our two apartments. I always thought Jeanette's husband had laid them, and it was his first bricklaying experience, maybe his last. I put the chairs on the bricks, where they teetered on the lumpy surface. I went inside and got down two coffee mugs. I always use the same one, but I had to wash the other one, as it had a dead moth in it. Then I poured the coffee in.

"Robin?" I said at her door.

"Yeah?" She came from inside somewhere. She had brushed her hair.

"Want to sit outside? I found some chairs."

"That sounds nice."

Slowly, carefully, as if recovering from an illness, she came out-side. She sat in a chair, and I handed her the coffee cup. "I hope it's not too strong."

"I like it strong," she said.

"Oh!" I said. "I didn't bring any milk or sugar."

"I have some," she said. She stood up and then turned around. "Oh. Do you want anything in yours?"

"No," I said. "I'm OK." It was real coffee, so I wasn't planning on drinking mine. I had bought it for the real-life act I had planned for Diana. The coffee was just a prop.

Robin went inside and put stuff in her cup. I heard her getting a spoon out of a drawer, stirring. She came back out, sat down, and took a sip. "Mmm," she said. She closed her eyes. "The kids went with Vic this morning."

"Oh? Really? His weekend, I guess, huh?"

"They'll be back tomorrow."

"You can live it up!"

"Luckily, I'm working all day. I hate it when they're not here," she said, biting her lower lip. "I just hate it."

"Well. You get a little free time for yourself, though, that must be—"

"I don't like time for myself," she said. "It just leads to think-ing, and thinking leads to regretting and worrying. I try to avoid free time as much as possible. For all the time that I'm not work-ing, I try to get a lot of videos."

I nodded. I decided to stop pretending that she was going to have fun without the kids, to stop acting as if I didn't know any-thing. "I understand completely. I spend a lot of time trying not to think myself. I'm something of an expert. But I have a whole row of guitars, instead of four kids. I'm not sure that they work as well." Without thinking, I took a sip of my coffee. "Hey!" I said.

"That's pretty good. I didn't know I knew how to make real coffee."

She laughed. A little. Sort of.

Then we sat there for a few minutes not saying anything. I didn't really have anything to tell her or ask her. I just didn't want to hear her crying. That was all that had brought us together, and so far, it was working. I drank the whole cup of coffee.

"What about you?" she said.

"What about me, what?"

"What are you going to do today?"

"Oh. Play my guitar. And, I don't know, work on some songs maybe."

She nodded and sat there a minute. Then she drank what was left in her cup. "Well, that was excellent. Thank you." She handed me the empty cup. "I think I'm going to take off now. I'm a couple of hours early for my shift, but Saturdays if I get there early, they usually put me right on. I can use the money."

"That sounds good."

"Enjoy your day!" she said, just the way they did in the grocery store.

"You too!"

She made a brief groaning sound. "I'll try."

I put the chairs back in the garage.

twenty-eight

When the kids came home one afternoon, Mike wanted a guitar lesson. Now Elise wanted one too. I no longer had a reason to practice being around children, but they didn't know that. We sat outside in the yard. I didn't want them to see that in addition to my hideous lamp shade, my lame TV, and my pathetic plant that was still sitting on the floor, I now had a whole bunch of new stuff crowded into the center of my place, some of it in boxes. I hadn't gotten rid of the old stuff yet, or set up the new stuff. Since I had recently lost the energy and motivation that a project of this scale would require, it might all just sit there for a long, long time.

"I have something for you, Mike," I said, "something just for you."

"What is it?" he said. "Is it a teeny, tiny guitar, because I want to hold it myself."

"Not a guitar. But you can hold it yourself. It's a whole other instrument." I went inside and got a bag from a music store from where it lay on top of one of the cartons. I came out and handed him the little bag. He pulled out the box that was inside. "It's a harmonica. I'll show you how to play it. Elise is big enough to hold this guitar, so the two of you can play a song together." I braced myself for his negative reaction.

"Like a band!" Mike said.

Good old Mike!

"Right," I said. "You got it. Because you know how in a band, people play different instruments? And I'll play with you too."

Mike put the wrong side in his mouth and blew. Nothing happened, and he looked crushed.

I turned it around for him. "OK," I said. "Now you can blow into the holes and make noise or breathe in through the holes and make noise. Try it a little. Good. Now, look at the top here. See those little numbers? Those are going to help you play songs. I want you to practice blowing through 4, then breathing in—that's called drawing—through 6 a couple of times. Right. Perfect." I turned on my stool to face Elise. "Now, Elise, see if you can make your fingers look like mine. That one, right there. Now push down so that the string is against the neck of the guitar."

"Ow," Elise said.

"Yeah, it's a little painful. If you practice enough, you'll get calluses and it won't hurt anymore."

"Like on the monkey bars," she said.

"Exactly. So press these fingers hard against there and then strum the strings with these fingers. Great. See how nice that sounds? Now I'm going to show you another chord, and then you can switch back and forth."

I worked with them for fifteen minutes. "OK, so that's all we'll do for today. I'll show you more whenever you want."

Elise stopped strumming and tried to give me back the guitar. Mike, taking his cue from his sister, took the harmonica away from his mouth to hand it over to me.

"Thank you, Mr. Good," Elise said.

"Thank you, Mr. Good," Mike echoed.

"You're welcome. Do you want to keep those a while to practice on?"

Mike looked at Elise.

Elise said, "Well, yeah. Can we?"

"Sure," I said. "Practice what I showed you and then I'll show you some more."

"OK." They started to rush home to show their mother.

There was probably something wrong with giving them the instruments to take home, I thought, something that, not being a parent, I had not considered. I tried to figure out what it might be. The harmonica and guitar were not dangerous, so that couldn't be it. Their mother might not like the noise? It might bother Jeanette upstairs? What could I say to cover my possible mistake? "Do your homework first!" I called after them.

The two of them stopped in their tracks and turned around to look at me. "We don't have homework!" Elise said. "It's summer!"

Oh.

I heard them talking excitedly to Robin about their lesson. Throughout the evening, I heard the instruments off and on. They sounded like a rehearsal for an experimental performance piece.

I put together my new desk and started working on the entertainment unit.

t w e n t y - n i n e

The next day I set up the TV and called the cable company to order service. Then I called the Salvation Army to pick up my old stuff. I dragged my desk out to the garage, went back inside, and started taking apart my old bed.

I was pretty exhausted by late in the afternoon, and I wanted to get out of the apartment. For some reason, I ended up at the beach, where I hadn't been in years. I sat on a wall and listened to the ocean for a long time. A Mexican family was cooking an enormous amount of food nearby. They had coolers, cooking utensils, grocery bags, plastic food containers, all arranged on and around a folding table.

Three young women and two men opened innumerable plastic containers of food and transferred it to the grill, to plates, to other containers. The food sizzled, and I could smell tomatoes and spices, meat searing over the flames. They had a radio on and a few teenagers danced intermittently. A grandmother sat in a chair drinking a Coke. I tried not to stare but just take an occasional glance between long gazes at the water. A man came over with a plate of food, offering it to me wordlessly with a lift of his eyebrows. I had sat there for so long that they must have thought I was hungry.

It looked good, sausages and peppers and fresh tortillas steaming on a paper plate. If I could have transformed into a member of this family, acquired a new past, present, and future by eating that plate of food, I would have gobbled it down gladly, meat and all. But I shook my head. "No, thank you," I said. He didn't say anything but kept holding the plate out. So I said, *"No, gracias, señor. Muchas gracias."*

"You sure?" he said. "Absolutely positive?"

"I'm sure," I said. "Thanks a lot, though. It's nice of you."

"You change your mind, man," he said, "you come on over and have some food with us. We got plenty. Too much. *Cerveza,* maybe?"

"I'm fine," I said. "Thanks. Really."

The man shrugged and walked away. I was embarrassed that my neediness was so visible, even to strangers, but not embarrassed enough to leave the sound of their voices, the generous swell of their laughter at a joke, and their huge and obvious enjoyment of the food, one another, and the night. I sat there and watched.

There wasn't much of a sunset, as it was overcast, just a glow through the clouds for a few minutes before daylight disappeared. The barbecue fire seemed to brighten as darkness settled in.

These are normal people, I was thinking. *This is how they behave. I can't have what they have.*

Why can't I?

Because I let my brother die! I don't deserve it.

There was a searing, sizzling hurt inside of me, as if with this sentence, this self-assessment, my insides began to barbecue themselves.

You think that not having a life yourself is payment for what you didn't do that night? I considered. *Maybe not sufficient payment, but it's all I have.*

What if it wasn't anybody's fault? What if it was just an accident, something bad that happened for no particular reason.

I could stop feeling guilty.

I tried to imagine this, life without guilt. Guilt had settled in with me a long time ago and made itself at home. I thought of it by turns as a friend, as a familiar old roommate I couldn't get rid of if I tried, and probably most accurately, as a nasty, exhausting, high-maintenance pet that I had somehow gotten stuck with and that was destined to outlive me. Then there were times when guilt seemed almost like a body part, an extra appendage that I had to wash, protect, keep warm. Any way you looked at it, guilt was always with me.

How would I get rid of it? I wanted to know.

I couldn't come up with an answer to that one. I thought about what Ellen had said the other night about the photo album. What if I could simply start a new life from where I was this minute? It might not have anything to do with selling songs or buying a house or furniture.

The beach was getting cold and foggy. I wished I had a sweatshirt. I wished I had a guitar, my security blanket. Of course, I would have felt like a giant dork sitting on a wall at the beach, strumming a guitar, but I was just about desperate enough not to care. I waited until the Mexican family had started to pack up and my physical discomfort had become sharper.

On the way home, I went to the donut place that everyone says is so great. All these years that I've lived here, I never tried those donuts that people talk about all the time. I didn't know what possessed me now, except maybe that the place was lit up and looked warm. I wanted to know if the donuts were really *that* good. I wanted to know that minute. I bought a chocolate twist and a crumb. I ate them. They were good. I got back on my motorcycle and started for home. Then I thought about the Mexican family and their food. If I had a family, I would buy them donuts. Ellen wouldn't eat one, of course. Maybe I could pretend that my neigh-bors were my family. I drove back and bought a dozen chocolate-glazed and a dozen plain-glazed. I parked in the garage and took the donuts inside. I looked at them for a full five minutes before I went back out, up the stairs, and knocked on Jeanette's door.

"Jeanette," I said. "It's Tom Good from downstairs."

"Oh, what is it, dear?" she said from behind the closed door. I could hear her starting for the door with her walker. "Is it a water leak? I don't have anything running! Not that I know of."

"No. Nothing's leaking." Guilt, my faithful old pet, clawed at me as I realized that I had never been up here in all these years except to report a problem. "I just—I got some donuts. Would you like some? A donut? Or two?"

There was a pause. "Oh, my lord!" she said, sounding startled.

I could hear her moving around behind the door, unlocking it. She had gotten a lot slower in the time I'd lived here.

"I'm in my nightdress, dear!" she said. "I hope you don't mind!"

"No, it's, I—" I stammered. "It's OK. I'm not that sensitive."

Finally, she opened the door. She looked at the box and put both hands to her cheeks, a cartoon of delighted surprise. "I've heard about this place! How did you *know* I love donuts more than life itself? How *did* you know?"

"I just had a feeling," I said, improvising on the spot.

She took two. "You have made my day!" she said. "Are you moving or just curious?"

"What?" I said. For a second, I didn't follow her train of thought. "Oh, the house across the street, you mean..." I pointed at it. "I was interested, but it was sold. Somebody else bought it."

"It wasn't meant to be then!" Jeanette declared. She opened her mouth wide, and half a donut went in at once. "Mmm!" she said, little sugary clumps at the corners of her mouth.

"See you!" I said. I went downstairs.

"Thank you again, dear!" Her mouth was still full.

I had a lot of donuts left.

I looked at my watch before I knocked on Robin's door. It was only a little after 8:30. It seemed later. I knocked three times. "It's Good!" I said from the outside. "I have donuts!"

The door opened. Robin was in her overalls again. "Hi. Oh. Donuts? The kids will be so excited!" she said.

I handed her the box.

"Oh, not all these!" she said. "What about you?"

"I had some," I said. "Back at the—"

"That's very generous of you. Kids, Mr. Good brought you donuts!"

"They're for you too," I said.

"Oh, no! Not me. I'm trying not to. I'm so fat!"

"You're not," I said. "You look great! You're gorgeous." I meant it. Who knew where these thoughts came from? I never said stuff like this.

Robin probably wasn't used to hearing it either, as she immediately turned a deep red. "Come in," she said. "Come in for a minute and sit with us. Would you like to?"

I went in. In all these years, I had never been inside this part of the house. There were toys and pieces of toys all over the place. There were naked, headless Barbies; hundreds of red, white, green, and blue Lego pieces that didn't add up to any building, vehicle, or even recognizable geometric shape; little fat plastic people in bright colors; trucks; blocks. There was a nearly empty dollhouse with, instead of dolls and tiny furniture, a coloring book and two crayons in its living room. Then there were books, pajamas, shoes, socks, and sweatshirts on the floor and on the furniture.

"Well, it's a mess, of course!" Robin said. "It's a small space, and if I nag them too much about being neat, they can't have any fun! Can I get you something to drink?"

"No, I, no, thank you," I said.

Maddy and Elise were playing a board game, Mike was watching television, and Ray was playing with some little bears, whispering to them as he moved them around the floor. The kids all looked up at me, surprised.

"Mr. Good brought donuts," said Robin.

"Good," I said. "Just plain Good is fine."

"I want one!" Ray said.

"Thank you! Thank you! Thank you!" said Elise.

"I want chocolate!" Maddy said.

"Whoa," said their mother. "There are more than enough here, and I want you to slow down and come with me to the kitchen. Everybody sit down at the table." They each had a certain spot at the table and went to it without hesitation. First, Robin handed out napkins. Then she opened the top of the box. "Ray, what kind would you like?" she said.

"Chockwit," said Ray.

Robin put a donut on his napkin. "Maddy?"

"Chocolate, please, thank you," Maddy said, probably hoping that using both would speed the donut's delivery.

"Good girl," Robin said. "Elise?"

"Chocolate too, please," Elise said.

"Mike," Robin said.

"Same. Please. Thank you," Mike said, reaching up for a donut. "You're welcome! Excuse me!" he added. The other kids laughed.

"Now, what do we all say to Mr. Good?" Robin prompted. She went to the fridge and got out a gallon jug of milk that was about half-empty.

"Thank you, Mr. Good!"

Now I was embarrassed. "I have to tell you something," I said. "I'm called 'Good,' just plain old Good. Not *Mr.*, OK, do you think we can change that? Because I really—"

"OK, Just Plain Old Good!" said Mike.

"Mike," said Robin in a warning voice, but his sisters were laughing. Ray concentrated on his donut. "Yes, we'll call you Good, if that's what you prefer."

I nodded.

"Why don't you sit down?" Robin said. I noticed she didn't call me anything now. Maybe she was just going to avoid using my name altogether. She pulled a chair in from the next room.

"Oh, well, actually, I have to go now. I just wanted to drop those off. I'll see you guys, OK? When you want another music lesson, just let me know, OK?"

"Tomorrow?" Mike said.

"Tomorrow's fine," I said.

"That's so nice of you," Robin said.

"Not really," I said. "I enjoy it."

I left in a hurry, as if I had something really important to do, as if someone were waiting for me.

I took the two steps over to my door, opened it, and went straight into my closet.

thirty

Once you've popped through a certain membrane of familiarity, like it or not, everything starts to be different. Now when I think about our lives as neighbors, there was the time before the donuts and the time after. On a time line of us as neighbors, there would be a chocolate donut above a black line marking that moment when things changed.

The day after the donuts, Robin made cookies and left some by my front door. *She thinks she has to pay me back,* I thought. I ate all the cookies and left her a note: "Thanks for the cookies. They were good. Good," it said.

The next day I got a coupon for SeaWorld when I bought gas. I left it in an envelope in their door. "Thought you might be able to use this. Good."

Robin sent Elise over with a bag of ripe avocados. "These are from our grandmother's yard," she said.

"Oh, thank you!" I said. "Doesn't your mom want some?"

"We have about a million of those things. Only Mom likes them."

"Tell your mom thanks. And your grandmother."

I made guacamole every night for three days and saved the pits.

I bought some pots and soil. I left a note, "Maybe your kids would like to plant the seeds from those avocados you gave me.

They were good, by the way. Good." I left the potting soil and the pots on their step. The seeds were in a plastic bag with a little water.

A couple of hours later, I heard the kids outside. There was a little bickering. "You did that on purpose!" "That one's mine!" "Hey! That's not enough!" Softly, their mother's voice wove in and out of their smaller, sharper ones. "That's it." "A little more." "All the way up." "Now water." "Yours is just right. Fine. Yeah. Stop. *Stop.*" Water was running, splashing on the bricks in front of the door.

When someone knocked on the door, I jumped. I got there in three steps, opened it.

"Hi, Mike."

He looked up, his head tilting way back. "My mom says you can come over for dinner."

"I'm a vegetarian," I said quickly, as if this ruled out dinner.

"I'll tell my mom." He disappeared inside his house.

A minute later there was another knock on the door. I opened it. "She says we're not having any meat anyway."

I thought a minute about what to do. When invitations come from next door, you have to be willing to follow through with your excuses. If you say, "I'm working," you have to actually leave the house at 5:20 and not come back until after 2:00. If you say, "I'm not feeling well," you'd better be able to fake some good, believable symptoms and stay in all evening. If you say, "I'm having guests," you'd have to find someone to come over at a moment's notice and be willing to put up with them for the evening.

"What time?" I heard myself asking Mike.

"Six-thirty," he said.

"See you then."

The post-donut age had begun, for sure.

I brought ice cream. Robin's mom opened the door. I hadn't expected this. Inside me, a family of cornered squirrels scrambled, frantically scratching and clawing to get free.

"I—" I said. "Hello. I'm Good."

"You sure are! You brought ice cream! That's pretty good right there," she said and took it from me. "I'm Liz. I don't think we've ever officially met in all these years. Come on in." Liz looked like an older, larger version of Robin. Her hair was as straight, but the color was flatter—more gray. She wore a loose-fitting shirt with a T-shirt under it and jeans, just like Robin.

Behind her, Robin was sliding a pan into the oven. "Hi, Good." She didn't look at me. She was busy with the oven. "Whoa! That's hot! I don't think the dial has any influence on the actual temperature anymore." She closed the door to the stove and stared at it for a moment.

"Just turn it way down and check in a few minutes," Liz suggested.

"I guess it will be done faster this way," Robin said. "A gas microwave!"

Liz deposited the ice cream in the freezer. "Here," she said, pushing a pile of lettuce on a towel toward me. "Make yourself useful. Tear this up and put it in this bowl. It's awfully quiet in the bathroom. I wonder what's going on." She left the kitchen. A few seconds later, there was a scream, all the kids at once, it sounded like, and then a lot of laughter. A few minutes after that, Maddy, Mike, and Ray came out in their pajamas. Elise was in shorts and a T-shirt. Maybe she was too old to eat dinner in her pj's. I wouldn't know.

When dinner happened, it seemed that each kid was having something different. Ray had a peanut butter and jelly sandwich. Mike had grilled cheese. Elise and Maddy had spaghetti with butter.

There was a chilis rellenos casserole that Robin, Liz, and I ate. The conversation was mainly about food. "Can I have some more milk?"

"What do you say?"

"I'm done!"

"Good brought ice cream. If you want some you're going to have to do better than that."

"How many bites do I have to eat to get the ice cream?"

"Mom! I'm done!"

And so on. No one asked me what I was up to lately. Or anything.

I planned to stay about fifteeen to twenty minutes after dinner, just so that I didn't seem unfriendly. But before I knew it, Elise was asking if I knew how to play Parcheesi, and Mike wanted help with his Legos.

"Well," I said, "I guess I could—"

Robin said, "Kids, don't make him play with you!" To me, she said, "I'm sorry, Good. I'm sure you didn't count on—"

"That's OK," I said, "really. I haven't played Parcheesi in a long time. I'm way out of practice." I sat down on the couch with them.

Ray climbed into my lap and started sucking his thumb. To the other kids, Liz, and Robin, this was probably no big deal, something Ray did all the time. But I had never had a three-year-old in my lap before. I pictured someone who knew me well walking in right now and finding me here like this. I pictured a bouncer from The Club somehow finding me here. "Good! Man! What's this?" I pictured myself shrugging, baffled, in response.

I looked at Robin.

"Well, Ray!" she said. "Nothing like making yourself comfortable!"

Ray leaned his head back and looked up at her silently. His eyes blinked in slow motion.

"Just give him to me, if you want," Robin said. "He's heavy."

"No!" Ray said through his thumb. He pressed his head firmly into my chest.

"I'm OK," I said. He was heavy, but in a nice way. He smelled like chocolate and something else I couldn't quite place. Buttered carrots, maybe.

"Don't forget I got a movie, you guys," Robin said. "Do you still want to watch it?"

"After this," Elise said. "I want to win!"

"*I* want to win," Mike said, joining the game. "You always win!"

"Maybe this is your night," I said to Mike.

Maddy won. She concentrated hard on counting out her moves, deciding which piece to play each time. It took a long time. She didn't make a big deal about sending another player's guys back to the start. She just quietly progressed until all her men were home. Then she said, "Ta-da!" with both index fingers pointed at the ceiling.

"Oh, man!" Mike said. "One of my guys never even got started! Lookit! He's still in the thing!"

"Next time!" said their mother.

"That was a great game!" I said. One of my legs, the one with Ray on it, was asleep. "I guess I better get home and let you guys—"

"*No!*" said Mike.

"Aren't you going to watch the movie with us?" Maddy wanted to know.

Ray's eyes flickered, and he gripped the front of my shirt with his fist.

"Oh," I said. I couldn't do this. I would get claustrophobic and antsy with all these kids and a horrible children's movie playing. I should get out of here right away, before I start to get desperate.

"Well," I said. "Maybe I could stay for a little bit of the movie. The beginning, maybe. A couple minutes." I shifted Ray to my other leg.

The movie was about dinosaurs trying to escape some kind of disastrous climactic change caused by a meteor hitting the earth. I tried to pay attention, but the next thing I knew, I was opening my eyes. My mouth was open and all dried out. Robin was rewinding the video. Maddy was asleep with her head on one arm of the couch, and Mike had his head on the other. I was in the middle with Ray draped across me. Oh, my God! What was happening? It was as if I'd been drugged or hypnotized or something! Could there have been something weird in the food?

Liz was putting the game pieces back in the box.

"Hmm," I said, running my tongue over my dry lips. "I fell asleep." I couldn't feel my feet.

"I don't blame you," Elise said. "That was so boring! And I usually like dinosaur movies."

Robin said, "Let me take this guy off you." She lifted Ray, who was as limp as an old bath towel, and carried him off. I shook life back into my feet and legs.

In a few minutes Robin came back. She said, "Could you take Maddy to her room? I'll show you where she goes."

I looked at her. I didn't carry kids. I could not remember ever carrying a single child in my life.

"I have this thing with my neck," Robin said to her mother. She started rubbing her neck. "It's—you know when you're getting on the freeway and you have to look over your shoulder? My neck kills me when I do that!'

"Maybe you should go to the doctor," Liz said, picking up the Parcheesi box to put it somewhere.

"Oh, sure, like I have time," said Robin. "First door on your right," she told me. She was picking up toys from the floor and throwing them into a basket. "I'll clear a path. It's the bed closest to the door."

I looked down at the sleeping little girl. *What if she wakes up as soon as I touch her?* I thought. Would she cry? What if she cried? What if I somehow lost my grip and dropped her on the floor? Robin and her mother didn't seem to realize that picking up a kid did not come naturally to everybody. I stood there for a second. *Just grab her under the armpits and start walking,* I told myself. I did. She was light. But it was her shape that made it difficult, those dangling arms and legs and the length of her body. A sixty-pound ball of concrete would have been easier. I could certainly see how doing this on a regular basis could give you neck problems. I carried Maddy to her room. There were pictures of Pink on one side and unicorns, puppies, and kittens on the other. I put Maddy on the animal side and covered her with a flowery comforter. Robin was at the door. I suddenly worried that I had done this wrong, her head at the wrong end of the bed or something.

"Could I impose on you to help me with Mike too?"

Another one?! I was thinking. "Sure thing," I said.

Elise slipped by me in the hall. "Good night," she said quietly. "Thanks for the ice cream."

"You're welcome," I said. Sometimes you wish people wouldn't be so grateful. It makes you feel so guilty for all the nice things, big and small, hundreds of them, thousands, maybe, that you haven't done over a number of years.

I carried Mike into the room where Ray was already sleeping. There were a lot of cars and trucks on the floor. I stepped on something with wheels that went shooting across the room.

"Sorry," Robin said. "It's dangerous in here."

"No harm done," I said. It had just startled me. I lowered Mike onto his bed. He let out a quiet grunt as he hit the pillow. I pulled up a comforter with traffic signs on it. I looked over at Ray, who was sprawled on his back in the shape of a star, arms and legs spread, as if open for anything that came along.

This got to me somehow, and I had to say something quick before my throat closed up on me. "OK," I said. "Well."

"Hey, thanks for coming," Robin said as I came out. She was on the floor now, picking up toys on her hands and knees.

I started out.

"Thanks for the ice cream," said Liz when I got to the kitchen.

"Thank *you* for dinner." I headed for the door.

"The kids love you," Liz said over her shoulder.

"Well, they're making a big mistake," I said.

She laughed; she thought I was joking.

At home, I went to the kitchen and put my ear against the wall. I heard the water running and plastic clattering, toys being thrown into the basket, maybe. They weren't talking about me or anything.

thirty-one

I had spent the evening at Robin's again. Her mom had brought the kids dinner from McDonald's, a special treat. There was some Happy Meal toy the kids wanted for their vast collections, some piece of plastic representing a character in a movie they hadn't seen. The rest of us had pasta and tomato sauce. I had brought chocolate cream pie from a bakery down the street.

Anyway, it was much later, after McDonald's and pasta, and they were all in bed. Robin's mother had just left, and I was about to get going too.

Robin and I were in the kitchen. She was folding laundry and had just picked up a towel with a picture of Goofy on it when it happened. At first, I didn't know what it was, didn't see it coming, and didn't recognize it when it arrived. In a way, it was like the sudden precipitous onset of a devastating virus. There was nothing I could do to stop it or to change its course. It simply happened to me; it came over me with a power all its own, and there was not a thing that I could do to fight it off, postpone it, or diminish its severity. It was like falling, too, like coming to the edge of something, and having just enough time to gasp or say, "Oh, shit!" before going right over the side and dropping fast in a free fall into a deep abyss. When I did finally clue in to what was happening, when I could identify it, name it with absolute certainty, I realized that this had nothing to do with any of the things I had always thought it had. It wasn't about the size or shape of body parts. It wasn't about faces, not even eyes. Neither voice nor mannerisms had any bearing on it either, and it wasn't about intellect or taste in books, music, or movies. It had nothing to do with timing or life circumstances. I was under the control of something outside of myself, outside of any kind of force that I had ever heard of. I had fallen in love with Robin, my next-door neighbor.

As Robin placed the Goofy towel on top of a neat stack, I took a breath that seemed to be the first in a long, long time. Then I reached up and took her hand. I stood, and she looked at me, surprised. She had this kind of half smile on her face, and I wasn't exactly sure what it meant. I didn't stop to ask. I leaned forward to kiss her mouth.

"Uh, no," she said, stepping back into the refrigerator. "No, thank you. Sorry. No. I mean, don't. Please."

"*What?*" I said. I was a little startled, as if waking up from a dream in a place I didn't remember closing my eyes.

"Listen," she said. "I'm sorry. I'm going to be blunt. I'm not interested." She said it softly, even patted my hand, to let me know that she didn't mean to hurt my feelings. But, clearly, there was no uncertainty there, no softness, and no room for a change of heart.

I said, "What do I have to do?"

She said, "Nothing. We're not going to get romantically involved. At all. Ever. No way." She picked up another towel.

"OK," I said. "What would I have to do to change your mind?"

She laughed.

"Seriously. I'm not going to go away."

She shook her head. "No. Not happening."

I stood there staring at her, and it was like I saw this door to another world, and I wanted to walk through it. I just wanted to be next to her, I don't know, hanging up Christmas stockings and shopping for a new dishwasher. I said, "What if I marry you?"

Immediately, she said, "Well, that would be pretty stupid, wouldn't it?" I thought she said it unnecessarily harshly. "I just told you I'm not interested. Why would you marry someone who's not interested in you?"

I said, "But I'm . . . I'm interested in you."

There was a huge silence. She folded a T-shirt: Mike's. She folded another T-shirt: Elise's. She started on a sheet.

"Robin?" I said.

"What?"

"Could you just think about it?"

She said, "No. I couldn't. Not even for one minute. You picked the wrong person. You have made a mistake. I forgive you. Now let's forget about it. Pretend it never happened. Go home, Good. Please. Could you go? Now?"

I stood there.

"*Go!*" she said. She pointed to the door, the way people did with dogs.

I went.

I had lived in my apartment alone for all these years, and I don't remember ever being lonely until now. I had been horny. I had been bored, and I had been depressed. There was that very bad time after Diana left when all I wanted was for her to come back so that I could try to be what she wanted. This was different. This was worse, far worse. Even I could see that up to now I had existed as a kind of ghost, a stick figure, a shadowy sketch imitating a living man. Now I had had a glimpse of what it felt like to be flesh and blood, a real person. For the first time, I experienced a massive ache, a deep longing for another person, an individual, *specific* other person, whom I knew pretty well, and who was on the other side of my kitchen wall. All of a sudden, I felt incredibly small, microscopic, and powerless beside this huge thing that was being in love with Robin.

How did people survive being in love? This was much too much for me to bear. I wanted to just curl up and close my eyes. I did this, made myself into a small helpless shape in one corner of my bed. But when I did, I found that a movie of Robin was playing on the backs of my eyelids. Robin was bagging groceries in her Vons uniform and her name tag that said SERVING YOU, ROBIN, SINCE 2000. Robin was loading her kids into the car. Robin had just washed her hair, hadn't had a chance to comb it out, and was microwaving mini pancakes. Robin was laughing because of something Ray said. Robin was crying because Vic had left her after he promised to stay forever. It was a perfect, beautiful montage of Robin. I could have written a musical score for it if it weren't for this burning, scorching, ripping pain that was shooting straight through me. I wasn't going to make it. I was going to die of being in love with Robin.

I had entered a new subphase of the post-donut era, which involved Robin's avoiding me. Any idiot, including me, could see that. She must have been doing her laundry in the middle of the night or even at her mom's house, and supervising her kids from the kitchen window. She must have stopped walking with them down to the 7-Eleven to waste their allowances on candy. She must have started sending Elise out to get the mail and take out the garbage.

OK. This was what people did when they didn't want to see you. I knew that. I had done it myself, switching bartending shifts to avoid a waitress or a singer-songwriter who had made the mistake of developing feelings for me. I did it sometimes to Jeanette to avoid her twenty-minute stories, to keep from having to carry something for her, buy something for her, or walk her somewhere. *God,* I thought with shame, *I had even done it to Robin.* Sure, avoiding people was what people did in certain situations. But she couldn't stay away from me forever; we lived in the same house. I had that going for me. I had that one fact on my side. I could wait. I could be very patient, if I had to be.

Starting a new life wasn't just a matter of wanting one and buying new furniture. Improvements had to occur on the inside too. I could do that. One day when I was going to the grocery store, I went up the stairs to Jeanette's place, and I knocked on the door. Jeanette snatched back the curtain with one of her clawlike hands, as if the other hand might be clutching a crowbar. When she saw it was me, her face changed from narrow-eyed suspicion to confused welcome.

"Good morning, Jeanette," I said when she opened the door. As a matter of fact, it was morning. I had been getting up at seven for a whole series of days now.

"Well, for goodness sake! It's Good! What are you doing here? Is the house on fire? Did I leave the water running in the laundry room? What's going on?"

"Nothing, Jeanette," I said. "Nothing at all. I'm going to the store and I wondered if you wanted anything."

"Well," she sputtered, a hand to her chest. "I . . . indeed I do! I'll go and get my list."

Now I'm in for it, I thought. *She's going to give me a whole lecture on sizes and flavors and her digestive system.* I was up for it though; I could handle anything Jeanette threw my way.

"Are you going to Robin's store, honey?" she said.

"Yes," I said. "As a matter of fact, I am. It just so happens. Coincidentally."

"She knows what I like. Just give her this." She handed me a list written in shaky, loopy letters on a piece of lined paper torn out of a spiral pad.

This was going to be easy. I didn't even have to think up a reason to look for Robin, because Jeanette had given me one. I would simply find her and ask for her help in getting Jeanette's things. Perfectly legitimate. She would see how nice I could be, getting groceries for an old lady. We would talk. We would make plans.

I got to Vons at around eleven o'clock. I went to customer service and asked for Robin. The manager's name was Alex, and he had been serving you since 1991, I saw from his name tag. "Is Robin here?" I asked him. "I need these groceries for an elderly lady who lives—"

"Robin's on her lunch break," the guy said.

"Already?" I said. I looked at my watch again.

"She starts early."

"True," I said.

The song that was playing was "Rocky Mountain High" by John Denver, which reminded me of pushing the radio buttons fast in an old VW bug that my parents bought me when I had completed all the requirements to graduate. I hadn't wanted to learn to drive; I put up a fight. And I didn't want anything that seemed like a present or a reward. My father said, "Tom, seeing you suffer isn't going to help any of us feel any better about losing Jack. Do you understand?" I took the keys he handed to me. The car smelled like all the VW bugs I'd ever been in, and in reverse, it said, "Merrr?" the way they all did too.

"Alex, override on 8, please. Alex," said one of the checkers over the PA, interrupting John Denver.

"Excuse me," Alex said. He hustled down to checkout stand 8, handed over a card in a plastic case. The checker scanned the card and handed it back. Alex hurried back to his post at the customer service desk, where I was still waiting.

"When will she be back?" I wanted to know. Now I was listening to "We Got the Beat" by the Go-Go's, remembering the apartment I had before the one I had now, where people complained about my guitar playing. The closet was way too small there.

"About eleven-thirty," Alex said.

I nodded. "Thanks."

I'd have to kill some time. I went to a bookstore nearby and leafed through biographies of musicians until it was time for Robin to be back. Then I stayed another five minutes so it wouldn't seem like I had been waiting for her.

I went to the customer service desk again. There was someone else there, Kelli, serving you since 1982, which was a hell of a long time. "I was wondering where I could find Robin?" I said.

"She's stocking dairy. Just go to the big dairy case."

"Thanks," I said.

Alanis Morissette, "Ironic" was on, and I was back eating Thanksgiving dinner at Ellen's. She had invited people from work without telling me, so I wasn't speaking. This was the other me, the old Good, not the new Good.

Way in the back of this enormous store was an entire wall of every imaginable dairy product and some dairy-free products. I didn't see Robin though. I looked around. No store employee in sight at all. I looked back at the dairy case. Milk cartons were moving. Someone was back there, stocking from behind the case. "Robin?" I said to a gallon of low-fat.

There was a pause. "Yeah?"

"Hi," I said. "It's me, Good."

No answer.

"I was wondering if maybe, possibly, you could help me with something? Please?"

"What?" She didn't sound like she wanted to know.

"Jeanette gave me her grocery list? And she said you know what she likes?"

There was a pause. "You're shopping for Jeanette now?"

"Well, I was coming anyway, so I just thought I'd ask her if she needed anything."

"Right," she said. "What's on the list?"

"Yogurt," I said. I tried to see her in the small gap between two rows of half-and-half, but all I saw was the shoulder of a big black jacket. It must be awfully cold back there.

"OK, look to your right. She likes the Jerseymaid lemon, and they're on sale, two for eighty-nine, so get six."

"Oh. OK. Bread?"

"She likes Dutch dill. It's the bottom shelf of the bread, next to the English muffins."

"OK, could you show me? Because I don't think I've ever seen that."

"Sorry, we're really swamped back here. If you can't find it, get Angel."

"Oh, yeah. I guess I could do that."

"Was there anything else?"

Her voice came out from a different place. She had moved. Here I was talking to the Reddi-wip, and she was down by the egg substitutes. I moved a couple of steps to the left. "Raisin bran."

"Kellogg's." It was the flavored coffee creamer talking to me now. I moved again.

"How do you know all this?" I was trying to stretch it out.

"I've been living in that house a few years now. So I've been doing Jeanette's shopping for, well, all that time."

"I see. Well, thanks for your help. I guess I'll go get the stuff now."

There was no answer from the dairy case, so I walked away.

I got the six yogurts. I walked to the bread and had to stare at it a long time until I found the Dutch dill. I went back to the dairy case. "Did you think at all about the other night?" I said to the hazelnut-flavored creamer. "Did you consider what I said?"

No answer.

"Because I meant it. I know you said you weren't interested, but I'm going to do my best to change that. I'll grow on you, I will. You'll see." The creamer didn't say anything. I looked both ways and then I leaned closer. "You have to believe me," I whispered urgently. "All I want is you!"

"Who are you talking to?" said a man's voice from behind the butter.

"Oh!" I said. "Sorry. I was talking to—I wasn't—I was just—never mind. I'm leaving."

"Good idea!" said the voice.

thirty-two

Ellen was wrong. You couldn't just change things starting now. If your life wasn't going to work, it wasn't going to work in a huge, sweeping way. Every little feeler that you sent out to get your new, better self to take root was going to hit a rock or a puddle of toxic waste or just shrivel up all by itself. Ever since I started this program to get a real life, everything I set my sights on as a goal ended up being out of my reach. I was stuck with myself.

I picked up a guitar, as usual, and I started to play. I played a song I'd written a long time ago. There were many problems with the song. It sounded childish, far too simple. Songwriting was another thing that I was bad at.

I just needed to put myself back on my program, that was all, push myself harder. I just needed to force myself forward out of this rut.

I was on my way to Ellen's on the freeway in my car. There was a little slowdown as I got closer to Mission Valley. I hope there isn't some game or concert at Qualcomm Stadium that I've forgotten about, I was thinking. Then traffic stopped completely, and I was sitting under that enormous bridge that connects the 8 to the 805. How much concrete did it take to build that thing? I was thinking. How long were they working on it? Were there people who had to work under it every single day for months at a time? Personally, I wouldn't want to do it. In fact, I didn't want to be sitting here at all. Now my heart started to beat faster, and my hands started to sweat. I looked at the car on my right in which a woman was talking on a phone. She laughed, nodding, and took a sip from a coffee cup. On my left, a gardener's truck was overloaded with burlap sacks of yard clippings. Two men sat inside staring straight ahead, sipping from Big Gulps. I certainly didn't want to eat at that moment, I can tell you. I just wanted the car in front of me, a gigantic bronze-colored SUV, to move forward. Even a couple of inches would make me feel better. I couldn't see through the windows to find out what kind of people were in there. If I had those dark windows, I would feel so boxed in, I would just freak out. In fact, I was freaking out right now anyway, and my windows weren't even dark. Sweat started to roll down my temples. What if I sat in this traffic so long that I ran out of gas? What would be the fastest way out of here on foot? Would there be any way to climb down off this thing, or would I have to walk a half mile to the exit? I turned around in my seat to look behind me: cars, lots and lots of cars just sitting there, spewing exhaust all over the place. How come the drivers all looked as though nothing was wrong? This was horrible! If you wanted to torture somebody, make them really suffer, this would be the place to put them, right here on the underside of this huge freeway, boxed in by about a million cars, with nowhere to go. If I were having a heart attack right now, could an emergency vehicle come up this way? All the cars would move over just a tiny bit and open up a lane, but would it be enough room?

Now my heart was really thumping. My shirt and face were soaked. There were little puddles on the steering wheel when I released my hands. *I can't stand this,* I was thinking. *I am not going to make it.* I put my face against the steering wheel and continued to sweat. I took a deep breath. Then I said to myself, *You won't be here forever. Sooner or later, you will move.* I lifted my head. The car in front of me had moved one foot. It was still rolling forward. I moved a little. Then we were up to 5 miles an hour with a pretty big space between us, then 10, and before long, I was going a full 23 miles per hour with room enough for a garbage truck between me and the next car.

When I got to Ellen's, my shirt was soaked and my hair was stuck to my head.

"Tom?" she said. Her eyebrows dipped toward each other in concern.

"I'm stuck," I said. "I mean, I *was* stuck. In traffic."

thirty-three

I was coming in with groceries when I heard Robin calling me from the upstairs window. "Good!" she yelled urgently. "Good! Hurry! Jeanette fell! She can't get up because of her arthritis. You have to help me pick her up!"

I put my bags down in the middle of the front yard and went bounding up the stairs, two at a time. Jeanette was sitting in the middle of the kitchen floor. She smiled up at me sheepishly.

"Well, it's my knight in shining armor!" she said in that crackly voice. "It's my own fault! I know better than to walk around in my hose with no shoes! Slipped on the darn linoleum! What was I thinking? If you each take one side, I'll be off this floor in a jiffy." She put out her elbows.

"I heard this tiny voice," Robin said, "and tapping, like knocking on a door, but it was coming from my *ceiling*. It's good you tapped, Jeanette, or it might have taken a long time to figure out it was you!"

"Hold it, Jeanette," I said. I squatted down on the floor. "Before we try to get you up, is anything hurting you?"

"No!" she said, as if it were a dumb question.

"Do you think you blacked out?"

"Blacked out! Well, for the love of Pete! No, of course not!" she said. I had hurt her feelings. "I slipped, that's all. My darn feet are so bad today, I didn't even want to put my slippers on. Then my hose slipped on the linoleum, and I couldn't catch my balance. Blacked out? Good lord! My legs are stiff, is all. I'm just not limber enough to get up. I ought to take a yoga class down at adult ed. That's how you get—"

"Do you think you hit your head anywhere?" I said.

"No!" she laughed at me. "Now, would you please get me off this floor?"

"OK, one more thing. Just squeeze my hands," I said. I think I saw this in a movie or something. She had a strong grip on both sides. I looked at her face, which looked exactly the way it always did, like an old turtle, wearing a lot of lipstick. "I guess you're all right."

"I'm fine! Of course I am! May I please get up?"

"I'm just going to go behind you here and grab you around the middle. Robin, you don't have to help, but can you get her walker? When I get you up, Jeanette, you can just grab the walker for balance, OK?" Robin scurried into the living room and pushed the walker in. I crouched behind Jeanette and hooked my arms under her arms. I was careful not to get anywhere near her saggy old chest. "Ready now? One. Two. Three!"

A teeny, tiny old lady is surprisingly heavy when you have to get her up off the floor. I pushed us both upright with my legs. For a split second I thought we were both going to go crashing right back down. Then I thought how complicated everything would get if Jeanette got injured. I'd have to bandage something. No! This had to work in one try. I pulled all my strength together for the last quarter of the way. I froze there, holding her tight for a second. Then I said, "Ta-da!" like Maddy winning the Parcheesi game.

Jeanette lunged for her walker, grabbed it, held it tight.

Robin clapped. "All right! You did it! Good job, guys!" These were the same words she said to her children all the time. I'd heard her say it a thousand times, but now that everything had changed, it made me ache.

Jeanette smiled. "Thank you, my dears. I'll be just fine now."

Robin said, "Let's get you over on the couch. You can rest there. Did you eat anything?"

"I'm going to go," I said at the door. "My groceries are—"

"Thank you, honey," Jeanette said, slowly rolling her walker and shuffling her feet across the floor to the couch. "Maybe a piece of toast with—do I still have honey?"

"I'll check. That's it, sit right there, and here, put your feet up."

Oh. They were finished with me. I went downstairs and picked up my slumping sack of groceries. My ice cream was going to be a mess.

thirty-four

Elise and Mike were finishing another music lesson outside. I had given them each three notes to play. My harmonica was around my neck in a holder, and my guitar was in my lap. I had demonstrated each of their parts several times. They had tried to do what I did, but so far made mistakes each time. Progress was slow. Now Elise was hunched over the guitar. I couldn't see her face, but I would have been willing to bet that her tongue was sticking out, a habit of hers when she was working hard. Mike had his eyes squeezed with the effort of trying to remember the three holes I had told him to blow through in sequence. I was holding my breath.

Then they both played the correct notes in the correct sequence! "You did it!" I said.

Elise jumped, startled out of her concentrated trance.

Mike smiled.

"Can you do it again?"

They both took deep breaths and did it one more time.

"Brilliant!" I said. "Do you want to try it once more, or something else?"

"Something else," they said together.

"OK," I said, "let's try three more notes."

Behind them, I could see my sister's car pulling up. What was she doing here? This almost never happened.

As my sister got out of her car, then locked it and walked toward us, I played three notes on the guitar and then on the harmonica.

When she saw me, saw what I was doing, her mouth dropped open. She didn't call out to me but approached very quietly.

"OK, guys," I said. "We have a visitor. This is my sister, Ellen." The kids turned around.

"Ellen, this is Elise on guitar and Mike on harmonica."

"It's nice to meet you both," she said.

"Nice to meet you," they muttered. They looked at each other and then at the ground, me, their door.

"Do you guys want to take a break now, while I talk to Ellen?"

They didn't answer but got up and silently went into their house. It surprised me how dramatically their behavior changed with the addition of just one person.

"What was—are you giving them lessons?" Ellen wanted to know when they were gone.

"Well, yeah." The way she looked at me made me embarrassed about it, as if I had done something weird like eat a flower off the bushes or something.

"That's great," she said, but she was still looking at me funny.

"Yeah," I said. "So what are you doing here?"

"Oh, yeah," she said, remembering. "I bought this sewing machine on eBay, and I wanted you to help me get it home and carry it into my apartment."

"A sewing machine? Since when do you sew?"

"Well, it's been quite a few years, but you know awhile back when we were talking?"

"You mean—"

"I was saying that, starting now, you should just start being the person you want to be. So I was thinking about it, and I wondered if there was anything that I wanted to do that I hadn't been doing."

"OK."

"Back in college, I made a quilt. A small one, a really simple one. And it was kind of lousy. It had lumps, and the things that were supposed to be straight were crooked. Nothing lined up or came out anywhere near the right shape, but I've always wanted to make another one. Who knows why. I have all these books about quilts and quilt calendars and quilt note cards, and I'm always looking at quilts in stores. So I mean, why always *want* to do something like that? Why not just do it? What could be stopping me?"

"Uh . . . The fact that you don't have a sewing machine?"

"*Exactly.* So I went on eBay, and I typed in the kind of sewing machine I was looking for—just a really simple one—and I restricted my search to the San Diego area. And guess what! I found one! And it's in a table! It's really old! And so I bid, and I won! It's just the cutest thing! It looks brand-new, and it was made in 1949! All I have to do is get it home. So could you help me with that?"

"Sure," I said. It was the least I could do. "When do you want to do that?"

"Now."

"OK, sure," I said. "I just have to finish the lesson with these guys first. Because we were right in the middle of—"

"Fine, yeah. Go ahead. I'll just watch."

I didn't know how to tell her that this wouldn't work. I didn't want to hurt her feelings, but the kids wouldn't play in front of her. I was shocked to realize that they felt comfortable with me, while they would be shy and silent around my sister. "No, you know, I think it would be better if you went inside my apartment and just kind of, like, waited, because they don't know you and—"

"Oh! I'm sorry. God, what am I thinking? They don't know me from a hole in the wall. I wouldn't want them to feel uncomfortable! I'm a stranger, and they don't—"

"Nothing personal, it's just—"

"Got it!"

Ellen went inside my apartment, and I called the kids. "You guys! Let's finish our lesson, OK?"

Mike came to the door and looked both ways as if he were about to cross the street.

"Ellen's going to wait for me inside my apartment. You ready? Where's Elise?"

"Right here," she said, coming through the kitchen. "Are we going to do more?"

"Yeah, where's your guitar?"

"I'll go get it!"

Mike sat down again in his seat and took his harmonica out of his pocket. A few seconds later, Elise joined him.

"Now," I said, "where were we? OK, Mike, listen to this."

We finished our lesson. It took only fifteen more minutes. Elise's hands were still pretty tender, and Mike's attention span was short. But they were making progress, which I found almost as amazing as the fact that they kept coming back for more.

"OK, you guys are great!" I said. "Now, practice whenever you can, and we'll have another lesson in a couple of days."

"Thank you, Good," they said together.

As soon as they were inside their own house, I could hear them calling, "Mom! Listen to this!"

"Ellen," I said. "We're done out here."

"Tom!" she said. "Your place!"

"Oh, yeah, I got some new—"

"It looks so much better! I love the kitchen table. And you have a working color TV! You've come a long way! Do you have cable?"

"Yeah," I said. "The works. So where's the sewing machine?"

"It's in Bonsall," she said quickly, not making eye contact.

"I think it will fit in your car if we put the backseat down."

"Bonsall! That's, that's, like, well, it's far!" I thought a minute. Dinners Ellen had made me came to mind, time she had spent with me when I was at my worst. I always begged Ellen to ask me to help her do something. I said, "But I'm not doing anything, so what the heck."

She smiled.

It was a good thing to see my sister smile. About something I'd said. It didn't happen all that often. I opened the trunk. "OK. Let me see if I have any junk back here." I took out a denim jacket and some trash. We lowered the backseat. I had never been to Bonsall. I had to dig out a map, which I handed to Ellen.

Ellen was giving me directions as we drove. "OK, get in the right lane. Now turn right. She said to look for a bridge over a—there it is—now turn right. OK, now it's, oh, these condos on the right. This driveway. Great. It's the fifth garage door. There's a parking spot!"

She opened the door before the car stopped moving. She said, "Come on."

I followed her to the front door. She rang the bell.

A woman in her sixties opened the door. She had curly gray hair and wore a jogging suit. "Is this my sewing machine girl?" she said.

"Yes. I'm Ellen. This is my brother, Tom. He has a bigger car than I do, so he drove me."

"I'm Kathy. Nice to meet you both. Come in." We followed her into the condo, which was neat enough for a military inspection and contained quite a few old black sewing machines. There were needlepoint pillows here and there with sewing machines, needles and thread, and pincushion designs on them.

"Here's your baby!" Kathy said.

This ancient black sewing machine was perched on top of a wooden cabinet with three righthand drawers. It reminded me of an old black-and-white textbook photo about the industrial revolution.

The cabinet looked like a desk, except for the sewing machine. "Here's how she folds up," Kathy said. Gently, she tipped the sewing machine forward into the top of the cabinet. A piece of wood covered the opening. "Pretty neat, huh?"

"Wow," Ellen said. "Wow! I've always wanted one of these!"

This was the first I'd heard of it.

Her hands were pressed to her cheeks and she was shaking her head as though she had just won a million dollars.

"Let me show you some other ones, just for fun. Did you see the one that I listed yesterday?"

"The 401A?"

"Yeah. She's a beauty. Want to take a look?"

"Of course!" Ellen said.

This could be a while. I looked for a place to sit down without messing anything up. Not finding one, I stood in the middle of the room. I ran my hand over the top of the sewing machine cabinet, as if I were interested in the finish. I tried to picture my sister sitting there, sewing something. The things you don't know about people!

She had to look at twelve sewing machines that were stationed all over the woman's house.

"Where do you find them all?" Ellen was asking in awe.

"You have to get up early every Saturday morning and get out to those garage sales! You have to hit those swap meets without fail! But it's a labor of love, let me tell you!"

"How many sewing machines do you think you've sold on eBay?" Ellen wanted to know.

The inside of my head was screaming, *"Who cares?"* On the other hand, I hadn't seen Ellen this happy since—well, I couldn't remember when.

"About a hundred," the woman calculated, "maybe more."

After hearing more information about old sewing machines

than I ever imagined existed, my sister and I each took one end of the table, turned it on its side, and loaded it into my car.

Kathy was standing there with a screwdriver. "Sure you don't want me to take those legs off?"

"Not necessary," I said. "But thank you."

On the way home, my sister kept looking fondly back at her sewing machine.

"What's up with you?" I wanted to know. "Since when did you get so nuts about sewing and sewing machines?"

"It's just something that I always wanted to do. I mean, I've done a little bit of it. In junior high, we had to take home ec. I made this hideous skirt. But quilts are different. I just like everything about them. The way they feel, the way they look. You know how many different patterns you can make with triangles?"

"No idea whatsoever. So why didn't you get a *new* sewing machine. Surely, the ones they make these days would be better than that old—"

She gasped. "You mean you don't just love that sweet little beauty? You don't just adore the way it looks? You'll just have to wait to see the way it sews."

"Honestly, I never—"

"Triangles are really my favorite thing. It's so amazing! You wouldn't believe how much you can do with triangles. Flower baskets and pinwheels and Ohio stars."

She'd lost me. It didn't matter, though, because she didn't really care what I had to say on the topic of triangles. She was off in her own little quilt world, and she was so happy there that she didn't notice she was all alone.

At her place, she'd cleared a space for the sewing machine table. She set it up and plugged it in. "I'm so happy!" she squealed and threw her arms around me.

I drove home thinking about my sister's newfound joy. If everybody had something that made them that happy, life would be better all around. Wouldn't it?

I kept thinking about happiness, where people find it, and how little it has to do with the things you expect it to.

Jeanette was that way about her "projects." Every year, she would bring me hideous things she'd made as Christmas decorations. I had to display these in plain sight in my house because she would be sure to stop by to check if I was using the thing. Once she made me a Christmas tree entirely out of hard candies. She stopped by three days later on the pretext that she had gotten some of my mail in her box. But I knew she was checking to see what I'd done with the Christmas tree. Fortunately, I hadn't gotten around to throwing it in the trash. I saw her little gray blue eyes darting around my apartment looking for the thing until she spotted it on my kitchen table. She showed me the directions she'd followed from some magazine. "Easy Christmas Tree Table Topper!" was what the article was called.

She explained that you had to start with a Styrofoam cone. I wondered where in the hell you would get one of those, but I didn't ask her, as I was afraid she might actually tell me. It would take a long time. She would give directions and everything, blanking out on street names. She showed me the supply list and the steps numbered one through sixteen. When she paused, I figured she must be done, so I said, "Well, you certainly did a lovely job." I thought I sounded completely insincere, as if I was just trying to get rid of her, which I was. But somehow this inane comment made her look as happy as she could be. Now that I thought about it, though, I wished I had something like that. I wished I could affix something to a piece of Styrofoam and be satisfied and pleased with myself for days. I really did.

thirty-five

I stepped through my front door to take my garbage out back. There was Robin, snapping a picture of me. Jeanette was behind her, smiling.

"What's—"

"First day of school, Good!" Jeanette said. "You wrecked the picture!"

To my right, the four Gunther kids were lined up in front of their door. They all had fresh haircuts and new sneakers.

"I'm sorry," I said to Robin. "Let me get out of the way."

I went to stand with Jeanette.

Robin said, "One, two, three." They all made their fake photo smiles. She snapped the picture.

Jeanette clapped. "Now, here's something for each of you! It's for recess, now! I want you to save it for recess!" She gave them each a package of Fig Newtons.

"Thank you, Jeanette," they all said. They looked at their mother, who smiled and winked at them, letting them know they were doing the right thing by not announcing they didn't like Fig Newtons or handing them back.

"You're welcome!" Jeanette smiled.

"OK, now get in the car!" Robin said. "We can't be late on the first day!" She put the camera into her big purse.

"Bye, everybody," I said. "I hope you—Good luck, I mean—I hope you get nice teachers!"

They all climbed in the car. Jeanette and I stood by the side of the driveway, waving as Robin backed out.

"There they go!" said Jeanette.

"There they go," I said.

A heavy, sad feeling settled over me then. What was it? A lingering memory of not wanting to return to school? Hard to say.

I went to the trash can, and Jeanette started back upstairs. "Have a nice day!" she said.

"You too, Jeanette," I said.

That evening my phone rang. I was watching something idiotic on television at the time. I still didn't turn it on very often, but it was there if I wanted it. I had more than a hundred channels now, all in color, of course.

"Hello?" I said.

"Hi," said a little kid's voice, and I thought at first that it was Mike. But he never called. He lived next door—why would he? Wrong number, maybe. "It's Jack," said the voice.

I know this is crazy, but first I thought of my brother, Jack, as a child, calling me from when we were small. Human brains are so easy to fool. And then I remembered the other Jack, my kid, Jack.

"Well, hi," I said, and then I panicked. "What—are you—is everything OK?"

"Fine, thank you," he said. "How are you?"

"Where's your mom?"

"She's right here. Do you want to talk to her?"

"No, I—no, that's OK. How are you? Oh, you just said you were fine. What's up?"

"I wanted to call you. I have to ask you something."

"Sure. Shoot." My heart started pounding. "Why didn't you try to find me?" he would want to know. "Why didn't you ever get me any birthday presents?"

"OK," he said. "Hang on a second." I heard papers rustling. "OK, um, at my school, there's this thing?"

"Yeah," I said.

"It's—my class is learning to play music, and I thought you would want to come. Because you like music."

"Of course!" Did I say it too loud? Was I too enthusiastic? "When is it?"

"It's, um"—more paper sounds—"December second."

"It just so happens that I'm free. What time?"

"Um... It's, oh yeah, here it is, ten-thirty. Do you want the address?"

"That would be great, yeah."

He told me the address.

"What instument will you be playing?"

"Recorder," he said. "We're learning three songs."

"Great," I said. "I'll be there. I'm looking forward to it."

"OK," he said. "See you. Oh, wait. My mom and I were watching this movie?"

"Yeah," I said

"And there was this song? My mom told me you wrote it."

"Oh, well, yeah," I said.

"She said you don't do that anymore."

"Sure I do," I said. "Every day."

"Oh."

"Do you want to hear a tape of some of my more recent songs?"

"Yeah," he said. "Sure."

"OK," I said. "I'll make you a tape."

"This is going to be my first time playing anything," he said, back to the recorder. "We just got them today, so I don't know if I'll really like it or anything. I don't like to practice things."

"I see," I said. "I can understand that."

"You can? But you probably practice all the time."

"But I'm old. When I was your age, I almost gave up the guitar because it was too hard. I wanted to sound like George Harrison, and I didn't."

"Who's George Harrison?"

"Guitar player. Anyway, my brother talked me out of quitting."

"I didn't know you had a brother."

I had to bring that up, didn't I? Just when things were going so well. Now I was going to cast this big black shadow over the whole conversation, depress the kid the first time he'd ever called me. "He died," I said. "A long time ago. I don't think your mom and I ever talked about him."

"Was he nice?"

"He was very nice. He was an excellent musician too."

"Oh," he said. "What was his name?"

"See, this is kind of weird. You're going to find this pretty surprising. His name was Jack."

"So I'm named after him."

"No. Your mom named you, and, see, your mom never heard of my brother."

"That's weird."

"Yeah," I said.

"OK, well. I'm going to go now," he said. "I have homework."

"OK, hey, call me back anytime!" I said a little desperately.

"Yeah," he said. "Bye."

"Bye."

That was good. That was hopeful. We had contact. I couldn't sit down. I was too excited. I called Ellen. "He called me!" I said. "The kid called me!"

"Jack?" she said. "He did?"

"Yeah," I said. I was laughing. "He invited me to hear him play his recorder at school. December second!"

"Wow, he gave you plenty of lead time."

"Yeah," I said. "Today was the first day of school."

"It was? Oh, yeah."

"They just got their recorders."

It took me three days to put a tape together. "Self-Destructive Tendencies" wasn't on it. I chose ten songs that I thought a kid in the sixth grade would like, not that I knew much about it. I just didn't put on any slow ones or sad ones. I made a copy for Mike and Elise.

I mailed the tape to Jack in care of Diana.

thirty-six

Ellen had me over for dinner and to show me the quilt she was working on. She was taking a class at an adult-education center called the Institute of Affirmation. "It's every Monday night," she explained. "You just bring in whatever you're working on, or they help you start something. It only costs seven dollars! That's all! Some of the ladies have been going for years. There are old ladies, middle-aged women, a few teenagers. No men, not even one. The teacher is so nice. So helpful and supportive."

I looked at Ellen's pieces. Complicated. There were all these little squares sewn together to make bigger squares. It kind of made my head ache when I thought of all the cutting and sewing and lining up that went into it.

"Yikes," I said.

"Yeah, well, it's not done yet. There are these ladies in my class who have made hundreds—literally hundreds—of quilts. Can you imagine that? They're so good. I'll probably never get that skilled. But I'm improving. It feels good to me just to hold the fabric." She squinched her eyes shut with pleasure. "Then I like to spread it out on the floor, and stand on the couch to look at it from above." She arranged all the squares in a pattern on the living room carpet. Slipping out of her shoes, she hopped up on the couch to look down on the design. We both stood silently for a moment and admired her work.

"It's really excellent," I said.

Then she showed me all the mistakes she'd made. "See right here. That didn't quite meet up right. See that? This is supposed to be a point, and it's flat. And over here, I don't know why I got this puckering. And look! This strip came out just a little too short and I had to add this! So annoying!"

I didn't see anything wrong with any of it. "It looks fine to me," I said. "But it looks so hard! How do you know how to do all that? And how can it be fun when it's so complicated?"

"It's not hard. Really."

We were having burritos, which I had picked up on the way. After we were finished with the quilt topic, I put one on each of our plates. Ellen poured Diet Coke from a big bottle for her and water for me. She sat down.

"Ellen," I said. "Something happened. Something big."

"You told me. Jack called. It's great. Now you can—"

"This is something else. And it happened awhile ago. Listen. I'm in love." She put down her burrito. "I am. I'm in love." I nodded, confirming what I had just said. Then I put both my hands over my face, as if someone had turned a bright light on me in the middle of the night.

"Diana again," she said. She sighed, as if she didn't know what to do about me, hopeless me.

"No, not Diana," I said. I didn't uncover my eyes when I said this. "You know that woman who lives in the front of my house?"

"With all the kids?"

"Robin," I said.

"Isn't she married with three kids?"

"Divorced with four."

"Oh. So what are you moping about? Love is supposed to make people happy."

"She doesn't want to have anything to do with me. She avoids me now, and we live in the same building."

"And this is the first time that's ever happened to you? Ha! You've lived a charmed life!"

I didn't answer that.

"So you see her every day, she doesn't want to have anything to do with you, and it hurts."

"I see her, I can hear her. Sometimes I can even smell her dinner."

"So move," she said.

"You're so helpful. God. I'm not going to move. I want to see her. I want her to change her mind."

"What are her reasons?"

"Reasons? She's not interested, that's all. No spark, I guess."

"Oh. That's a tough one. Impossible to argue with that one. And she's got all those kids to think about."

"I know that. But I *like* the kids. They're excellent."

"But you can see what she's thinking, can't you? She's not the only one involved here. Plus, you're single at your age. That doesn't look too good, I'm sorry to say."

"Would it be better if I'd been divorced six times?"

"No. It would be better if you had been divorced once. About two years ago. And *she* left *you*. That would be ideal. So what are you going to do about it?"

"I'm going to wait. I'm going to be this exemplary neighbor, this undeniably excellent, completely normal, nice guy. I'm going to make myself irresistible."

"Good luck with that." She took a big bite of her burrito.

"You're not being supportive."

"I'm being realistic. I think you should try to see things from her point of view. She's got four kids she's trying to raise by herself. It's probably really hard to make it financially and keep track of what everyone is doing. She's trying to keep everybody afloat. It's *hard*. And then here comes this late-forties, never-married bartender, who's had quite a few girlfriends in and out of his place over the years—girlfriends she's seen arriving and departing, remember—and suddenly he claims he's in love with her. To her, this is not the perfect situation. I mean, if you were Robin, would you want to give you a chance?"

"I'm not a bartender anymore."

"Oh, even better. Here comes this *unemployed,* late-forties bachelor who—"

"Ellen, you're not getting this."

"No, I think *you're* the one who's not getting it, Tom."

"I've started a new life. I'm different."

Ellen didn't answer.

"Really. I have. Well, you too! Don't you feel different now that you bought that sewing machine and started making that quilt? A lot of other things are possible all of a sudden!"

"Sure, but—"

"So, me too! It's like you said! You decide who you want to be and you change! I changed! Doesn't she see that?"

"I guess you have to prove it to her over time or something."

"That's what I'm going to do then. I'm going to prove to Robin that I'm a whole different person!"

"Well, OK," she said. "I hope you do."

We finished our burritos. People should believe you when you tell them something. Even if it's completely unexpected. Even if it's out of character and seems impossible.

t h i r t y - s e v e n

Someone was banging on the door. "Good! Quick!" It was Robin.

I had just stepped out of my closet, where I had been playing guitar and where I couldn't hear anything. She might have been calling me for hours, and I wouldn't have known. I was at the door in two seconds flat, my heart pounding, my mouth dry. "What is it?" I said. "What?" I pictured the four kids, fevers, blood, broken bones.

"Jeanette!" Robin said.

"What?"

"I heard a thump, and I went running up there, but there's no answer."

Oh God, I thought.

"You have her key," Robin said.

"I do?"

"Yeah, remember her daughter gave it to you once, just in case?"

"Sure," I said. Miraculously, I did remember, and I knew right where it was too. I grabbed the key out of a kitchen drawer. "Here, OK. Let's go."

Jeanette was on the floor in her nightgown and (thank God) a flannel robe. "Hello, dear," she said to me. She sounded a little drunk, and she was leaning awkwardly on one elbow.

"Jeanette, what happened?" Robin said, crouching on the floor beside her.

"I fell. It's theesh darn slippersh my daughter-in-law gave me. No traction. It'sh jusht like lasht time. Now, if you two would help me up, I'd be mosht grateful."

She was definitely slurring.

"Jeanette, your mouth is drooping on this side," I said. "Do you feel that?"

Robin and I looked at Jeanette's face. The right corner of her mouth was definitely lower than the left. Did it always look like that?

"Yeah," Robin said. "Good's right. Your mouth looks droopy over here. Does it feel different?"

"I'm fine," she said. "Jusht lift me up, would you? Pleashe?"

Robin looked at me, her eyes wide. "I think she's had a stroke. She doesn't sound right. She's slurring"

"Jeanette," I said. "Squeeze." I held her right hand. Nothing. "OK, now the other side." She squeezed my hand hard. "Do this one." I pointed at the first hand. Nothing.

I said, "We're going to have to call 911."

"I'm fine!" said Jeanette. I had offended her. "Don't do that! They're going to charge me an arm and a leg!" Jeanette said.

"Call her son first," said Robin.

"Robin, he lives in Sacramento. This is an emergency. Call 911. Really. Right now."

"OK, I'm calling. You sit there with her."

Robin went to the phone. Jeanette and I listened while she gave the address and described the symptoms.

I sat down on the floor behind Jeanette, while Robin dialed. "Jeanette," I said, "would you like to lean on me? You look a little uncomfortable, on your elbow like that. Here, just..." I put my arms under her and scooted her back against me. Essentially, she was lolling in my lap.

"Oh," she sighed with relief. "That feelsh much better. Thank you, dear. You're turning out to be a nishe man, after all."

"What do you mean by—"

"They're coming!" Robin announced. "Can you hang tough for a few minutes? I'm going to go downstairs and check on the kids. Then I'll wait out front and flag down the ambulance."

"All right, dear," said Jeanette. "We'll be fine here."

"Maybe you could get her a blanket first," I suggested.

"Right," she said. "Why didn't I think of that?" She trotted to the living room and came back with an afghan in baby colors. She draped it over Jeanette's legs and stomach.

"Thank you," Jeanette said quietly.

From the door, Robin looked back at us. "I'll be right outside. Hold on. Just a few more minutes. Jeanette, I'll call your son from downstairs, from my phone."

As soon as she went out, Jeanette asked me, "How long are they going to take? Hash it been a long time?"

"No, not long at all. About a minute, Jeanette. I've got you, OK? You're going to be all right."

"You're very good to shtay with me." She patted my arm with her left hand.

"My pleasure," I said.

It crossed my mind that she could have another stroke any second, that she could die right here while I was holding her. She must have been scared, sitting there on the floor, about to be taken away in an ambulance. *I won't let her go*, I promised myself. *I will hold her, no matter what, even if she dies right on me.* To my surprise, it was kind of peaceful, kind of cozy, like holding Ray on my lap when he was tired.

I saw the flashing lights through Jeanette's living room curtains. "Here they are," I said. "The ambulance is coming."

Soon two paramedics were thumping up the stairs with Robin leading the way. One was a woman about thirty years old with a stubby ponytail and lots of hair that had fallen out of it around her face. The other was a guy, about my age, but with gray hair.

Somehow I had always thought that paramedics would treat an ailing old person with tenderness and care, kind of like animal lovers talking to pets. But these two were all business. Did we know what kind of medication she was on? Who was her health-care provider? Who was her primary-care physician? What time did she fall? They asked Jeanette her name and age and who the president was. She got everything right.

It all took much longer than I thought it would. There was a lot of back and forth about hospitals on walkie-talkies. There were a lot of questions, and there was paperwork. In the middle of it all, Jeanette's son called. Robin had her cordless phone upstairs. She had left him a message.

"A stroke, they think," Robin said into the phone. "Her right side is weak... No, she can talk, but she slurs.... Yeah ... Alert, completely lucid.... Sharp Memorial.... OK. You're welcome."

"What'd he say?" Jeanette wanted to know. "Is he coming?"

"Yes, he's leaving right now, but he's driving, so he won't be here until close to morning."

"All right." Jeanette sighed.

Finally, they had her loaded on the stretcher and were about to take her down the stairs. They put a blanket over her, which made her look small and almost childlike. Couldn't they at least give her shoulder a little pat to make her *think* they cared about her?

I said, "Wait! I'm going with her. I'll stay with her until her son comes in the morning." I took this in the way I would a plot development in a movie. Hmm, what will happen next?

"What?" Robin said.

"Yeah," I said. "They're going to do tests and stuff. We can't let her be alone. It wouldn't be right. What if she wants something or has a question."

"If you're sure you can—"

"Yeah," I said. "I'm sure. I have nothing going on. No one is waiting for me."

The paramedics were moving her out the door. "You riding with us?" said the woman.

"Yes," I said. I was really doing this.

"That'sh very shweet of you," Jeanette said. "You're really turning out to be a very nishe man."

"Thanks, Jeanette," I said. At least someone noticed the changes I was making!

I was following the gurney down the stairs.

Robin trotted out to the street behind me. She had bare feet, I noticed. "OK, Jeanette. I'm going to call the hospital tomorrow and find out how you're doing."

"I'm fine, dear. You take care of the children. I'll be fine."

They loaded her in. I was standing outside the door, holding the afghan.

"Good, how are you going to get home?" Robin asked me.

"I'll figure out something. Go inside. The kids are probably scared about the ambulance."

"Let me know what's happening."

"Yeah, I will." I climbed in the ambulance. One of the paramedics closed the door.

"I've never been in an ambulance before," Jeanette said. Her eyes were closed.

"Me neither. What an adventure, right?"

"Whee," she said in a very tiny voice.

We took off.

thirty-eight

Jeanette didn't come home right away. I went to visit her in the hospital. Robin put together these little care packages for me to take to her. She left them on my doorstep when I was out, with notes like, "If you see Jeanette, would you give her this? She loves chocolate, and I don't think they'll have it for her in the hospital. Also, here are a couple of magazines I thought she would like and her *TV Guide*."

I took the stuff to her. Every time, she looked a little alarmed to see me. "What are *you* doing here?" she always said.

"Hi, Jeanette," I'd say. "Robin asked me to bring you a couple of things."

"I love Robin! Robin's a sweetie!" she said.

"She is, yeah," I said.

I kept the visits short. "Well," I'd say, picking up her candy wrappers. "You need your rest."

Robin didn't avoid me anymore after Jeanette went into the hospital, not that this was a huge improvement. She pretended that I hadn't said what we both knew I had. She pretended she didn't know that I was in love with her. She was as remote as a person could be after you've professed romantic love to her and dealt with an emergency together. "Good morning," she would say as a greeting. Or, "It sure warms up when the sun is out." These were exactly the kinds of comments that drove me nuts. Personally, I would have preferred it if she had just walked by me and hawked a gob at my feet. I can't stand it when you don't know what someone is thinking.

The day Jeanette was due to come home, Robin's kids made a banner. At first it said, WELCOME HOE JEANETE! Then I noticed that Robin had taken the sign down again, and Elise and Mike were out with markers, squeezing in the missing letters, a green M and a blue T.

I should probably do something too, I thought. I bought a flower arrangement at the place near the 7-Eleven. I didn't want her to think I didn't care. They gave me a card to go with it. "Welcome home!" I wrote. "Good." That looked weird. Would she even know that "Good" was the signature? I squeezed in "Tom" before the "Good," just like the kids with their mistakes.

When I got home, I ran upstairs with the flowers and set them down in front of her door.

A little while later, Mike knocked on my door. "My mom said to tell you that Jeanette is not coming home today."

"She's not? Why not?"

"No, she's going to—what's it called, Mom? That place?" he yelled in through their door.

"A nursing home."

I could hear her fine. She could have told me the whole thing herself without moving.

"Yeah, she's going to a nursing home for a long time."

"For a couple of weeks, honey, not a long time," Robin corrected.

"Oh, for a couple of weeks."

"Thanks for telling me, Mike." I stepped out and went to Robin's door. Poor Mike shouldn't have to be the go-between. "What happened, Robin?"

Robin was pouring pasta into boiling water. She did a little
hop backward so the hot water wouldn't splash on her. Then she
stirred with a wooden spoon. I could have stood there watching
her all night.

She said, "Her daughter called. She said they were concerned
that Jeanette was still a little frail to be here full-time, even if her
daughter stayed with her. So they're doing the nursing home as an
interim step."

"I see," I said. "So she hasn't had some kind of a setback?"

"No," Robin said. "I think they just didn't want to rush her."

"OK, well." I shrugged.

"The kids were disappointed too, but we don't want her coming home before she's ready, do we?"

"No," said Ray without looking up from his coloring. "We do
not!"

Robin looked at me, as if wondering what I was still doing
there, staring into her kitchen.

I nodded. "OK, then." I went back to my place.

At home, I wrote Robin a song. It was a dorky, corny thing to do,
but I couldn't help myself. She would never know it was about her,
of course. It was about how I saw her every day with her kids, how
I knew she had too much to carry, couldn't I just carry something
for her, just to her door? Then there was a verse about how I could
hear her through the walls, and I knew that she could hear me.
Couldn't I come into her part of the house just for a little while?
It was dumb, but it had a nice chorus about how I promised I
would leave her alone, and I promised I wouldn't complicate her
life. I made a tape of it. Then I copied it onto its own cassette. I
put a couple of other songs on there with it to flesh out the tape.
When Mike came over for his lesson, I gave it to him to take home.
He could listen to it at night when he couldn't sleep, I told him.

thirty-nine

When The Awful Thing happened, I watched it live on my new TV on one of my many cable channels. If I had not been on the Brand-New Good Program that had taken place over the summer, I would have slept through it and heard about it later. As it was, I could have been watching a soccer game live from Austria or a program on how to cook mussels in white wine. But I tuned in to find Katie and Matt live. Once it happened, I was caught, unable to tear myself away from the live coverage for the rest of the day.

"She called me on her cell phone. She said she was OK," said the mother of an office manager, staring frantically into the camera, "and since then I haven't heard from her again." "It's our anniversary. I have a present for him," a young woman sobbed. And, "I'm alive. I don't know why or how, but I'm alive. I don't know who was holding my hand. I want to know your name! I want to say thank you, but I don't know who you are!" This young guy broke down on camera. He had an earring, and he worked in the mailroom of a big company. White dust and smudges of black were on his face. His forehead had dried blood on it. The reporter, who was a mess, with her hair all over the place and her shirt dirty, put her arms around the young man, and she was crying too, as she softly patted his shoulder.

It was noon before I realized what was happening to me. I was in the bathroom, pulling toilet paper off the roll, scolding myself for not having Kleenex. *Normal* people have Kleenex for when they cry.

Cry. I was crying. Crying? My brother was dead, Mr. Smeltzer was dead. Diana was gone. I had a kid I hadn't seen until he was eleven. Robin didn't love me. And lots of people had just died suddenly for no good reason. No good reason at all.

I saw suddenly and clearly that my brother, Jack, had also died for no good reason. No one had helped him. No one was there with him. He must have felt so alone. *I* had felt so alone. Still did. Now I was sitting on the floor in the bathroom, sobbing. The whole world seemed so sad. And so pointless. How could people keep going every day? I had no idea.

The TV stayed on for four days. Sometimes I went to sleep, but I didn't turn it off. After a few hours, I'd wake up to watch, just to make sure nothing else had happened while I had my eyes closed.

The fifth day, I felt a little better. Then immediately I felt bad for feeling better. I took a shower and got dressed. I was going to the store.

The first thing on my list was Kleenex. (I had a list!) I bought three boxes on sale. I don't believe I had ever bought Kleenex before, and here I was, buying in bulk. Even when I had a cold, I had always used toilet paper, napkins, and paper towels. I bought groceries. I bought cleaning supplies.

When I got home, I decided to write a song about my brother. No, I didn't decide; the song just arrived whole, and I wrote it down. It was coming fast, and I had to hurry to put the bags down and get a pen. It was almost as if I had already written it and memorized it. It was about trying to recall what he was wearing the last time I saw him and what the last thing I said to him was,

and how he answered. There was a part about how no matter how many times I tried, I couldn't get the picture of his whole face in my mind just the way it had been when he was alive. Then there was a part about how I was sure that he was going to walk through the door a minute or two from now and then this bad part, this sad patch was going to be over. It wasn't a slow song in a minor key; it had a catchy, simple chorus, and it was easy to sing. You might think this is strange, but this was the first song I'd ever written about my brother. It took me only an hour, and most of that was playing it over and over to myself, listening to it. Honestly, when I had finished the song, I felt better. And it was pretty good too. Next thing you knew, I might just find myself sitting down to listen to the *Layla* album straight through. You just couldn't tell what might happen.

I called my sister. We had been talking all week. People all over the world had been calling one another and expressing their love. My sister and I didn't do that exactly. Instead, we said things like, "You OK?" "Yeah. You?" "Yeah, well, not really." "Me neither." But now that I had finally written this song, I thought, we will really be able to communicate.

"Hi," I said when she answered. "It's me. Are you OK?"

"No," she said. "You?"

"Hell no," I said. "I'm a mess. Listen. Why don't you come over for dinner?" We hadn't gotten together since the thing happened.

There was a pause. My sister was too polite to say, "What?! Since when do you invite me over?" But I could imagine that her mouth had dropped open. I added, "I'll cook you something, and we can, you know, talk about . . . it."

"OK," she said. "I accept. I'll show you what I've done. You know that four-patch set on point? Since you saw it, I've been working on it all the time."

"What?" I said.

"The *quilt.* You saw it when I first started. It's helping me cope. Remember? The sewing machine?"

"Oh, yeah," I said. "Right. The sewing machine. I'm with you now. Yeah, bring the quilt. I want to see."

There was another pause. "You do? Really."

"Of course," I said. I mean, what could it hurt to look at someone's quilt if it was important to her? I forgot to say anything about the song. I was going to, but then I forgot.

I had to go back to the store because of the dinner. Then my Vons card didn't work because I'd already used it the same day. They had to call a manager for an override. I hate when that happens. I was bringing in the groceries when Robin came home with the kids.

"Good's here!" Mike came running over and threw his arms around me.

"I'm getting a cookie," Ray announced and charged into my house.

"*Ray!*" Robin said.

"It's OK," I told her.

Elise said, "Welcome home, Good!" She and Maddy went inside their house.

"Were you on a trip?" Mike wanted to know.

"Me? On a trip?" I said, patting Mike's back with my free arm. "No. I've been right here. Inside my, you know, house."

"Mom said you weren't here, because we didn't see you! We thought you went on a plane somewhere and then couldn't fly home! Know what? A bad thing happened! Bad men killed people, but we're safe, Good, and we can go to school and we don't have to worry about a plane crashing into our school or people poisoning us or killing us or killing Mom with a box cutter or *anything*!" His eyes were wide with terror.

I put the bag on the ground. I squatted down and hugged him hard. I looked up at Robin, who was rubbing her hand over her face. Like most faces I'd seen lately, hers looked tired, pale, and worried.

"That's right, Mike," I said. "You're safe and so is your mom. But if you do worry, you'll tell her, right?"

"Or you can tell a teacher!" Mike said. He had been briefed.

"Sure. That's right," I said.

"Or your *dad*. Or your rabbi or Sunday school teacher. Or any adult you know well. Because they love you and *care* about you!"

"That's it."

"They have commecials about it," Mike explained. "Mrs. Bush is on Disney *and* Nickelodeon. I could tell *you* if I was worried, couldn't I, Good? *You're* an adult who cares about me!"

I nodded.

Robin said, "Mike, you can get a cookie too."

Mike went inside.

Robin was going to say something, but I went first. "I wonder if you and the kids would like to come over for dinner."

Robin was already shaking her head before I got all the words out.

"My sister is coming," I said. "She's bringing the quilt she's making. It's a four-patch set on point." I was just parroting what Ellen said on the phone earlier, desperately blabbing any crap that was in my head. I said, "It's been such a sad week I decided to do something with my sister. I—"

She opened her mouth. She was going to say no.

I said something else quickly to stop her from speaking. "You could bring the kids. Of course! I'll do all the food and everything."

This is easy to say when you're sure someone is going to turn you down.

Robin pressed her lips together, thinking. Then she said, "A four-patch set on point? That sounds nice. Do you know what size? I mean, is it for a bed or a crib or a wall hanging or what? Do you know what colors she's using? Or is it scrappy?"

"Oh," I said. "I have no idea. Ha! You have reached the end of my quilt knowledge. I don't even know what a four-patch set on point is. No idea whatsoever. But you can see tonight. When she comes. You don't even have to stay or anything. You can just look at the quilt for two seconds and then leave, if you want. You don't even have to talk to me. I won't even—"

"I have a frozen pizza for the kids," she said, thinking it over. "Mike was worried about you. I don't know why, but he somehow got the idea that you were on one of the planes, and then we didn't see you for a couple days—"

"But I was right here! Didn't he hear my TV?"

"Yeah, but he has a friend whose mother leaves theirs on when they're out, to fool potential burglars."

"I'm sorry! I should have made more noise. The poor kid. Why didn't you just knock on the door?"

"I don't know. We were so sure that you weren't home. Anyway. OK, we'll come. We'll be there. What time?"

"You're *coming?* You're sure? OK. Six?" I said. "I could make it earlier, if you want. Or later."

"Six is good."

forty

There was a knock on the door that I knew was Ellen—five soft knocks, the way she always does. When I opened the door, though, it was everybody.

"Oh!" I said. "You're *all* here," which sounded as if I didn't want them all to be there, as if they weren't welcome. So then I said, "Ellen, this is Robin. Robin, this is—"

"Tom," Ellen interrupted. "We've met. Many times."

"Oh, that's right. Of course. And do you know all the kids?"

"Elise, Mike, Maddy, and Ray," she said. The expert.

"Oh. Wow," I said. "That's impressive."

"Not very," she said. "Are you going to let us in?"

Everyone laughed, as though this were funny.

"Come in," I said, backing up to give them room.

Ellen was carrying a big plastic bag stuffed with things. At first I thought she had brought a lot of food. "What's in there?" I said, preparing to be insulted that she hadn't had faith in my ability to provide dinner.

"The quilt," she said. "Remember?"

"Oh," I said. "Right. The quilt."

"Let's see!" Robin said.

Ellen opened the bag and pulled out a huge thing with blue and yellow squares all over it. It had grown since I first saw it.

"Oooh!" Robin said, picking up the cloth. "It's *gorgeous!*"

The kids gathered around and took a look. Elise tentatively traced a seam with one finger.

"It's not done yet," Ellen said. "I still have to put the borders on and, you know, quilt it and everything. But it's gone faster than I thought it would, that's for sure."

I said, "I didn't know you could do that."

"I'm just learning," Ellen said to Robin. "I'm taking a class."

"Still," I said, shaking my head. "That's—that's a lot of... of work."

Robin and Ellen laughed, as if I were one of the kids saying something incredibly innocent.

Then they started talking about quilts, fabric, different classes you could take. What was this? They hardly knew each other. How did they have so much to say?

I went into the kitchen. I had actually made dinner. I didn't choose a very complex menu—spaghetti with sauce from a jar, premade salad that came in a bag, bottled dressing, and heat-up garlic bread. Unfortunately, the fact that they had arrived all at once had thrown off my timing. Now I got flustered trying to get everything ready at the same time.

I had never had this many people in my place at one time. My table was too small. Robin went home and got a beach towel and put it on the floor for the kids to sit on. I had a new rug, which had scared them all into taking their shoes off. "It's just a rug," I kept telling them. "Whatever gets on it, it's just a rug."

I had rented a movie, *How the Grinch Stole Christmas,* that I slid into my new DVD player for the kids. They had already seen it, of course, but that didn't seem to matter. As soon as Robin handed them their paper plates and pressed PLAY, they sat there silently chewing their pizza and staring at the tube. I felt guilty that they were so easily absorbed, as if I had drugged them to get them out of the way.

I managed to overcook the spaghetti until it was a gluey mass, but Ellen and Robin ate it anyway.

The two of them had hit it off immediately, almost too well, as I was completely out of the conversation.

"So is this your first quilt?" Robin wanted to know.

"I made one in college," Ellen said. "And I loved it. I wanted to do that for the rest of my life. Then I never made one again, until now."

"If you liked it so much, why did you stop?"

"Stupid, I know," Ellen said. "At the time, I was trying to get a high-enough GPA to get into law school. I thought if I made quilts it would entirely take me over, and I would be a failure. So I stopped."

"That's too bad. But you did get into law school," Robin said. "Right?"

"Yes," Ellen said. "And I hated it. I still hate law. Anyway, there's a flying geese class next month that I'm going to take. I can't wait."

"Aren't triangles hard to work with?"

They went on and on like this. You'd think we'd spend some time on the most recent developments in the unfolding horror story, but maybe because the kids were there, everyone decided to stay off that. Or maybe we all needed to be off that topic for now. The sadness and tension and worry were still there, sitting right at the table with us, but for the moment, the two women were looking in another direction, to something that attracted them and absorbed them, made them happy. Robin went home a couple of times to get books to show Ellen. Quilt books. She had a whole library of quilt books, it turned out. She used to make quilts, too, before she had kids, but since then she hadn't had time. Who knew?

They were talking so much, and I had so little to contribute, that I finally joined the kids on the towel. How could I mind? I hadn't seen my sister so enthusiastic about anything in a long time. And the movie was pretty good. But Ray fell asleep on the towel, and Maddy was curled up on my bed with a distant look in her eye. I could have closed my eyes and drifted off myself, but Robin stood up and said it was time for them to go.

"Oh," I groaned, as if I were one of the kids. "Now?" Immediately, I felt sadness and loneliness pinching at my chest.

Ellen and Robin looked at me.

"What?" I said.

"Nothing," they said together quickly, as if over the past couple of hours they had become a unit.

I knew what they meant. I never used to want people around, and now I did. I was different, and they noticed. After years of being alone and stuck, something had finally shifted inside me. Did you ever see one of those time-lapse movies about changes in landmasses? Subtle, imperceptible shifts in the earth push two plates together. Rain and wind wear away rocks, softening the shape of coasts and mountain ranges. Occasional strong earthquakes create surfaces that weren't there before. At the end of a few thousand centuries, you wouldn't recognize the place. I was like that. For years, I had seemed inert and immutable, but underneath, there had been the minute shifts going on. I'd had the occasional momentous event that shook my whole structure. Taken together, these experiences had been gradually edging me toward this moment in which I was finally different. I had changed, and change was good. Change was Good.

One thing about big transformations is that when they happened, it is hard to remember how different things were and what they were like before.

forty-one

My phone rang, and it was someone I didn't know. She said her name, Marjorie Something, but it didn't mean anything to me. "Jeanette's daughter," she said.

"Oh!" I said, "How's she doing? We're looking forward to getting her back! The kids made a sign and everything!"

"My mother passed away last night," she said. "In her sleep. She didn't suffer. There wasn't any pain."

"No," I said. "Jeanette? No!" And I started to cry right then and there. I had only recently realized how attached I was to Jeanette, and now she was gone.

The daughter was saying, "...very fond of you and Robin. She's at work now, I guess? I tried to reach her, but... Anyway, Mom was so grateful for all the help you gave her at the...at the end of her life." Now she was crying.

"I'm sorry," I said, all choked up. "I'm so sorry."

"Well," she sobbed. "She was old, but, but I wanted to keep her!"

My heart broke for this woman I had never seen. Death was just a bad idea, and there was far too much of it around. The daughter said she'd get in touch with us about the funeral.

I had to tell Robin. She would want to know. I drove down to Vons. She was at lunch, but I told Alex, the manager, that it was important that I find her.

"She usually eats by the fountain on the lower level of the shopping center."

"Thank you," I said.

She was sitting by herself, eating a salad out of a clear plastic container. She didn't see me at first. I stood there a few seconds, thinking about how I should say it, what words I should use. She had on her Vons shirt and her name tag and her black uniform pants. She closed her eyes and turned her face up to the sun for a minute. Then she went back to her salad.

"Robin?" I said.

She turned her head and looked at my face. After just a second, her whole expression changed. Her eyebrows went together and her mouth opened. She said, "Jeanette?"

I nodded.

She put down her plastic fork, put the salad container down next to her, dropped her face into her hands. When she cried, her whole body shook with each sob.

I sat down next to her and put my hand on her back. "I'm sorry," I said. "I'm sorry. I know she really liked you, and you did so many things for her." I handed her some tissues that I had brought with me for this reason.

She blew her nose. "I have to go home, Good," she said. "I hate this job, and I have to call my mom."

Sometime after The Awful Thing happened, Adam Blackburn from Point Blank called. He needed a song for a telethon to raise money for the children of the victims. He had tried to write one himself and came up empty. He asked if I had anything. "Maybe," I said, and I played "A Minute or Two from Now," the song I wrote about my brother, for him over the phone. He liked it, and he asked if he could use it. "Sure," I said, "be my guest." I taught him the song. I didn't think much more about it. One curious thing about transformation is that often when the biggest shifts occur, it doesn't seem like anything much is happening at all.

I was in bed asleep when the phone rang. "Honey?" My mother. "Well, it was wonderful. It was a beautiful song. You've really done it now, kiddo."

Slowly, it dawned on me what she was talking about. "Mom?" I said. "You're watching MTV?"

"Oh, Ellen told us your song was going to be on."

"Oh," I said. "How did she know?"

"Sweetheart, you told her."

"Did I?"

"Of course you did. Now, I've got to go. I need to call in my donation. I love you, sweetie."

"I love you too, Mom."

We hung up.

Someone was knocking on my door. I opened it, and Mike was there. "Good, you were on TV!"

"What are you doing up so late?"

"A guy said your name! He said, 'This song was written by our old friend Tom Good.' I was watching with my mom, and they told your name! It was the best song on the show! It was about a boy who wasn't home yet. Can you sing that for me? Tomorrow, because I promised my mom I'd go to bed right away if she let me watch the whole show."

"Of course," I said. "Tomorrow. Night, Mike."

"Oh, wait. Mom liked it too, Good. She said to tell you. Night, Good."

And for that, it was all worth it—all the pain, the hiding, the bad choices and false moves I'd ever made in my life seemed OK to me, because I had started to move forward. I had turned some of my life into a song. A real song that people liked.

f o r t y - t w o

George Harrison died.

I got a guitar in fourth grade because I wanted to learn to play like George. I learned to write songs by learning every Beatles song by heart. Since eighth grade, I had been a vegetarian because I read that George was.

I felt my heart tearing out again as I had so often during the last few months. But then a new feeling came. It came in the form of a little guitar riff that I heard in my heart and then in my head. The riff was saying, *Thank you!* And I wrote a song to George based around that riff. If I could have put a grateful celebration of every Beatles teaching—about songwriting, guitar playing, humanitarianism, grace, love, and peace—into one song, I would have. As it was, I managed a simple, worldless melody called "Thank You!" And that became the song I played first every morning to get myself grounded, my mantra, so to speak. (I first learned the word *mantra* because of George. You see? George had been with me all this time.)

Gratitude can take you a long way.

forty-three

I was at Corona Vista Elementary, sitting on a folding chair. I was twenty minutes early. I watched the end of a movie about sharks that some kids about Elise's age were watching. Then the movie ended, and those kids left the room. Parents came in and sat down. They all knew one another and talked and laughed. I saw Diana come in. I stood up, ready to go to her, to talk, to ask questions. But she gave me a perfunctory wave and sat near the front. Some kids came in and sat on the floor. A guy sat next to Diana, a nice-looking guy, who was all dressed up. The fiancé. He looked about as different from me as a person could: short, neat haircut; suit; polished shoes. I stayed where I was, three rows behind them. They leaned toward each other to talk. Diana talked to a lot of the other parents. The place filled up. People had to stand. I gave my seat to a grandmother and stood over on the side near some bookshelves.

Kids started filing in, sitting on the floor in front of the parents. These were little kids, though, kindergartners maybe. Then a group of older ones came, second-graders, first-graders? It was hard to tell. Anyway, there were hundreds of them. They kept filing in until it looked as though there was no way the floor could contain them all. A teacher stood up. "Boys and girls on this side, I want you to move over this way just a little bit more." She made a sweeping motion with her hand, as she took a few giant steps to the left. "And boys and girls on this side, please move this way." She swept with the other hand, did a giant side step the other way. There was a lot of wiggling. "That's right. We have another class coming in to see the program. Good. Great. Thank you." A new group of kids paraded in.

Next, a platoon of kids Jack's size marched in behind a large gray-haired teacher. They were all holding plastic recorders. "Good morning!" said the teacher as the students found their places behind her.

I was scanning the faces. I found him! He was searching too, looking all over the room, unsystematically darting his head around, from the right to the left and then back again. His eyes finally locked onto mine. He blushed and smiled at me. I waved like crazy before I considered how embarrassing this might be for him. I put my hand down and smiled. He smiled back. Then he found his mom.

"We've been practicing," the teacher went on, "as you must have heard at home." There was a ripple of chuckles. "I think you might even recognize the songs we're going to play." More chuckles.

The teacher turned around and knelt on the floor in front of the students. She lifted her hands. They all put their recorders to their lips. They played "Kumbaya." Right away, I choked up. Again. Almost anything could do this to me now, especially the words "moment of silence" and "loved ones" and lots of different kinds of music.

I had to sniff, and it was kind of loud. The woman next to me opened her big bag and handed me a pack of tissues. "Thanks."

She sniffed. I handed the tissues back. "Thanks," she said. "I usually only fall apart when they sing, but ever since this fall I—"

"Oh, God," I whispered. "They're not going to sing, are they?"

"I don't think so."

Next they played "You Are My Sunshine," followed by "This Land Is Your Land." I saw Jack looking over at me, and I managed to make my mouth turn upward in a smile. *Good job,* I was telling him. *I like it.*

They were finished. "Thank you all for coming!" said the big teacher. "You've been a wonderful audience. We hope you've enjoyed the program." She turned and led the kids outside. The parents were starting to leave in the opposite direction, out the front door. I saw Diana and her finacé heading out.

"Wait!" I wanted to call after the class. But they weren't stopping. I couldn't just let Jack go back to class without speaking to him.

I pushed through the crowd to follow the kids. They were going outside and branching off to go into different classrooms in portable buildings that occupied one end of the playground. I'd lost track of Jack, and now I didn't know which room he was going to be in. I stood in the middle of the blacktop, looking at the sea of kids. But he'd disappeared.

"Uh, Good?" the voice was at my shoulder.

I turned, and there he was. "Hi!" I said to Jack. "You were fantastic! That was outstanding!"

"It was?"

"Yeah, it was! Three songs! Whoa! How long did it take to learn those?"

"I don't know. It seemed like a really long time. Could you hear my recorder? Could you tell which one was me?"

"Loud and clear! Are you kidding? It was the best one! You sounded great. Right on tempo! I loved it."

"OK, I've got to go, or I'll get in trouble."

"Oh," I said. "Don't get in trouble! Can't have that."

"Good? Can I tell you something? I was kind of scared to play in front of you."

"Oh, no," I said. "God, that's—sorry I—"

"But I'm glad you came. It worked out. Mom said it would. See ya," he said, and he walked off.

Another kid, a boy I hadn't noticed at first, had hung back waiting for him. "Was that your dad?" I heard him ask.

"Yeah," said Jack. "One of them." He turned back and waved to me.

I waved back.

I was one of his dads! How about that? I got choked up all over again and hurried out to the street and my bike.

forty-four

Kmart was bankrupt. "Well, now, what the—" I said out loud the first time I heard the news on the radio. That must be wrong. Kmart couldn't just— Then I kept hearing it over and over again. How could they have let that happen? On the news that night when I sat down to watch CNN, Kmart was the big story. People were talking about it in line at the grocery store. Every day, there was another story about it on the radio. "Will Bluelight go out forever? Increasing competition from retailers like Wal-Mart and Target..."

Panic surged through me. *What about my T-shirts? What about my socks?* I was thinking. A lot had changed recently. Surely there was this one thing, just one small thing, that could stay the same.

I drove to the Big Kmart on Clairemont Mesa Boulevard, the one I always went to. I went straight to the T-shirts. There were only three packages in my size, all white. I don't usually buy white. I didn't think I had since I was eleven. I looked at them for some time, pulling the packages forward in the rack as if they might be hiding something. An old man shuffled over. I worried that he was after medium pocket Ts! I had no choice! I grabbed all three packages off the rack. I would have bought more. I would have bought hundreds, if I could have. But there were only three, which I held tightly all the way to the checkout stand, as if someone might want to take them from me.

As soon as I'd paid, I drove over to the mall, to Miller's Outpost. As long as I was doing my shopping, I might as well get some more things, a couple pairs of jeans and maybe a sweatshirt. At least there was Miller's Outpost. I could count on that anyway. Miller's Outpost was where I had been buying my jeans for, well, forever. OK, it wasn't called Miller's Outpost anymore. Last time I was here, the store name had changed to Anchor Blue, for some reason. Marketing, probably. Maybe the name sounded better to teenagers or something. Who cared what it was called? The important thing was that the jeans were the same. I parked where I always parked, walked past Macy's and the toy store, and then came to Miller's Outpost or whatever it was called.

I should say that I came to where it used to be. There was white paper on the inside of the windows so I couldn't see inside. There was a sign saying that it had moved from this location. Gone!

My heart was thumping like crazy and I had to take some deep breaths, slowly. Something gripped me around the neck and threatened to choke me. I just had to sit down there by the dolphin fountain and think for a minute. What the hell was happening here anyway?

On the other side of the fountain, a boy who was about five was throwing coins into the water. He would pinch a penny between his thumb and his forefinger, squeeze his eyes shut tight, and then open them for a second before he hurled the coin into the water. He did this five times, then turned to his mother, a redhead in a T-shirt that said CLICK OK, and asked her something. She put some shopping bags on the ground and dug around in her purse for her wallet. Then she handed the boy some more change. He made his wish ten more times. Or maybe he made ten more wishes.

When the mother was out of pennies, they walked away. "I hope it works out for you," I wanted to call after him. Of course I didn't, as I didn't want to alarm them.

What had the boy been wishing for? A toy he wanted. No, it had to be something bigger.

I know what I would wish for him, I thought. I would wish for nothing unexpected to happen in his life. Ever. That would be a good wish. If the kid could get that wish, life on a smooth course with no surprises, he'd be doing pretty well. That's what I'd want for myself. I'd want to eliminate store closings; sudden, loud noises; price increases that I hadn't planned for; and of course, surprise deaths and other life-changing disasters.

Wouldn't I?

Of course, without surprises, I never would have felt the jolt of joy at hearing my own song on the car radio for the first time, way back when. I never would have felt that clutch of love at seeing Robin's neck bent as she folded a Goofy towel. And once you felt those things, there was no going back. I was forever trying to feel those things again, to re-create the feeling of those surprises. No matter how much my head tried to keep things the same, my heart would go on looking for more doses of happy coincidences and lucky accidents. You just couldn't stop your heart—it was addicted to surprise—no matter how much your head tried to avoid it.

And you couldn't just wish to avoid the bad surprises and have lots of the good ones, because who knew which disasters were going to turn out to be miracles? For years it had seemed to be a bad one that a family with small kids had moved in next door. Now, another surprise, that turned out to be good. Surprises were tricky. You just never knew what you were getting.

I stood up. I stayed there a minute, looking at the money on the bottom of the fountain. What did they do with it all, and whose job was it to fish it out? I reached into my pocket and took out a dime. I looked around to see if anyone was watching. No one was. "Good surprises," I whispered to myself and threw the dime into the water.

Then I walked into the Macy's men's department and bought seven shirts. They were all different. There was a maroon polo; a green one; a tan button-down long-sleeve; a denim one; a plaid short-sleeve; a dark blue long-sleeve T-shirt with a yellow number 28 on it, for some reason; a purple turtleneck that was on sale. I paid and went into the dressing room to put one on, the number 28, which I wore home. 28, I thought. Why not?

forty-five

Sometimes I think that writing "A Minute or Two from Now" was what caused my life to finally move forward, but I guess it wasn't. It was everything that led up to it too.

The song took on a life of its own, earning lots of money for the children who lost parents in the disaster.

It's not as if I was never sad again or anything. Being sad only really started with the song. Before that I had just been kind of a zombie. And the good thing about being sad is that, afterward, you appreciate feeling happy a lot more. Emotion is a relative thing. That's all I've got figured out so far.

It wasn't long after the dinner that Robin and Ellen signed up for a quilt class together. If I had been able to sew, I could have been with Robin in a heartbeat. They'd work over at Robin's, cutting pieces of fabric apart and sewing them back together in geometrical combinations, blocks. Ellen would come over and get me to ask my opinion. Then they'd lay the blocks out on the floor in Robin's living room and squint at them, deciding which arrangement they liked best. Sometimes they had to stand on the coffee table for an aerial view. "Oh!" Mike said once, watching them rearrange the pieces. "It's like a puzzle."

"Exactly!" said Robin, and she hugged and kissed him. I wished I'd said that.

The quilts seemed to occupy more and more time. Ellen quit her job. "What?!" I said. "You *quit*? Why?"

"I'm going to take quilt classes for a year and then start my own business."

"Selling quilts?" I said. "You're a well-trained, experienced lawyer!"

"So?"

"So . . . so that's what you do for your *job*! You can't quit! You're only fifty-two!"

"Am I allowed to change my job, if I feel like it? I believe I am. I don't like being a lawyer. You have to argue all day, and I don't like to argue."

"Kind of late to be reaching that conclusion, don't you think?"

"Personally," she said, "I think the timing is perfect. If there's one thing I've learned lately it's that people should be doing what they enjoy with people they like."

When she said that, I just stood there for a minute, staring at her like an idiot. She was right, of course. It was just a little hard to adjust to the idea of my stable, lawyer sister with the big-time, serious job becoming some kind of seamstress, doing crafts projects all day. No fair! I was supposed to be the unstable one with the offbeat job!

"I don't know about you, but I've had it with working for a purpose that's at odds with my personality. I've always wanted to do this. When I started sewing on that little black machine, that was it for me. I just don't want to do anything else." I stared at her without saying anything. "It's just a change, Tom. And—"

"Don't tell me! Change is good. OK, OK."

A few days later, someone knocked on the door. I thought at first that it was one of the kids, but you get to know the knocks. This was someone who didn't knock on my door every day.

It was Robin, holding a bright multicolored lump of fabric.

I was so surprised I could barely choke out, "Hi."

"I finished my quilt." She said it so quietly, it almost sounded like a secret.

"You—and you wanted to show me?" I never felt so honored. "Let's see." I was speaking quietly too, as if there were a sleeping baby in the room.

She handed me a corner, and she took a corner. We stepped apart and the quilt opened.

There were lots of hearts on it. They were made of different colored pieces of purple, blue, and red fabric cut up and sewn back together. In between there were pieces of dark blue fabric with a darker blue, flowery pattern.

"Wow," I said. And then I said it again, more softly, "Wow."

"It's—it's just a quilt," she said, her cheeks reddening.

"No, it's not. It's beautiful. It's got hearts on it, and it's fuzzy on the back here."

"You think so?" she said.

"That it's fuzzy? Yeah, nice and soft. What's that on the back? Like pajamas, right?"

"Yeah, the backing is flannel. But no, I mean, beautiful. You think it's beautiful?"

"Beautiful it is. Oh, yeah," I said without a doubt.

"This didn't come out right." She picked up a corner and explained how the points were supposed to—I don't know, something—and didn't. And then she proceeded to show me all the mistakes in the quilt. This took some time. She said there were twisted seams and mismatched points and quilting stitches that veered off course. There were parts that weren't symmetrical, parts that she had taken out and redone so many times that they got stretched and couldn't go back to the right shape, and parts that weren't the right distance apart. It was all invisible to me, but I listened to all of it and nodded, as if I could see it. Then I said I wouldn't have noticed it if she hadn't shown it to me. I said, "If you look at it one way, it's hearts in a square, but if you look at it from another, the background is the main thing and it looks like diamonds." I held it up and looked at the patterns, and then I tilted my head the other way.

"Oh!" she said. "You can see that? I mean, that's the way it's supposed to look, but I wasn't sure that the fabrics I picked were the right—"

"And the colors. Wow! How did you have time to make this?"

"I have a whole lot of vacation days," she said. "And a little while after the disaster happened, and you know, Jeanette, I started thinking that I couldn't face going in there and stocking dairy and working the register the way I normally did. I didn't want to stay home and watch TV or not do anything at all. I wanted to focus on something that would take all my attention. I wanted to do something that would last, that would make me feel good, that would be, I don't know, pretty. So this was it. This was what I decided to do. I worked on it all day when the kids were at school and then again at night too. It helped. It really did."

"It's incredible," I said.

"Well, good," she said and she turned to go to the door.

"Wait!" I said. I picked up the quilt. "You forgot your quilt." She shook her head. "No, I—What? It's yours," she said.

I was so shocked, I think I actually took a step backward.

"Didn't I say that when I first came in? I thought I did. I made it for you. To have. You wrote that beautiful song, and it inspired me."

I stood there with my mouth open. "But it—you worked so hard, and it took so long, and it's so *nice*—I—"

She laughed. "Not that nice. My next one is going to be better. I'm hoping—"

I had choked up again.

"Good?" she said. "Are you OK?"

I nodded.

"Should I—what should I do?"

I shook my head and motioned that she could go. She went.

I sat down on the bed and sobbed into the quilt. Then I worried that I would ruin it, so I got a tissue. I hurried back to it; I didn't want to be away from it too long.

I slept with the quilt that night, like a kid with a special blanket. I had it all wrapped around me tight. And I didn't wake up in a sweat, not even once.

The next day there was another knock on the door. I didn't even consider that it could be Robin two days in a row. But it was, and she had soup. She had made it. Herself. She stayed and waited for me to taste the soup. I swallowed. "Mmm," I said. "Wow."

"You like it?" she said. "Really?"

"Really," I said.

"See, I wasn't sure about the hot sauce. Some people don't like it. I tried not to put in a lot, but if I didn't put any in, it would be, like, kind of blah. So I just put in a little, about half what I normally do."

"It's great. I love hot sauce. Hot sauce is outstanding."

"Oh! Does it need more? I can go get it. It's right by my—"

"No," I said. "It's perfect." To prove it, I kept eating.

"So, do you feel better today?"

"I do, yeah." I said this quietly. "I love the soup . . . the soup is really . . . tasty. It's great. Thank you. Did I forget to say thank you? Sometimes I am so rude. I'm sorry. I really am. God. Sometimes

I'm an idiot. And thank you for the quilt. Did I say thank you for the quilt?"

"Yeah," she said. "And you're welcome."

We both looked over at my bed, where the quilt was folded at the end. I don't think I had ever folded a homemade quilt before.

She smiled at me, and my eyes filled with tears, which immediately spilled over. I looked around for a napkin or something. When was it going to *stop*?

"Oh, Good!" she said. "I'm sorry! I'm making you cry again! Am I depressing you? Sorry. I'll go." She took a step toward the door

"No!" I said a little too urgently. I took a step after her and managed to grab her hand. I hadn't touched her since that night I lost my head over the laundry. I fully expected her to jerk away and maybe even give me a hard shove. But she didn't. She stopped walking and squeezed my hand. Then she turned around and leaned forward. She kind of pressed her face into my shirt. There was a lot I would have liked to do at that moment, but unfortunately in the hand that she wasn't holding, I was holding a bowl of hot soup.

"See you tomorrow," she said. She stood on her tiptoes and kissed my cheek.

Robin came over a couple more times. Once she brought me some cookies and once she asked if I wanted anything from the store. Then, after I said no, she stood there for a really long time, not moving and not saying anything.

I said, "Robin? Are you OK?"

"Uh, yeah," she said. "I just—oh . . ."

The kids had started yelling, "Mom, come on!" from the car.

"Oh," she said. "I have to go." And she left.

· · ·

Later that night she knocked on my door.

I said, "What's the matter? Is everyone OK?"

"Yes," she said. "Everyone is fine. They're all asleep."

"Oh," I said. "That's good. I thought—because it's so late that maybe—"

"No," she said. "Nothing like that. They're fine. Everything is fine. We're all . . . fine."

"OK," I said.

"Can I come in?" she said.

"Uh, sure."

"I think I can hear them from here if anyone—"

"You can," I said. "Absolutely."

"Really?" she said. "Have we been—"

"Not at all!" I said quickly. "Not a bit!"

"Good. Because I wouldn't want to—"

"Of course not. You haven't. Ever!"

"So," she said.

"Do you want to sit down?"

"Sure, thank you," she said. She sat on one of my chairs. There was this long silence. Then she said, "Don't you get it, Good?"

"Get what?"

She sighed and rolled her eyes. "The quilt? The soup? The cookies?"

I looked at her and blinked.

"I like you."

"Thank you," I said. "I like you too. I know I haven't always been the best—"

"Good! I mean I *like* you, like you. You know, as in *like* you, as in let's go out on a date, as in without the kids, as in kissing, et cetera, et cetera, *that* kind of like you."

"Oh!" I said. "Sorry, is *that* what all the visits were about? God.

How stupid can I be?"

"Well, pretty stupid, I guess," she said.

"But what about all those times you told me to leave you alone?"

She rolled her eyes again. "I changed my mind," she said. "It happens, OK? I mean, you started behaving in a whole different way, and then, well, I changed my mind. Geez, it's not that complicated."

"No, it's really not," I said. Then I kissed her.

And from that moment, I wasn't alone anymore. Ever again, as it happened. From then, there were people around all the time. Kids and grown-ups, even animals. I'm not complaining. It was just a big change is all, a huge improvement, let me assure you. After stagnating for years and years, doing the same thing day in and day out, all by myself for the most part, suddenly everything was different; not one thing was the same as it once was.

forty-six

At first, I really didn't get the attraction of cutting up and sewing little pieces of fabric together. In the first place, it's difficult and takes a long time. Plus, it's expensive. Ellen was sinking a hundred dollars or more into materials for these things. Then she had to make them herself! And I mean, what for? You can go get a blanket for a few bucks any old time. Try Target! They even have quilts there that *look* homemade! But of course that wasn't the point. I personally would not sign up to make one, but I guess I do get it. Now. After thinking about it for a long, long time. I mean, I like the results. Sure, I love to look at them, and that's a good thing, as they are all over the place around here—on the beds, on the couches, on the walls, and even in the car. The shower curtain is a quilt! The kids wear quilted patchwork jackets to school! We live in a colorful, stitched together, padded world.

I've written some more songs. I showcase them at The Club every few months. Each song is the accumulation of all my experiences up to now, plus some embellishments, plus some other stuff that I make up completely. I can rearrange the pieces in an infinite number of ways, like the blocks of quilts—log cabin, flying geese, courthouse steps, and delectable mountains—that Ellen and Robin make.

They started a business together. You might think that the business is for selling the quilts they keep cranking out all the time. That would be a perfectly plausible idea. The quilts are beautiful and cozy and well made, and there are lots of them. But it's not a quilt-selling business. Their business teaches *other* people how to make the quilts. You would be amazed at the number of people who want to make quilts, more every week, it seems to me. Robin explained it to me. When everything is going crazy, either on a personal level or a global level or both, you want to have something that you can control, something that you can be in charge of and make sure will come out right, even if you have to do it over countless times. So that's what they do: they help people make things that come out right.

For this and many other purposes, Robin and I bought a house in the mountains. We moved there before we even got married. It started out as an ugly, beat-up old cabin on a large piece of property. But we've changed it and added to it and built so many studios, bedrooms, extra buildings, and creature comforts that it's hard to remember anymore what the original place looked like or, for that matter, what we saw in it. Robin and Ellen have a separate work space with tables, a design wall, and equipment for up to twelve quilters at a time. Their business is called Heart Patches. The business logo is a purple and red heart shape that has been cut apart and sewn back together with uneven stitches. They have a business motto that adorns their letterhead, mugs, sweatshirts, not to mention quilts. The motto is "It's a hard world—let's quilt it!" They sell franchises, shops that are now located in shopping malls throughout California and seven other states, where you can buy quilt stuff and make Robin and Ellen's designs.

They say they want to be the McDonald's of quilts. Don't try to point out to them that McDonald's is everything that quilt making is not—fast, cheap, and without individuality. I've mentioned that.

And I've mentioned that McDonald's emphasizes uniformity where Heart Patches encourages uniqueness. "Oh, you know what we mean!" they say, waving me off. "We mean we want to be everywhere all the time." Twice a year, they move to a huge space in San Diego for quilting seminars for their franchise owners.

Robin and I and the kids live above the quilt studio. Even our kitchen is upstairs. Jack visits us. Although he doesn't want anything to do with music, he was pretty pleased when Diana signed up for a quilt class and made a reptile quilt for his room. Ellen has her own little building down a short path from the main house, sort of a one-bedroom cottage. I've got my own studio way at the back of the property in what we think used to be a stable. We put in a skylight and enough power for a medium-sized airport for all my gizmos and gadgets.

The kids tend to alternate between these locations and their swings and slides that are sprinkled under the oaks. Mike has his own guitar, specially sized for a kid's small hands. I designed it for him myself.